The West Coast Affair

A novel by

Peter Richards

This book is a work of fiction. Names, characters, places, organizations, incidents and dialogue either are the product of the author's imagination or if real are used fictitiously, and any resemblance to actual persons living or dead, events, corporations or locales is entirely coincidental.

National Library of Canada Cataloguing in Publication Data

Richards, Peter, 1939-
The West Coast affair : a novel / by Peter Richards.

ISBN 1-895332-28-1

I. Title.
PS8585.I1855W47 2003 C813'.6 C2002-911156-0
PR9199.4.R52W47 2003

—

Printed in Canada by Friesens

Cover Illustration by Cim MacDonald. West Coast artist

Book Design by Desktop Publishing Ltd. Victoria, BC
desktoppublishing@shaw.ca

To all whose life's work is to care.

1

> In a somer seson, whan softe was the sonne,
> I shoop me into shroudes as I a sheep were,...
> ...Wente wide in this world wondres to here.
>
> *The Vision of Piers Ploughman-William Langland*

A summer tragedy and a family deserted, a western odyssey and a newborn child, a change of identity and a policeman's journey.

"Bist ee goin' down town?" A twenty-five year old man, sunburned and sweating in the hot, late morning sun, called out as he pushed a wheelbarrow full of gravel along a railway track. He wore a flat cap and baggy black pants. A heat haze rose from the rails behind him, shimmering over the banking on each side over dried grass charred with burned patches sparked from the coals of passing trains. The only other sound, apart from a bird singing high overhead, came from the clink of harnesses in a nearby field where a hay cart, loaded with hand- tied sheaves, was being pulled by two cart-horses towards a winding country road. An older man, shovelling fill under a railway sleeper, looked up and leaned on his shovel.

"Ah?" A slow interrogative affirmative came in reply.

Bill, now in his sixties, still lived by the advice given by his father who had been in the Crimean War eighty years earlier; 'Never volunteer for anything,' he told him, ' wear a balaclava in winter and a cholera belt in summer and you'll live for ever.' That was the message his son remembered, even though the flannel belt and the woollen helmet his father wore in winter, covering his face and frightening the town's children, had failed to help him to live through the Great War. Bill therefore waited non-committally for the expected request for a favour. He looked under his peaked hat at Alec Coles, the younger man, who approached panting from his exertion in the heat.

They both worked for the Great Western Railway and caps were standard issue. The flannel belt Bill was wearing laced around his waist was not; but he was convinced that it prevented chills as well as cholera, even on a hot summer morning.

"Will ee gemme a pink'un?" When he was not working, and often when he was, Alec followed the horses. He held a silver threepenny bit in his hand, still in his pocket and felt its milled edge with his thumb, blackened as much from smoking cigarettes as was the rest of his hand from the tar off the wooden railway sleepers they had been replacing. He took the coin out and looked at it for some time before reluctantly passing it over to his friend when he had nodded assent. He read the Latin abbreviations round the head of King George V without comprehension and turned it over and read the date; nineteen twenty-nine.

"It's a new one," he said as he watched it leave his hand into his friend's pocket.

"It's still only worth thruppence."

"If they don't 'ave a Pink'un I'll 'ave a Citizen. An' I'll want change."

"Mean bugger."

Alec looked to see if Bill was being serious, saw his face crease into a smile and said, "You wait till I get a big win and I'll show you who's the mean bugger. But you can keep the change an' 'ave a pint o' Stroud on me if you want." He mimed fawning generosity, touching his cap with his blackened forefinger.

"Fine lot of beer I'll get for tuppence." Bill laughed and put an oil-stained jacket over his shoulder as he walked off down the railway line a short distance before stopping. "And check them points afore Cardiff's 'ere," he called back. The Cardiff to Paddington express would be pulling into Gloucester Station at eleven twenty-two and would make it there to the Charminster cutting within twenty minutes.

"I tightened them bolts like they're welded together..." Alec's protestation of a job well done was cut short by the older man.

"An' if the Newent goods comes from Cissester 'e'll 'ave to wait in Cranbourne siding till Cardiff's through. Points is on disconnect 'member an' you'll 'ave to give 'im the ol' 'eave 'o yoursel'." Hearing a steam train making heavy work of the gradient half a mile away he added, "An' if I ain't mistaken 'ere 'e comes. Better tuck 'im in quick."

Alec waved, threw the switch to direct the train from the main line to the siding and called out as Bill walked off down the line in the direction of Charminster.

"You goin' near bookie's?" He reached into his pocket, counting its contents and calculating risk.

"Na. Missus'll kill 'ee if I go there for 'ee. An' maybe me too." Bill knew his friend was spending too much in the betting shop but as a man, couldn't advise him himself and made Alec's unknowing wife the tyrant who might do so. In fact Myrtle didn't know of her husband's weakness, never being privy to information about his wages. In any case she would have been too occupied with her young family to worry about it, as long as there was enough left to pay the bills.

A few minutes passed before the engine of the goods train, spewing smoke and steam, headed into the siding together with the first three of its cars and Alec took the opportunity to go to see Fred in the signal box half a mile back down the line. Fred had a wireless and might know the early running at the Cheltenham races. Alec had put a lot more than threepence on Carrick Gold to win at eleven to two and the result mattered. If the race was on the wireless he wouldn't have to wait for the pink sports newspaper the next day to find out if he was rich.

In the signal box it was cooler out of the sun and he could no longer hear the bird high overhead. Perhaps it had stopped singing.

—

Fay Plunkett's sleep was restless. It was a hot sultry night in Gloucester in the summer of nineteen twenty-nine and she was disturbed by a confusion of dark images which filled her mind and boded ill for her mood on waking. Disjointed thoughts and pictures of irrelevant happenings appeared before her over and over again, but their very existence protected her at least in her sleep, from an overwhelming sensation of anxiety and a black depression. Otherwise this mood, lying in the deep well of her subconsciousness, had filled all of her waking hours during the past month.

That night the darkness was absolute and the air oppressive and close, as if it were crying out for the release that rain might bring. Thunder rolled over the Malvern Hills to the north and close by a mosquito's whine conjured in her dreams images and sounds of the screams of demons, these ever increasing to a roar, which woke her suddenly with a premonition of catastrophe. A train was crossing the metal bridge over the river Severn close by, rattling and clanking, its wheels vibrating against the rails in a cacophony of sound accentuated by the steam bursts driving its wheels and thrusting pistons.

Now awake, she saw a half moon shining through the one window of the apartment which she shared with her husband and now too, with her one-month-old baby girl, Anna. Jim Plunkett lay beside her in the bed snoring noisily. The blackness and hopelessness that had filled her days for the past weeks then returned, but sleep would not and she lay back on her pillow listening for the chimes of the cathedral clock, measuring time until her baby woke for feeding at daylight. Then, although the sun was clearly lighting the nearby cathedral tower, their room remained sombre inside, matching her mood. Some of the windows were still bricked up because of the window tax, leaving them in a permanent semi-darkness.

She got up to make sandwiches for her husband who was going on a business trip to London. She felt some relief about his being away, even though it would only be for a day.

—

At Gloucester station as the express train from Cardiff to London approached the up-line platform a slim man, about twenty-two years old and dressed smartly but cheaply, crossed the footbridge and checked the time of his watch against the station clock as he waited for a second class carriage. It was eleven twenty- three and the train was on time. His ticket, folded into his hat-band had been bought by his employers, Messrs. Avery and Blundstein.

He would normally travel third class but on this day he had an assignment. He carried a briefcase containing only some sandwiches and a blue package closed with a wax seal, which he knew contained five hundred new five-pound notes; payment for a deal brokered by his employers.

He sat on the up-line side of the carriage so that he could give a prearranged wave to his wife as the train left the station.

"Serve her right if I sit on the other side," he brooded when he saw that he had a compartment for himself. Things were not going well at the Plunketts'. Ever since their baby had been born, his wife had seemed angry and cried much of the time. His reaction to her distress was less than understanding or sympathetic. 'Surely she could at least try a little harder,' he often thought as he walked reluctantly home from work to their Westgate Street apartment. 'She doesn't have to work ten hours a day for a pittance, like me.' Jim Plunkett wallowed in a self-righteous and self-directed sympathy which spared little thought for others.

But it was good to get away if only for a day, so he waved as they had arranged as the train moved by and in that momentary glimpse of her, standing with their baby in front of a worn, soot- covered brick wall next to an advertisement for Bovril, he saw the picture of her which would remain with him for years to come. His wife's eyes, haunted by the hollow look of depresssion, did not confirm any warmth of feeling as she waved. He thought though that Anna smiled at him for the first time just then, as she was held in her mother's arms there at the railway station, although smuts, smoke and steam obscured a clear view of her and he could not be certain.

A train journey can often mellow the chronic anxieties of everyday life. Provided that people have the good fortune not to meet someone they know, or perhaps someone who wishes to know them, passengers can sit in solitude and yet be surrounded by a crowd of others and can daydream of what they will. They usually do.

That day Jim Plunkett was daydreaming alone in his compartment. He was not fully awake, yet not asleep either because he did notice someone walking along the railway line wearing a flat cap and carrying a jacket flung over one shoulder. He noticed the man because he was wearing one of those woollen belts that they used to wear in the army. Jim Plunkett thought then that he was glad he had not been old enough to go to war. His mind imagined what it might have been like to hear the rattle of Gatling guns and the shouts and cries of men in combat; of men going 'over the top' when the whistle was blown; of men dying in their hundreds from bullets, with gas from smoking canisters of phosgene and chlorine tearing at their eyes and lungs; of men dying alone in the emptiness of the mud of another country.

They were speeding up, the rhythm of the wheels on the rails increasing in tempo and, as they approached Charminster, he heard the whistle blown.

'What must it have been like to risk your life like that?' he wondered and was relishing the safety of the railway carriage until his imagined sound of machine-guns rattling like the train's wheels, became a palpable vibration for a fraction of time. A second later he felt a violent shaking like an earthquake and then there followed a screaming explosion of broken metal, glass and released steam, as his compartment compacted from front to back, causing a great fissure to tear transversely through the roof and down both sides. Jim Plunkett was thrown violently into the air, out through the hole in the roof, down an embankment and into a thicket where he struck his head heavily against a tree.

Dazed but still conscious, he looked up at the track above him and saw that the second class carriage, broken in the middle, was supported at each end by the carriages which had compacted it and that the central break was elevated like a bridge. Even as he watched, fire funnelled up to the top from both ends as gas from fractured pipes and cylinders used for heating, exploded and filled the air with smoke and fire. Trapped people shouted for help in the tangled metal. Some screamed in the flames. Some, already free, were helping others and trying not to see or hear those who were helplessly trapped as fire approached. He choked on the acrid fumes of tar burning on the track, but this only partly hid from his senses the horrifying smell of smoke from burned clothing and flesh mixed with the sweet scent of apples baking in the inferno of the Newent goods- train.

Jim Plunkett tried to climb the embankment to help but fell back into unconsciousness just as he saw a young man in a flat cap and baggy black pants running along the track. He was shouting out, "No, no, my God no!" He held a pink newspaper. There were tears streaming down his face.

—

Alec Coles had been listening to Fred's wireless in the signal box. The commentator's voice had risen with the excitement of the approaching finish.

"And with half a furlong to go it's Carrick Gold with Newton Clip on the outside, ahead by a short neck. And now a late challenge from Ayala in the blinkers with Ian Younghusband using the whip. If he can hold on it will be an upset for the bookies." The voice increased in speed and tone to describe the race to the finishing post, now only a few yards ahead of the field.

Alec's mental images of the race, now focused by the

radio commentator's words, transported his mind those few miles to Cheltenham. He knew the track, could picture the race and the proximity of the finishing post and could imagine the thundering hooves carrying his hopes of winning a small fortune. Then he felt a vibration through his feet on the floor of the signal box giving a confused reality to the picture in his concentrated mind.

"That'll be Cardiff," Fred said, the signal box now shaking as the express train passed.

If there are any moments in a person's life which later might be included in a collective subconsciousness of the universe, Alec Coles' contribution would have occurred at that time. The moment would stay with him for ever and he would be destroyed by it.

'That'll be Cardiff,' Alec heard and he remembered the points where he had worked that morning. They had been switched to 'disconnect' and the signal lied. The goods-train from Cirencester on its way to Newent had stopped in Cranbourne siding, 'tucked out of the way' as Bill had advised and because Alec had not switched back the points to the main line after its passage, the Cardiff to Paddington express was now following it in to oblivion at sixty miles an hour, its wheels carrying hundreds of tons of steel, wood, gas and unsuspecting humanity.

There were a few moments as the train went past while Alec collected his thoughts from their flight to the Cheltenham race-track. The memory that he had forgotten to switch the points back from the siding to the main line then struck him like a physical blow to his stomach, surging a flow of adrenalin from his gut to his fingertips. In an instant he saw that his error was final and that he could only watch while the results of his carelessness played themselves out to their inevitable conclusion before his eyes.

At the realisation of the enormity of his mistake Alec

Coles could only say, "And Carrick Gold was second." But Fred Oldsby didn't hear him. An explosive screeching crash preceded the appearance of a plume of smoke, steam, dust and metal fragments rising above Cranbourne siding a half-mile away.

—

Unlike Fay Plunkett's disturbed sleep that night, an ocean and a continent away in the Pacific Northwest region of Canada, Henry Wilson had slept well. He and his wife had paddled their canoe all the previous day and now, sleeping the sleep of the exhausted, they lay under a blanket, rested but feeling cold and uncomfortable just before dawn. The canoe, a dugout carved from a cedar log, was upturned across two rocks close above the highwater mark in Bishop's Bay, an inlet sheltered from tide and weather by surrounding mountains. Dew dripped onto his uncomplaining arm extended beyond its cover, but it otherwise protected him as well as his wife lying beside him. Martha lay in a half sleep, turning from side to side and thinking of their newly-born grandson in the south.

It had taken them six weeks to paddle north from Vancouver, crossing the Queen Charlotte Strait above Vancouver Island. They kept close inshore to avoid bad weather and then stayed in the inland waterways of the western coast where they visited friends and relatives in Soo-ma-Halt near Rivers Inlet, after the crossing past Egg Island. They also stopped to visit at Bella Bella, Bella Coola, Namu and Klemtu. Now although they could be home in less than two days, they saw that the oolichan fish were running and decided to join the other Haisla people from Kitamaat who would be heading down the Devastation Channel. They would be going towards the Kitlope river for the oolichan harvest at Wash-wash, the summer village below Keemanu, the whistling mountain.

Oolichan, small herring or smelt-like fish, rich in oil, swarm in their millions into the coastal inlets every year where their arrival is eagerly awaited by salmon, eagles and bears as well as people. Henry knew that they could probably catch up with the villagers at Rix Island and get a tow the rest of the way to Keemanu, provided that they made an early start the following morning.

The summer village was only used during the oolichan run. Its wooden buildings were dwarfed by the immense vertical rise of Keemanu, the Whistling Mountain named after the noise made by the winter's wind when it blew strongly over its snow-covered peaks and ridges. It stood by the Keemanu River which joined an inlet from the ocean ending five miles further on at the Kitlope River. Oolichan, called candle fish since they could be dried and burned like a candle because of their rich fat content, had their oil extracted at the camp in vats where they were boiled to produce oolichan grease. This delicacy was much sought after by the native peoples as far away as the Hazleton mountains. It was carried there along the oolichan trail over the mountain passes or along the Skeena river.

The night before, when they arrived at Bishop's Bay, Martha had cooked oolichan scooped from a nearby creek and the campfire still smoked from the remains of their meal.

Later that night their sleep in the quiet stillness was disturbed by a movement in the earth beneath them. It had an almost imperceptible range but reflected massive power. Lying asleep on the ground, it woke them both although they felt it for only one or two seconds and it had stopped before consciousness returned to explain it.

"It was an earthquake," Martha said.

They spoke to each other in the Haisla language.

"No," Henry laughed, "it was an old grizzly bear after our supper leftovers. Look what he did to my arm!" He held up a dew-covered wet sleeve. Martha kicked him and laughed.

"It was an earthquake." She turned to go back to sleep.

"It was that Weejit turned himself into a grizzly bear to give us a fright." Henry joked about the legendary Haisla raven figure of mischief, said to be capable of such transformations.

"It was an earthquake. I don't see ravens here. Go to sleep!"

Under the canoe Henry picked up some dried grass and twigs which he had saved there from the overnight dew. He threw them on the campfire and as the smoke turned to flames he studied the sloping arch of the canoe above his head. He thought of the time when he and his son had shaped it with an adze from a cedar log. He could see the lines made with each stroke, still visible on the inner surface from where he lay. He wished those days back again. Tom had changed after the government residential school and seemed to be angry all the time. Henry and Martha didn't understand his moods now, but at least in the schools he had learned to read and write. They both wished Tom hadn't gone to the city though, wished he wasn't angry so much, wished he would talk more and were sorry that he had left his wife before their new grandson Dave was born.

In the north-west, dawn encroaches only slowly on the night so that a faint lightening of the eastern sky behind the mountains revealed only their ridges, somberly at first and only later with more clarity. Henry could then make out rockfalls and streams in more detail at the higher levels. Below these at the treeline, around three and a half thousand feet above him, he could now make out the first outline of the forest edge as it glistened when the brightening sky behind it reflected through the morning dew on the cedars, firs and spruce trees above. Then beams of sunlight shining through these trees over to the mountains across the bay, illuminated the morning mists above them in linear patterns of blue and grey haze.

The warmth, promised early in the orange glow to the east, would take an hour or two to arrive before the sun would rise above the mountain ridge and flood into the bay where they had spent that night. Henry reached into his bag and brought out some bread and smoked salmon and put a pot on the fire to boil water from the creek.

The water of the bay, glasslike, was almost undisturbed by the slowly rising tide but an occasional ripple there hinted at the rich life hidden below the reflections of the mountains painting its surface. A crow flapped its wings noisily at the top of a nearby spruce tree and a bald eagle cried across the bay as if complaining at the delay of dawn. Patchy mists clung to the tall cedars around them and across the bay in the early light he could see mists rising from the natural hot springs at the water's edge and hanging in the trees higher up, dripping moisture to the ground. He was close to home.

Martha awoke. "It was an earthquake," she said.

Henry nodded. "Maybe," and then, "maybe Weejit or a grizzly." She threw a small pebble at him and laughed.

Henry stared at the pot as he waited for the water to boil. Then some concentric rings rippled its surface for a few seconds. A rock fell into the sea nearby making a loud splash in the early morning quiet.

"I told you. It was an earthquake."

Perhaps aware of the spirits within, they both looked into the darkness of the forest, yet to be awoken by the morning sun. They had felt earth tremors in the past and this was no different.

"Yes, it was,"Henry said softly.

—

Only a few miles to the north, but half a lifetime later in nineteen seventy-five, the fading light of a November afternoon was diminished further by grey clouds and rain driving heavily down on the previous night's melting snow. Kitamaat village on the Pacific northwest coast was preparing for winter. A yellow taxi splashed through the deep puddles scattered within the packed ice on the road. Rain and the snow now falling with it, was accentuated by the car's headlights which briefly illuminated a workshop room in a wooden cabin. This lay close to the water at the end of a road running alongside an inlet from the sea, the Douglas Channel. The taxi circled and came to a stop outside.

The town of Kitamaat was separated from Bishop Falls across the water by a saltwater inlet and on days like this one, by low cloud and poor visibility which obscured the one mile crossing to the aluminum plant and the nearby townsite.

"You got a visitor." A man with an expressionless face made the observation while the proprietor, who had also seen the taxi's arrival, attempted to shield the low light in the room, but to no avail. The visitor, a man in his sixties, well-built and upright had seen the light as he approached the cabin and had paid the taxi driver. He knocked twice firmly on the door on which a sign read: 'Jonas Davis- Wood Carver'.

Jonas intended to say that he was closed for the day. It was getting late. However the man who came in when he opened the door had a powerful presence and a friendly manner which made his planned rejection impossible.

"Late in the day I'm afraid. I won't keep you long." The visitor had an English accent and obviously anticipated the reaction he might receive.

"Come in and shut the door," Jonas said as he gestured for him to to sit down. The visitor was a big man who seemed to fill the door frame. He wore a raincoat under which could be seen a shirt and tie which looked out of place in the workshop. On his eyebrows and grey hair there were snowflakes which melted and ran down his face as he looked around the room, heated by a woodstove which crackled in one corner.

The cabin was built of logs in the style of the Pacific Northwest and there remained in it the lingering aroma of cedar and smoke. A shelf on one side was filled with model constructions of buildings, boats and bridges intricately constructed from thousands of matchsticks. On the walls there were exhibited a number of wood-carvings of very high quality.

"I'm looking for someone and wondered if you might be able to help me," the visitor said, looking at the carvings as he spoke. "Have you heard of an 'Aloisius Stubbs'?" he asked. "I'm Frank Watson, by the way. I've come from London to look for him."

Jonas shook his head and looked round at the man with the mask-like face who, sitting in one corner away from the light, had not been noticed by the visitor until he did so. There was no response.

"Did you carve this?" Watson turned to Jonas and held out a wood-carving of a salmon which he had brought with him. "It's excellent work. Look at those abalone shells and the lines of the body and fins." Jonas noticed that his enthusiasm was genuine.

"You know about carving?" he asked.

"I do some myself but I think I'll give up now. My work's the poorer for comparison with yours."

Jonas reached for the carving. "Yes. That's mine. It's signed on the back. Where did you get it?"

"It belongs to Hector Stubbs, Aloisius' brother. He's in jail." Watson walked round the carvings looking at each one carefully. "Are they for sale?"

"Most sold already," Watson heard in reply and looked disappointed.

"What about these matchstick models? Do you do those too?" Watson was fascinated by the detailed construction and appreciated the amount of work involved in them. "I might like to buy one."

"You can have one." It was Dave Wilson who spoke. He had remained in the shadow of the corner of the room until then and when he came forward Jonas introduced him. Dave offered a choice to Watson who noticed a huge scar across his left cheek and his absence of facial expression. He couldn't fully understand the meaning of the offer without interpreting Dave's expression or conversing longer and as Dave withdrew to the corner again it was Jonas who said, "He likes you, or he wouldn't give it to you. He makes them all the time."

"Thank-you, I really appreciate that. We'll talk about it again later before I go." Watson nodded to Dave in recognition of the gift he had offered and turning again to Jonas asked, "Have you ever seen this man?" He held out a photograph of a thin man with a pointed face and eyes which looked as if they belonged to a small dog.

Both Dave and Jonas nodded. "It's Kitchener," Jonas told him.

Watson had difficulty restraining a laugh. "So Aloisius Stubbs renamed himself after the Kitchener's Arms."

"What's that?"

"That was his favourite pub in the Old Kent Road until he had to leave in a hurry. Where is he now?"

"Probably dead. No one saw him after the earthquake. He worked at the dam site where it was flooded. That was nearly five years ago now." Jonas looked at Dave for confirmation as he said so. Dave nodded.

Watson thought for a moment and said, "Then I've finished what I came here for." However his policeman's mind, for that indeed it was, still wondered why Aloisius Stubbs the forger, also known as Scratchy, and now apparently, also as Kitchener, would choose Bishop Falls to live in when he was on the run.

He asked as an afterthought, "Did anyone know him well here?"

"Don't think so. No one really liked him," Jonas explained.

"He knew Harris." It was Dave's voice, unexpected from the shadow.

"Who's Harris?"

"Dead too. The earthquake. Not seen after.They found his car," Jonas took over.

"Who did Harris know here who I can talk to about him?" Watson asked.

"His wife. Maybe people at work. He kept himself to himself and didn't see many people." Jonas seemed to know about Harris but it was Dave who added, "He knew Doctor Anna."

"Is she a medical doctor? Was he a patient of hers?" Watson asked.

Dave said "Yes," and after a pause, "but he knew her from before." Jonas looked at him enquiringly and Dave stopped talking, withdrawing again to the corner.

The following day Frank Watson called on Doctor Anna to ask her if she had met Harris or Kitchener in the past. She told him that she had first seen Harris in hospital in Vancouver years before and that she was a friend of Maria, his wife. She said that she had never got to know Harris well because he had always kept a distance from people. He had no close friends.

"Harris wasn't shy or withdrawn in that sense," she told Watson. "In fact he was quite the opposite; outspoken and dominating. I wondered if he was trying to hide something and always felt uncomfortable when he was around. Kitchener was a patient of mine. He had been very ill and wasn't seen after the earthquake and the tsunami wave which came with it. Harris visited him in hospital once," she said to Watson. "That seemed strange to me at the time. I don't know why, but they just seemed to be people who were so different that I wouldn't have expected it."

Watson assumed then that these contacts were the source of Dave's suggestion of a previous acquaintance between Anna and Harris.

After talking for nearly three hours to Jonas and Dave that evening, Watson took the matchstick longhouse model out into a taxi. He liked Dave. The story he had learned was incomplete. He knew that.

The snow was falling heavily when he left and the taxi would have difficulty making it back to Bishop Falls around the winding coastal road if he had gone later. Jonas had told him that in the Haisla language, Kitamaat means 'people of the snow'. He looked past the windscreen wipers, laden with snow, to the road in front almost obscured from view. 'That's apt,' he thought. Then later, 'But who did Harris know? And why Scratchy Stubbs? Why here of all places?' The questions would keep recurring until he resolved them. It was like having to finish something already started, like a matchstick model made in fine detail which has to be completed. He looked at the longhouse model; Dave's gift, and wondered whether there might be a connection there worth following but dismissed it as too unlikely.

2

Ac as I beheeld into the eest an heigh to the sonne
I seigh a tour on a toft trieliche ymaked,
A depe dale bynethe, a dongeon therinne,
With depe diches and derke and dredfulle of sighte.
The Vision of Piers Ploughman-William Langland

A tower in a western city and thoughts of the east, some devious plans and an inquiring mind, and a death and thoughts on unforgiven mortality.

"Morning Mr. Harris. Top floor?" A uniformed elevator attendant stood aside to admit a middle-aged man who ignored him after nodding assent. Susan Meyers, accompanying her employer from the ground floor, stepped in after him and discreetly raised and then lowered her eyes a fraction, in sight only of the attendant, as she handed Harris an appointments list dated September the first nineteen hundred and fifty- six. She knew it wouldn't be a good day at the top when he ignored the list and impatiently slapped the side wall of the elevator with the back of his hand.

"Damned thing's slower every day. You, what's your name? Can't you get anyone in Vancouver to fix this thing?" Harris addressed the elevator attendant.

"I'm Tom Wilson. I'll see if the Otis people can come today." He looked directly at Harris as he spoke and it was Harris who looked away to see that they had passed the eighteenth floor and were arriving at the roof suite of offices, marked 'Harris-McQuaid. Construction Engineers'.

Her employer pushed his way ahead leaving Susan Meyers to follow, saying as he did so, "Get me the Douglas Channel File and if the minister calls tell him I'll call back when I can. But make sure he'll still be there. It's important that we talk."

Harris always made himself difficult to contact, even when he was soliciting work or a favour for himself. In fact he had developed to a high degree of finesse the knack of appearing to be giving a favour, when in fact he was receiving one. People who knew him a little, and no one knew him well, coined this as a figure of speech; a Harrisism.

"I'll fetch the file now sir. Would you like coffee?" There was no reply so she would have to bring some anyway.

By all outward evidence Richard Harris' business was successful. He employed ten draftsmen and engineers and as many office staff. At fifty-two he was now greying at the temples and gaining some weight, although without excess of it. His clothing reflected both his wealth and his indifferent taste. The latter could be seen also in his office furnishings that were expensive without style, modern without decorative embellishment and entirely functional.

From his office window he looked out at the Lions Gate Bridge which he had just crossed on his way from his home on Vancouver's North Shore. There his wife Maria kept house and worried about their son John who had just finished university in Kingston and was now an intern at Montreal General Hospital. His high-school graduation photograph was on Harris' desk. It pictured a serious youth who expressed a degree of rebellion with a boot-lace tie beneath his cap and gown.

Harris stared across to the Lions Gate Bridge, a suspension bridge high above the harbour entrance linking Stanley Park and the main city of Vancouver to the more residential area on the North Shore. His mind was on other matters. He was not an entirely happy man as could be seen by his abrupt manner and insensitivity to people around him.

"Leave it there." He indicated the desk and Susan Meyers left the file and a tray with coffee before leaving the room.

Harris looked out across the water to the bridge and returned to his reverie. Some workmen near the raised central part of the span were burning off some old paint and a plume of smoke rose into the otherwise clear morning air. In his mind he was transported back by this scene thirty years in time and many miles in distance to the Gloucestershire countryside, to a time when his life had been for ever changed. The change he had often likened in his own mind to that of a Phoenix rising from the ashes. This poetic vision of himself however he could share with no one, but it reinforced an idea he held about himself that everything he did was pre-ordained and that he was not therefore guilty of any misrepresentation or misdeeds.

Susan Meyers called on the office intercom. "Mr. Harris, it's Mr Davis on the line. He's going to Ottawa shortly. Can you talk to him?"

"Put him on." Harris, abrupt as usual in his relationship with his staff then changed his tone as he spoke to the caller. "Ah, Frank I'm glad you called. How's Mary? I hear you're off to Ottawa again. I sometimes wonder what you are up to over there. I'll have to have a word with Mary about all that I think. Look, I want to see you about the Douglas Channel project you're planning. I'd like to help. I think I can. No, don't decide now, we'll talk about it later. The bridge or the dam. We could do either, or both if it comes to that. I'll get someone up there to look it over and get some concept plans done for when you get back. If you think it might work for you we'll do some costing and go from there. Yes, of course I know it will go out to tender but I'm sure we can come to an understanding." Harris never allowed other people to interrupt him when he was talking. "We'll talk about it later. Good luck in Ottawa."

He terminated their one-sided discussion, put down the telephone and stared back at the bridge from his office window. The smoke had gone by then, but he remembered the past again and recalled the arch made from the compacted carriage, smoking in the middle and remembered Jim Plunkett, the young man who, thirty years before, had awoken from unconsciousness with a headache in a wooded thicket beneath a railway embankment. Then his waking memories were the sounds of heavy equipment lifting the broken railway carriages, the shouts of the railway crews and the moans of those still trapped four hours after the crash. These were followed by the realisation that he was lucky to be alive and had survived a major disaster. There was blood on his scalp, now congealed on his neck and hands and this had made him start from his confused state. He sat up and saw his brief case in the cleft of a tree only fifteen feet away. He was hungry and remembered that it contained some sandwiches and his mind, not yet rational amongst the surrounding death and chaos, chose the commonplace to consider. They were made from jellied eels; young eels or elvers made into sandwiches.' He thought of the eels migrating down the River Severn and across the Atlantic Ocean where they would feed and grow after an odyssey of freedom in the warm Caribbean waters before returning. He liked jellied eels.

'Freedom. Yes, freedom,' he thought. The very shape of the River Severn's estuary opening out to the Atlantic and the New World had always fascinated him. 'But, for me, how?' he had often thought and he thought the same again there, in the thicket beneath the embankment and then yet again when his eyes lit on the other package in his brief case. It was wrapped in blue paper and sealed with a wax seal. He remembered its contents and why he was there. He thought of freedom; freedom from the boredom of his work as a clerk with little prospect of promotion, freedom from his failing marriage and the wife he thought he had loved but knew that he did so no longer and freedom from the responsibility of the baby girl with her red hair and the ugly red birthmark behind her ear.

Jim Plunkett looked at the blue packet in a moment of indecision. Some railway workers were moving closer to him, searching alongside the line and his thoughts were interrupted by their words as they approached. Something stopped him from calling out that he was nearby. He couldn't tell what it was. One of the workers, his face coloured a strange mixture of black and white from the oil and tar smeared on a complexion made ashen by the work he had been doing, spoke to a newcomer to the crash site.

"The fire burned right through these two carriages and anyone inside will have gone up in smoke. We'll never know who was there or how many, poor buggers. There's just ashes and steel left now."

'Just ashes and steel.' Jim Plunkett thought about it. He was free to decide. The question was black and white; the answer yes or no. He looked again at the blue package in his hand and chose then to remain there where he was until nightfall, beneath the broken train, the carriages and twisted rails and the collective grief of hundreds of people.

The human mind has a great propensity for rationalisation and self-delusion. Perhaps Harrisisms first occurred at that time, for Jim Plunkett elected to enter a life of lies, deceit and selfishness which he was able to rationalise in his mind into a conception of one of doing good for others.

Jim Plunkett became Richard Harris.

—

Richard Harris remembered then, all those years later, how he had had to change his identity and had made his way to London with sympathetic truck-drivers concerned about the narrow escape he described for them. He had been directed through a pub in Camberwell Green, to a flat close to the green itself where he was able to move in with no questions asked, when he paid the appropriate rent in advance.

It was a basement apartment with some light in the day time filtering from small street-level glass blocks on one side, but otherwise unlit. Water ran down one of the walls where some old wallpaper hung freely from a drier area above and mice and rats had chewed the pieces that had fallen to the darkened concrete on the floor. There was an outside toilet shared with other occupants of neighbouring flats and this, having no light, could be used at night only by leaving the door open to allow the light from a street light to shine in over a wall. The kitchen included a gas stove but there was no refrigerator and a cold water tap over the sink was the only source of water. It was an inauspicious start for the Richard Harris he was soon to become.

"You 'ere again then?, Don't you 'ave a 'ome to go to?" The thin man with a pointed face had been in the Red Lion's public bar on several occasions when Jim Plunkett spent his evenings there to avoid spending time with the rats at his flat. "Will you join me for a drink? Aloisius Stubbs at your service. What'll it be?" Aloisius had seen that Jim had no obvious shortage of funds yet had discovered that he lived in a very cheap flat. He must, he knew, have something to hide, something that no doubt could be turned to his own advantage.

Jim Plunkett was pleased to have any company at this point and had been beginning to wonder about the wisdom of the path he had chosen for himself. Caution advised that he use an alias after his disappearance and he answered, "I'll have a stout and bitter and thankyou for it," and added awkwardly. "I'm John Smith. Pleased to meet you."

Aloisius Stubbs smiled. He was sure he would know if someone was really called John Smith and his years of training as a petty criminal specialising in forgery told him that this man was not. After four pints of draft bitter mixed with stout, Jim failed a test when he didn't respond to an off-hand question directed to 'John' from Aloisius as he looked past him at the wall. It was time for Aloisius to make his move.

"You know, it's no' every day you meet someone who you take to righ' away but oi think we will ge' along really well." Stubbs spoke with a Cockney accent. "In fact oi think oi can be of some 'elp to you if you so require it."

"Help? Why? What for?" Jim Plunkett looked uncertainly at the other.

"'elp to make you a real John Smith if that's wha' you wan' a be. It migh' cost you a bi' o' the ready bu' you'll be pleased I guarantee."

It was Stubbs who persuaded Jim Plunkett to take on the name of Richard Harris whose family had committed him to the Maudsley Hospital up the hill from Camberwell Green. He was unlikely to be discharged. Later, a visit under Aloisius' direction to Somerset House in the Strand enabled Jim Plunkett to obtain a new birth certificate in the name of Richard Harris. Books with names and birthdates covered the shelves on the walls and to look through all of the Harris's would have taken most of the day. However knowing the date of birth of the unfortunate man in hospital enabled him to find the birth entry quickly and for half a crown he obtained his new identity.

Half a stolen crown for a new identity! This Phoenix' rebirth was based on questionable morality but the new Richard Harris was determined to make good.

Two weeks later, at the Red Lion, Aloisius brought in a passport in the name of Richard Harris. It indicated that the owner was an engineer.

"All my own work," he said proudly. "By the way my friends call me Scratchy. It's because of the fine pens I use when I work. I'm afraid they're a bi' hexpensive."

Harris paid up and moved north of the river Thames. He didn't want to leave a trail that anyone might follow.

With a more salubrious apartment and a new suit, Harris later met Maria whose father worked at the Portuguese embassy in London. She was impressed by his apparent wealth and his occupation as an engineer and soon agreed to marry him and together they moved later to Christchurch on the English south coast where their son John was born. There Harris learned about Bailey bridges; temporary transportable bridges for emergency uses. It was this knowledge which helped him later in wartime when he enlisted in the Royal Electrical and Mechanical Engineers and where he learned the basics, and only the basics, of bridge construction. He went with the Allies through the Normandy landings and then on across Germany, repairing or building temporary Bailey bridges across rivers to enable the armies to move across the continent.

As is often the case in wartime, he found himself promoted rapidly and developed a self-aggrandizing approach to his work which seemed to impress most people and which even persuaded him himself that he was as good at his work as any qualified engineer might be. The certificate of qualification cost a little from his London acquaintances, but by these means he didn't have to face the tedious and unpleasant necessity of studying and taking examinations to obtain it.

—

A sixty year old man reached for his calendar while eating breakfast in his home on Clapham Common, London. He lived alone. Cereal and tea were on the menu that morning as he only cooked once a day. Frank Watson leaned the calendar carefully against a model of a longhouse made from matchsticks and thought of Dave in Bishop Falls. He always planned ahead and tried to associate events in his mind both from the past and from the present. The calendar was for December nineteen hundred and seventy- six.

"Harris knew Scratchy Stubbs before he went to Canada. Perhaps he helped him in a time of need; professional need that is." He spoke to himself often when he was alone.

"Let me see now." He listed on a piece of paper; money, passport, birth certificate. "That'll do to start with."

He lifted his telephone and started making calls.

—

Richard Harris protected himself from any possible questioning directed from an uneasy conscience with rationalisation and denial.

'Of course I took the money after the train crash, but what was it to be used for in the first place?' he asked himself. 'If someone pays a large amount like that in cash it must be for something they don't want a record made of afterwards; something illegal. I did well to stop it before the process was repeated and no doubt will be rewarded for doing so one day.' He concluded that what he had done was praiseworthy and, in that he had had to leave his wife and child to effect the good deed, it reflected ill on his employers and a moral righteousness on his own part. That they were responsible for what had happened to him he was certain, but he was unable to confront them with the guilt he projected onto them lest his own part in the matter might become known. He therefore decided that he would forgive them.

This thinking, born from the generous heart he thought he owned, was part of Harris' survival strategy in the early years of his deception. Later, based on the self-affirmation that he was doing good for the community with the business he had started, there resulted in him an arrogant persona which recognised in itself a moral superiority over others. This was however anxiously seeking any hint from those same 'lesser beings' that they might be questioning his motives or his past. As a result Harris became known for having a bad temper. Employees quickly learned that he was never to be crossed, never to be questioned and never to be ridiculed, even in jest. Therefore, he never could be loved. Therein lay his weakness. He was alone within his world, alone within his family and alone at work.

With the passing years this solitude ate at his composure, weakened his drive and above all increased his vulnerability to self-accusation and that, being intolerable for him, he could only overcome with a hardening of irrational denial and projection on to others of his own weaknesses.

As a wife, Maria's position was unenviable. She became the object of his disordered behavioural thinking and eventually, in order to protect herself from his angry outbursts, she steered conversations away from such matters as Harris' past life, qualifications, childhood or parentage and in so doing became, vicariously, part of that behavioural pattern herself. She was now part of his secret; but only a small part, for he had never talked to anyone, including her, about his life before nineteen hundred and twenty-nine.

Twenty six years after that date, later in the day he had gone up in the elevator to the top floor of his offices with Susan Meyers and Tom Wilson, Harris found himself in hospital.

"Tell me how it happened." The intern took notes as she spoke to him. He had been too ill on arrival two hours earlier to take any kind of history from him.

"I had this sudden pain in the left side of my chest; severe, as if I had been run over by a steam- roller. It spread to my left arm and up to the left side of my lower jaw. I felt my pulse racing in my ears and then woke up in hospital here. That's about it," Harris told her.

"Has it happened before?" she asked him.

"No. Well, not like that, but it has come on a couple of times when I've been out walking, but then it went away by itself."

The intern wrote down 'some pre-infarction angina' and asked, looking at the brown stain on his thumb, "How many cigarettes a day?"

"Twenty or so."

"More likely the 'so' I think." She nodded towards his hand.

"Your parents, did either of them…". She was interrupted by Harris' emphatic, "No," and she looked questioningly at him, but as no further explanation was forthcoming she felt that she had to leave that line of enquiry when she noticed a speeding up of his heart rate recorded on the monitor at his bedside.

"Exercise?" she asked him.

"None really."

The intern knew that here was the classical heart-attack victim. He was going to have to change a lot if he wanted to live; that is, if he survived this time. She noticed also that there was something about Harris which she felt was familiar, but she couldn't recall seeing him before. She had spoken to Susan Meyers who came with him in the ambulance and who told her the little she knew about him

"I found him on the floor, lying on his gold cigarette case. There were files scattered around him on the carpet. He'd knocked the telephone off the hook as he fell and that's what told me something was wrong." Susan Meyers had gone back down in the elevator this time with Harris on a stretcher. She didn't raise and then lower her eyes then in Tom Wilson's direction, even slightly.

—

Across a hospital ward, curtains had been drawn hurriedly around a bed. Unable to sleep himself, someone had seen a patient slump forward from his elevated bed-head and had pressed the call bell at three-fifteen in the morning.

He now heard orders whispered urgently and saw shadows thrown onto the curtains from the enclosed circle of anxious staff, giving a fleeting impression only of the frenetic activity within. Then, more equipment was dragged under them, more staff, laboratory workers, a physician and a medical student arrived. Through the screening he saw an occasional glimpse of the patient there, his chest bared, tubes in his throat, a respirator, intravenous fluid lines and then a defibrillator, used after urgent whispers of warning prior to its discharge, to avoid the shock being grounded by the staff themselves instead of the patient.

The whispering then became louder, more insistent, until there was a collective realisation and a smothered silence followed behind the screens, telling of the unspoken ending.

Other people in the ward, awoken by the disturbance, tried to look away or to pretend that they were asleep or hadn't noticed as they tried to respect the last privacy of the man they had joked with at supper-time the previous evening.

The staff left one by one, looking to the front, avoiding other patient's glances, as if denial might negate the failure they felt in the face of the finality of death. Feelings of failure, self-questioning and even guilt showed on their faces, brought on by this ultimate terminal inevitability for all of humankind.

The intern left to talk to the patient's wife who had arrived from her home as quickly as her arthritis permitted. They went into a side room and closed the door.

—

Richard Harris couldn't sleep. That he had been admitted earlier in the day with the same diagnosis as the patient who had died certainly concentrated his mind on his own mortality. He always had a feeling of unease about himself; not about death but about his own identity, brought about by the life of fraud and deceit which he was living. This unease was accentuated by the closeness and unexpectedness of the death which he had just witnessed and which he had all but experienced himself earlier. He went over the day in his mind and remembered his soliloquy in his office about his past life. He had recalled the train crash, but this time had allowed himself to dwell on what might have been; on his first wife and the baby he had left twenty six years before. It was then that the pain had started.

Harris had no religious affiliation. He had been brought up as a Catholic. Church attendance was expected, but contraception was not he thought wryly as he recalled his first wedding's hurried preparation. He was now uncommitted; an agnostic; a Laodicean.

"In any case," he thought, "who would want a thieving bigamist, who's living a life which is a panoply of deceit and lies, to be a member of their Church?" and he surprised himself with this self-admission, brought about by his present circumstances. Age was weakening his denial and a hint, or perhaps more than a hint, of his own mortality then made him look back in discomfort at what he had been throughout his life.

"You still awake? You'll need your rest you know." A medical student walked by looking tired and still trying to grasp the significance of what he had just witnessed for the first time.

"I'm in for six weeks. Total rest," Harris reminded him. "They even have to feed me so that I don't overdo it, so I'll get rest don't you mind." He sounded thoughtful.

"This is the nineteen fifties," the student told Harris proudly. "You get modern treatment and you get better." He stopped, looked to where the curtain remained closed around the bed down the ward and smiled awkwardly at Harris. He was already part of the delusion that man could overcome all illness and, who knows, live forever.

"We can pretend things and go on pretending them until

we believe them ourselves," Harris heard himself saying, "but it doesn't make them true." 'Can this really be me saying this?' he thought to himself, and then aloud, "They're all pretending to themselves. Don't get me wrong. They all think they can do it. They mean well. In fact without them where would I be today?" He gave an expansive gesture.

"Did you know then that he...?" The student looked across at the closed curtains. He thought that they looked in the semi-darkness of the ward like a crypt in a medieval cathedral with railings and stone carvings hiding the statuary within.

"Died?" Harris finished the sentence for him and then answered it, "Yes."

"Did they come and tell you, to explain?"

"No. No one came. They just left."

"Everyone's upset." The student thought he should explain; support the home team.

"Yes." Then a pause, the electric clock on the wall humming quietly, the only sound for half a minute.

"But they should tell you," the student said and thought that they should talk to him and to each other about it as well. Something had happened. It had happened throughout mankind's time on earth, was timeless, part of his existence, yet he didn't understand it; feared it even.

Harris knew why. "They don't know what to say. It's better to say nothing at four o'clock in the morning rather than meaningless platitudes isn't it?"

"I guess..." The student didn't sound convinced.

Another pause followed; the electric clock like a third presence reminding them of time, ongoing forever.

"Are you...?" The student hesitated and looked at Harris.

"Afraid of death?" Harris had spent years anticipating

peoples questions before they were spoken. He did it unconsciously so that he would have more time to formulate a reply without giving away his secret.

"No. In fact when my time comes I shan't mind at all. I'll find it interesting really, finding the truth at last. 'Is there an afterlife?' and that sort of thing." Harris seemed to have no doubt that if there were, he would be included with the participants. "There are a few things I need to do first though so I'm in no hurry." He paused and then added quickly, "Well we all have some catching-up to do," and in so saying dismissed the topic lest he be asked what the 'few things' were. For some reason as he said this, his mind presented himself with a picture of a young man in a confessional box in a Gloucestershire Church.

Their conversation was interrupted by a side-door opening at the end of the ward. Light flooded the room briefly and the student moved toward it, unsure whether he should intrude.

3

Ac on a May morwenynge on Malverne Hilles,
Me bifel a ferly, of Fairye me thoghte.
I was wery forwandred and wente me to reste.
The Vision of Piers Ploughman. William Langland

A parting sorrow and unrecognised meeting, exhaustion and memories of a Malvern storm, dreams of the future, a shock in the present and a look back to the past.

"Fred knew it would be soon. He told me himself yesterday. He seemed to have had some kind of an idea that he was close to the end even though he seemed to be getting over it all." The deceased patient's wife seemed to have expected the news. She was certainly well prepared for it when the intern talked to her. They both stood now in the doorway, their shadows reaching into the ward along the beam of light stretching across the floor almost as far as the bed with the closed curtains, their voices lowered in recognition of the presence of the incomprehensible.

"The truth is that I expected to be sending him home before the end of the week so he certainly seemed to have some sort of a premonition about it. He was such a nice man. He kept everyone laughing all the time. We did everything we could." The intern, her empathy with the widow's loss combining with her own professional uncertainty in the face of death, now felt a need to explain, to be exonerated from a self-perception of responsibility for the failure evidenced by the body behind the closed curtains.

The older woman reached over. There were tears in her eyes but she touched the intern's hand and said, "It's alright," as she left the doorway and walked along the path of light to the curtains in the shadows. They parted to admit her for her last goodbye with her companion of fifty three years.

"He'll just have to wait for me for a while," she said to the medical student as she left. "He was always so impatient. It'll do him good." He thought that she looked a little straighter, as if her arthritis was not so bad as before. But it would be more than two years before her life could move on; before acceptance would overcome loss.

The intern would always remember that touch on her hand; a recognition of her needs by someone herself in the extreme of grief. Such a gesture was worthy of that.

She sat at the nursing station at the end of the ward, making notes, tiredness slowing her hand. It was the work for which she had trained during the past seven years, physically exhausting as well as emotionally draining. Unconsciously she brushed back her hair with her hand. It was auburn, curled and full and now swept back it revealed a small red birthmark behind her ear.

Richard Harris saw the movement, saw the birth mark without taking notice of it, and as he looked at her he thought she seemed familiar but couldn't remember where they might have met.

She finished the record she was writing and signed it, 'Anna Plunkett'. Neither of them knew at that time the association which existed between them and their lives and it would have been of great interest to Richard Harris if his thoughts had been able to accompany those of his daughter on their journey back through time where they went that night in her room, when sleep would not come to allow them rest. At times such as this Anna would look back at her past life as if observing it through someone else's eyes. She did this often when unable to sleep. It allowed her to distance herself from the reality of her memories so that she could recall unhappy times without pain and also bring back to consciousness the happier moments that gave her pleasure. The memory she recalled that night was brief but cherished; bitter and sweet.

She saw in her mind a day in nineteen hundred and thirty eight. It was late August in Gloucestershire. The year had been wet and harvests delayed and the complaints of the local people had reached such a degree that even strangers would approach each other to talk, as if to look for reassurance from outside their own circle, that the order of things had been changed only for the time being and that this was not indicative of doomsday. In fact the real threat they would have to face was to come from an altogether different source the following year, but this was not known to most of the people walking to Barton Fair across an old stone bridge over the River Severn from Westgate Street, near Gloucester cathedral.

In particular, the present could be seen to have much more immediacy for a nine year old girl, accompanied by an older woman, perhaps her mother. They seemed to have difficulty in keeping up with the rest of the crowd making its way over the bridge, which they crossed with an air of excitement to an open field bordered on two adjacent sides by a railway and the river. There, bright lights, music and coloured tents signalled that Barton Fair had usurped the territory of a herd of Herefordshire cattle, now lowing disconsolately in the far corner of the field.

A full moon was starting to wane but its light later on would be welcomed when breaks in the clouds hinted that the weather might be changing for the better. However the day had been hot and sultry and low rumbling over the Malvern Hills to the north and flashes of lightning in the distant early darkness warned that summer had yet to declare its presence with certainty. The older woman was now twenty yards behind her daughter whose face, alive with expectation and excitement about the scenes ahead of her, was so taken out of herself by them that she had forgotten her mother walking slowly behind.

"Wait Anna." She was wheezing, short of breath as she called again, "Come back with that torch. You'll have to slow down for me. I can't see where I'm walking." The voice was thin, as was its owner Fay Plunkett, who was poorly dressed with clothes repaired several times and whose shoes were worn down and scuffed. Her complexion was white; not the elective pallor of a wealthy woman, but that brought on by chronic ill-health and poverty. This showed also in a thinness of her features, particularly where the greater prominence of her upper cheek bone accentuated her hollow cheeks below. Her breathing, wheezing and faster than usual, would not support a voice loud enough to penetrate her daughter's excited concentration.

"Anna!" she called again, but this time her voice was lost in the loud rumble of a train crossing the metal railway bridge over the River Severn on its way from South Wales. It was carrying coal, steel, guns and more trucks for the army. She stopped, holding on to a wooden post supporting a barbed wire fence, put there to keep cattle from falling into the river. She remembered a visit to Barton Fair nine years previously, the night before her husband died. There were no guns or trucks then on the trains, just people, goods and apples. She looked down at the water, black except where the moon was reflected within. An eddy made by some night creature close to the bank, caught her eye. She watched for it to come up to the surface again. It did not. She stared at the blackness; pictured the creatures within. A feeling of horror and revulsion overcame her but she stayed holding on as if transfixed.

"Mummy, did you say something?" The mother looked round, surprised, when her child's voice called.

"Oh yes, I need the torch. Stay with me now Anna will you?"

"Hold my hand then. Are you alright?" her daughter asked anxiously.

"Yes."

Anna stayed with her then. She knew she was needed there when her mother looked like that.

"Come on then." Anna pulled on her hand. The carousel beckoned from the centre of the fair with jangling music and white horses going up and down carrying excited children past coloured mirrors. Some were holding ice creams, toffee apples or candy floss, others holding on for their lives lest they might fall. She could see the big wheel, bumper cars, clowns and swings. She could hear the shouts and screams of laughter above the sound of electric generators and coarsely amplified music. It was all happening at once there in the field, in the lights, away from the darkness.

Over the bridge the bells of the Norman cathedral sounded the half hour past nine o'clock. from the great stone tower reaching up into the darkening sky. The tower, still dimly lit above, reflected the last rays of the setting sun from a weather vane pointing to the west. Anna still remembered that final glint reflected from the evening light; a random image, perhaps irrelevant. Such are memories, at times evanescent pictures of uncertain reality or importance, and at other times matters of great consequence.

Her mother looked again at the river, shuddered, and allowed herself to be led away by a small hand pulling her away towards the life in the crowds in the field beyond the cathedral's tower.

Voices called out as they passed, "See the sheep with five legs, tuppence only. The fattest woman in the world and the smallest man, threepence. Knock down the coconut and its yours, five balls for tuppence. Shoot the ducks off the shelf, fish and chips, acrobats, hall of mirrors, ghost train, jellied eels..." Fay Plunkett remembered again that time nine years before. He had liked jellied eels.

The sadness of afflicted people forced to exhibit themselves for a living was apparent to the nine year old girl. When she saw a man with the bone shortening achondroplasia Anna smiled at him, but she thought then that he looked even more sad and she was glad when they left for the next attraction. Outside some Gypsies were dancing and playing music on drums and violins. The rhythm of their music increased in tempo slowly and deliberately, the melody repeating as it became louder and faster when more people joined in with dancing, clapping and stamping their feet. The Gypsies wore bright clothes of reds, blues and greens. Their caravans and horses, symbols of freedom and a carefree life when seen from the perspective of a nine year old girl, told of travelling to exotic places and lives of permanent excitement.

Fay Plunkett, oblivious almost to her surroundings as tiredness brought on by illness and depression took hold of her, was just aware of a young girl dancing in the middle of the grass in front of the music- makers. The child was lost in the rhythm of the music. She wore a scarf on her head which followed her movements as she stamped her feet, swayed and waved her arms, driven by the rhythm of the dance. Her dress flowed out as she pirouetted, her pigtails flying from beneath her green scarf.

'She's got knickers like the ones I made for our Anna from those kitchen curtains,' Fay Plunkett thought to herself and remembered then that she had not had enough elastic for the legs so that when she saw the design of her curtains calling her every time the girl pirouetted she was reminded that she had not been able to afford it. It was only then when she realised that it was Anna out there with her stove-pipe pants in the midst of the dancing, the music and in the world of people she thought were all happy except herself.

The drums and violins reached a climactic crescendo just as raindrops began to fall. Thunder rolled nearby and a lightning flash almost simultaneously told that a storm was upon them. The crowd moved toward the stone bridge. Anna stood still, not wanting to move, rain now running from her green scarf and from her smiling face as she looked upwards to the lowering clouds. She felt then as if she didn't want to move ever again and wanted that moment to stay with her always. It was then her mother's turn to come to her and to gather her up into her arms and her worn coat and to take her home. They crossed back over the stone bridge and as they did so, another train from Wales crossed the metal railway bridge close by making a vibration which shook the nearby walkway they were crossing.

"It's like an earthquake," Anna looked up in her excitement to her mother and continued, "we read about them at school. But they don't happen here; just in other countries."

Fay Plunkett was too ill to get out of bed the next day and the doctor came. She had to go to the infirmary so that Anna was sure she would die. She only knew of two other people who had gone there and they had both died.

—

"So what will you do when you grow up?" the doctor asked Anna sympathetically the next day, knowing her precarious social circumstances if her mother's pneumonia failed to improve.

"I'm going to be a farmer," she told him. She was fascinated by the straight lines and patterns which ploughmen carved from the green fields as red-brown furrows were turned from the earth by the plough. The horses, straining in their harnesses always seemed strong, reliable and uncomplaining. She liked horses. Anna had thought after watching them working one day that, 'a ploughman's life was certain, ordered and in control. They worked hard and were effective and you could see what they had done. They were effective, that's what ploughmen were.' Even when she was only nine years old, she felt a need to do something with her life which would be worthwhile.

"You could be a doctor and help people when they're sick, like your mother," the doctor told her. Perhaps he had recognised Anna's precocious understanding of her mother's needs and seen the supportive role played by this nine year old girl in dealing with her mother's prolonged depressive illness when there was no husband to do it in her place.

Anna had never seen a woman who was a doctor and couldn't imagine such a thing. "I'll be a farmer, I think," she answered him.

"I'm sure you'll be a very good one."

Anna had come to the hospital just before the 'crisis' when her mother's temperature was at its highest. Death from pneumonia was common in those days and that point in the illness known as the 'crisis' occurred when the temperature and sepsis reached a level where a patient would either succumb to the overwhelming infection spreading from the lungs, or would slowly recover, with the fever dropping rapidly when the immune system took control. There were then no antibiotics available to help. Anna's mother at this point was pale, sweating and incoherent and her strange words were frightening for a child to hear. The neighbour who had brought Anna that day, was crying.

"Don't worry, she'll be alright," Anna had told her and when, the next morning, the temperature had started to drop, she thought, 'Perhaps I'll be a doctor after all; one who has horses and just ploughs sometimes,' and later, in bed that night, a further soliloquy; 'I'll travel around the world like the Gypsies and dance every day and do whatever I want to and not listen to other people if I don't agree with them. And I'll learn to make those poor people at the Fair better, and I'll make people who are sad feel happy again.' She thought again of her mother in the infirmary as she fell asleep and dreamt of cotton wool and thermometers, of the smell of disinfectant, and then the feeling of rain and dancing and of pictures of horses and people and lights and darkness and ploughmen.

Nearly six hundred years before Anna's sleep that night a poet, William Langland, wrote of a ploughman who walked out in the Malvern Hills 'in a somer seson when soft was the sun'. He observed the idiosyncracies and hypocracies of the world of people around him as he travelled and saw, in his mind's eye, the world as a 'fair field full of folk' lying between the darkness of the nether regions below and the towers above of heavenly cities of light.

It was a storm from the Malvern Hills which dropped its soft rain on Anna's face that day at Barton Fair. When she grew up she became a physician, not a ploughman as she had hoped at first, but like Piers the Ploughman she did observe the human condition around her, both in others and in herself, as she travelled life's journey.

—

A nineteen seventy-six calendar still leant against the matchstick longhouse model in Frank Watson's kitchen. Rain beat against the window and washed London's soot and grime from the leaves of the plane trees around Clapham Common. Their branches, stunted by regular pruning, didn't reach far enough to provide cover for the boys running to escape the downfall from their game of football. Frank Watson, picked up the telephone as soon as it rang.

"I've got some of the information you wanted sir," he heard. "Richard Harris, at least the one born on the day you told us, apparently died in nineteen hundred and thirty at the Maudsley Hospital. Funny thing is that he got married the next year so something's up somewhere. Oh, and we checked with Petty France. He got a passport in nineteen forty- five. Didn't stay dead for long it seems."

"Thankyou Roberts. I'll be in touch."

Things were becoming decidedly interesting for the policeman.

A London Transport double-decker bus splashed into the inevitable puddle by the bus stop outside, its characteristic engine's noise not noticed by Watson as he was so accustomed to it being there in the background of his life. He couldn't sleep when there was a bus strike since it was the absence of the sound which was abnormal after all the years he had lived there.

A man, who looked as if he might be about the age when he would start his pension, stepped the three paces from the bus stop to Watson's door and knocked tentatively.

"Come in Hector and sit yourself down." Watson opened it to admit Hector Stubbs who had been released from Wormwood Scrubbs two days before. He had accepted Watson's invitation to call round to talk about Aloisius, his missing brother.

—

“What’s this then? Some people’ll do anything to get attention won’t they?” Two days after his father’s admission to hospital, John Harris approached his bedside, affecting a light tone when he saw that the older man’s patience was strained to its limit by his enforced rest.

“Had to get time to read a bit I guess,” Harris said, nodding toward a seat at his bedside for his son and then adding, “How did you get here so soon?”

“DC3 to Toronto, then on to Winnipeg, then Calgary and now here. I was lucky with connections. Cost a bit though.” He held out an open hand and smiled.

“Better see your mother about that. I’m not allowed to do anything. There has to be some advantage to being in hospital.” Harris had a rueful expression.

Did you really have a heart attack?" his son asked.

“They called it a myocardial infarction but I think it was all a fuss about nothing.” Harris had lived with denial all his life and this one was easy for him now that he was feeling better.

A young woman in a white coat came into the ward. “There’s the doctor. You can speak their language can’t you? Go and ask her if I can go home now.”

John Harris looked across at the intern as she visited a patient on the other side of the ward. She looked familiar he thought but knew at the same time that he hadn’t seen her before. He wouldn’t have soon forgotten a woman so attractive. He walked over to her.

“I’m Richard Harris’ son. I’m an intern at Montreal General and have come from back east to see him. I wonder if you can tell me how he is. He’s likely to try to leave as soon as he can so I’ll see if I can persuade him to stay.”

"Anna Plunkett," she introduced herself. "I'm pleased to meet you. We're going to have to work on him together to get him to stay."

"I'm John Harris. I'll see what I can do to help. How is he anyway?"

"Well he's certainly not the most accepting of patients." Her tone reflected the degree of understatement she was using.

"I'll bet he's the worst. Was it a bad one?"

"He can see we are talking about him so I'm sure he won't mind if I show you his cardiogram." She looked across at Harris who gestured towards the door when she did so and looked questioningly in her direction. "Your father had a big anterior infarct. Look, there was definite S-T elevation right across his chest leads when he came in. He was in shock and we had to use sympathetics to keep his pressure from going down into his boots. He's lucky to have done as well as he has and to be here to be able to complain at all."

"I'll tell him. He'll stay." The younger Harris' emphatic statement ended with an uncertain edge as he saw his father's impatient enquiring look.

"That'll help us. What are you doing in Montreal now?" Anna asked.

"I'm a surgical intern right now. I'm doing obstetrics after that. Then, who knows? How about you?"

"Psychiatry, perhaps anaesthesia and then General Practice. How long are you planning to stay? I get the feeling I'll need some moral support if your father's going to stay in for six more weeks." Anna looked across at the elder Plunkett who appeared more agitated as he waited for their conclusion.

"I'm here for two weeks now. I took my annual leave as I can't go travelling across the country too often for obvious reasons." John Harris remembered that he had to ask his mother for the air-fare he had borrowed. "By the way, your name, Plunkett, sounds French, so where did you get the accent?"

"It probably was French once but as you guessed, I'm English. I'm from Gloucester." Anna told him and thought to herself as she spoke, 'It's strange but I feel as if I've seen him somewhere before. But I can't think where it must have been.'

"Gloucester, that's where Edward Jenner came from. The smallpox man. I'm glad he didn't practice on me but it all worked out for the best in the end though didn't it? I've got an old book about him. I collect old books. Its a sort of hobby." John Harris found Anna easy to talk to.

Anna remembered the statue of Edward Jenner outside the infirmary where her mother died and she too had an interest in antique books and thought to herself how unusual it was to find someone with the same career who also shared common interests and who had a familiarity which she couldn't explain.

It was Harris who might have explained it; that Anna was his son's half-sister. But he was unlikely to do so just then as he had not yet recognised the intern who was looking after him and when he did, he would have to keep hidden from them anything which would lead to the secret of his past being exposed.

Richard Harris found the days in hospital uninteresting and interminable. The boredom of enforced incarceration wore on his limited patience and was relieved only by the arrival of barely interesting meals, visitors, usually his wife Maria or son John, and the completion of the daily nursing sheet. 'Temperature?, bowels?, respiratory rate?'

'Why is that always twenty per minute and not nineteen or twenty one he wondered? I must be a very regular sort of person.' Maria came most days with John although his son missed a couple of days during the two weeks and Harris noticed in passing that those days were the ones when Anna was off duty. He decided not to ask about it but his mind, having little else to do, wondered if the facts might have some association.

Harris' time of relaxation came to an abrupt end soon after however and that particular possible association was a major cause of his early departure from his hospital bed; not because he was considered cured, but because of a major threat to the secret of his past life. Harris suffered a shock to his equanimity which caused him to discharge himself from the hospital despite the seriousness of his illness and against the advice of his medical care-givers.

"This is Doctor Franks." It was Anna who introduced the new intern to Harris. "He's taking over from me now that I've finished here. I've told him you're a difficult patient and that he has to keep you in for another four weeks, or else.!" She smiled as she said this, trying to make light of the fact that she knew he was becoming increasingly impatient and unlikely to stay the course of his treatment.

"I'm moving on to another job now. Perhaps I'll see you again sometime? Good luck with the rest of your stay here."

She thought it was unlikely that their paths would cross in the future and Harris assumed that her comment was purely a matter of polite conversation, but he was to recall it with alarm later that evening. He was sorry she was leaving. There was that familiarity he felt about her which had been cemented by her ongoing care during the first two difficult weeks of his illness. He was not easily able to express gratitude but surprised even himself when he heard himself saying, "Thank-you for all your help," as she moved on to the next patient with Doctor Franks.

At seven o'clock that evening Harris was visited by his son who brought a book for him to read.

"It's called 'Magic Mountain' by Thomas Mann, and if you think you have troubles you should read this. It's about a man who has to stay in hospital for years. No it's not a horror story; it's literature." John smiled. Harris looked morose.

"Thank-you. I think." He took the book holding it as if it might cause him an injury and placed it carefully down on the other side of his bedside locker. "By the way," he said as he did so, "did you know that Doctor Anna's leaving? It's a funny thing but I never found out what her surname was."

"It's Plunkett. Unusual name isn't it. She comes from Gloucester in England. I knew she was leaving, and Dad, I have something I have to tell you. It's great news."

Chance and circumstance are responsible for much misunderstanding when their paths cross in a complex social world and this time they created a confusion of considerable magnitude. John Harris hadn't told his father before then that he was engaged to be married, in case it upset him in the critical stage of his illness when he would learn that his son was to marry someone from a very different background from his own. Harris associated Anna with the news he was about to hear and looked cornered, even frightened as he responded, "Well, what's this great news then?" He seemed guarded and introspective about this conversation with his son, almost as if he were threatened by it.

"I've got engaged," his son said simply, in turn uncertain about the reaction he was seeing in his father's face.

Harris visibly shrank back into the bed he occupied. He assumed wrongly that his son had unknowingly become engaged to his half- sister, Anna and this news, coming on so soon after his own realisation that she was in fact his daughter now living in Vancouver, required all the subterfuge that he could muster to avoid giving himself away. His mind, racing ahead of circumstance and events to pre-emt with lies and deceit the problems he might face if his secret became known, now found itself unexpectedly at checkmate.

His face, usually somewhat highly coloured, at first suffused brighter and then went pallid. He seemed to gasp, as if short of air. The intern was called and the resident came to see the new electrocardiogram being taken in response to Harris'reaction.

"He's got a lot of P.V.Cs. but no real evidence of new damage." The resident examined Harris and showed John the extra beats on the electrocardiogram which had shown up in response to anxiety. "They're not a sign of another heart attack. I think he'll be all right, but the problem now is that he insists on leaving. He's signed himself out. You understand that we can't stop him if he wants to go, but at the same time we can't be responsible for whatever might happen to him." The resident emphasised the word 'whatever'.

So Harris went home four weeks early. He shut himself in his room and was visited only by Maria. He stayed there for a week, sleeping only fitfully and at the end of that time, once he had wrestled with the realisation of what had happened and what he would have to do about it, he returned to being his old irascible self.

Harris accepted that Anna must be his own daughter by his first marriage and realised that if her mother was still alive he would be found guilty of bigamy as well as larceny and deception on a multitude of matters. But the difficulty which bothered him more than anything else was his mistaken understanding that his son from his second marriage was engaged to the daughter of his first. The odds against that happening by chance would be astronomical, but it seemed to be happening anyway, so Richard Harris called up all his abilities to ensure that the odds were even higher against any marriage actually taking place. He wrote her a letter, couched in vague terms, which might have interested Anna if she had in fact been engaged to his son, but as it didn't refer to her relationship with him, it lacked significance for her and was forgotten until many years later.

—

"Madam, I trust you wouldn't think it impolite of me to offer you a share in the taxi I am about to call for myself." He, moustached and wearing a tailored double-breasted suit, seemed to have charm. He looked up at the rain just starting to fall, at the packages she held and at the road, full of every vehicle imaginable other than the usually ubiquitous red London Transport bus.

She, well dressed, continental in style and appearance with the flapper designs still *de rigueur* for the London set in nineteen thirty-two, nodded gratefully after he retrieved a small package, blown from her hand by a gust of wind.

They, together, entering a time of change in their lives; a new direction for both.

"Richard Harris." Introducing himself, he bowed in the continental manner recognising her foreign origins.

"Maria Santos," she nodded toward him in return with momentary eye contact; an affirmative gesture.

—

Maria was born in the Azores in nineteen hundred and eight. Those islands in mid-Atlantic, passed by steamers and bulk carriers on their way to and from the West Indies and the United States of America, were an idyllic place for a childhood. The winter climate was mild, the summers warm, but not too hot and the pace of life a few decades behind that in continental Europe. Her mother had died in childbirth and her life revolved around her father. When his work took him to Lisbon, the move was exciting, but his next posting, in the Portuguese foreign service in London, was less welcome for the young woman, who didn't at that time have the language skills to adapt readily to their new environment.

London in nineteen thirty-two was crowded and in winter was cold, smoky, dirty and embraced a poverty which although far from Dickensian, was accentuated, in the eyes of the young woman from Sao Miguel, by the grey clouds and persistent rain which fell that year. Soon after her arrival she had experienced a London 'pea-souper'; a fog so dense that it was impossible to see across the road. The particulate matter causing this, carboniferous, sulphurous and acidic, clogged her lungs and with the complication of a respiratory infection, gave her the bronchitis which recurred throughout her life.

However, despite this poor start for her association with England, for Maria life was better than for most people. She lived close to the Portuguese embassy with her father and through connections in his work, had an enviable access to the life-style of the social elite of the capital city. Maria had studied music and her voice was trained to a degree which suggested that she might sing professionally, but the peripatetic lifestyle forced on her by her father's occupation prevented any career development in that direction. Nevertheless she was welcomed at many of the social events held in Kensington, Berkeley Square and the West End and was usually invited to sing.

She didn't however identify herself with the people she was visiting. That she was born in a poor area in the Azores was not obvious to them but she recognised her own roots as being different, felt that difference and maintained a degree of aloofness brought on by social uncertainty. It was this distance which she maintained that was often mistakenly interpreted as indicative of social superiority in the class-conscious milieu surrounding her.

On that day in nineteen hundred and thirty-two, Maria had been shopping at Harrods in Knightsbridge and was planning to walk to her friend's house a short distance away in South Kensington. Her packages redirected her to the bus stop and to her future.

Richard Harris recognised that she was attractive and possibly wealthy. He had changed considerably since the rebirth of his personality after the Gloucestershire train crash nearly three years previously. He had grown the moustache primarily for disguise after his own reported death in the train crash, when one day he saw one of his ex-employers across a London street. With their money which he had stolen, he had bought hand-made clothing which he wore with a trilby hat and an air of wealth.

"You are most kind. It would be a great help to me if you could assist me as far as Bedford Gardens." Maria was at the disadvantage that all foreign women have in another country of being unable to decipher the hidden messages transmitted by clothing style, speech, behaviour and a language which is not their own from birth.

He smiled reassuringly as she accepted his offer. They were married three months later.

It was soon evident that she had made a mistake, but pride and a realisation that she had a responsibility to try to make her marriage work, prevented her from telling her father that his suspicions about her chosen man had been well-founded. When later her father was transferred to Angola she stayed behind with Harris. Her father died of malaria two years after this and she decided then that the marriage must have been the Lord's will and that she would try to make the best she could of her life with this strange man with secrets and an angry heart. She learned early on in their life together that he would not allow himself to be questioned about his past and that his sensitivity about such enquiries bordered on the extreme. She learned also that he didn't have any further financial resources and that when her own savings had been used up there would be little left for necessities. They moved several times to cheaper apartments, usually at night time, but only after he assured her that the accounts had been paid in full.

The depression was underway and work was not easily found for an engineer, as Harris described himself. One morning he spoke from behind his newspaper at breakfast, "We're moving to Christchurch," he said in response to an unrelated question of Maria's. He often disregarded her communication, possibly as a means to make her feel inferior or more dependent on him in their situation where he himself was obviously a failure.

"Christchurch? Where's that?" Maria was pleased at the prospect of a change.

"It's on the south coast."

"What are you going to do there?"

"They need engineers at a military establishment there. They need someone with know-how about bridges so they asked me to help." He lied glibly about his imagined accomplishments. In fact he was to be a trainee mechanic and the job was offered in response to a well-exaggerated curriculum vitae and some references written by Scratchy Stubbs.

Their departure from their latest apartment was sudden and finite. Harris told Maria that he was settling the account with the landlord while she was packing their suitcases and together they then carried these to a bus stop on Vauxhall Bridge Road. They waited for one of the London Transport buses which just might have been the one which, by its delay, caused their meeting twelve months earlier. They looked out of the bus' windows as they crossed Vauxhall Bridge and then as it skirted the south side of the river Thames when they passed the Houses of Parliament on their way to Waterloo, Harris looked across the river and said, "Damned fools. They don't know what they're doing. If they did we'd all be in better shape." There was always someone else he could find to blame for his misfortunes.

In Christchurch, the Harrises lived in a small upstairs apartment in Portfield Road, close to the military engineering works. He went to work every morning except Sunday at seven-thirty. On weekdays he arrived back at five-thirty and when at home never discussed his work with Maria.

"It's secret," he said one day soon after their arrival, "and if word gets out to the enemy it would seriously jeopardise the safety of the country as a whole. We're involved in the development of highly complex military equipment. It's vital that information on the work isn't discussed in the community." Harris continued the illusion that he was a gifted engineer and Maria had no reason to disbelieve him.

"Any contact between the wives of the employees is strictly forbidden," he lied to her. "We even change our work descriptions to avoid letting secrets out," he added to obviate the risk that his deception over his status at work might become known to her and cause him to lose her trust.

In fact it was true that Harris' work was classified as secret. The mobilisation of the German army was stimulus enough to keep it so, but release to the enemy of Harris' knowledge as a trainee mechanic was unlikely to bring the country to its knees, even if he were to discuss his work at the King's Arms every night.

With this restriction on social encounters together with her different background and absence of known contacts in the area, Maria was lonely in Christchurch. She walked around the old town, the Priory Church, the gardens, quay and the Norman Keep. It was to the old Priory Church that she was drawn daily, where she experienced a peace which would sustain her through the loneliness. The challenge to her well-being from that however was met by the arrival of her son John at the Royal Victoria Hospital in nearby Boscombe. She endured a long and difficult labour culminating in a Caesarian Section operation for the birth. Her recovery was slow and it was several months before her strength returned and she was able to walk to the Priory Church again. Harris was sorry that she had started wandering about again rather than staying indoors. He was not a sympathetic person.

That Richard Harris was a liar of consummate proportions was true. But he could only achieve this high degree of proficiency with a comparable level of intelligence. This in fact he had.

He rapidly learned all there was to know about Bailey Bridges and was promoted because of his practical abilities. When war was imminent in nineteen thirty nine, the staff were checked for 'foreign' connections. At what she thought was a chance meeting Maria was asked about her husband's work as a mechanic.

"I don't know what he does at work. We don't talk about it." Her response resulted in high recognition for her reliability and further checks on them both, which might have included a check on Harris' birth certificate, were omitted and considered unnecessary. Had it been checked they might have found that the real Richard Harris died in nineteen thirty. But they never knew. Nor did the erstwhile phoenix, the new Harris, for that matter.

—

"Mum, there's something I want to talk to you about. Something important." Her son John had his anxious tone and Maria guessed that what would follow would involve her being a go-between with him and her husband. She guessed that he wanted to talk about his engagement. He hadn't mentioned it since Harris' reaction in the hospital a week earlier and she had thought it best to wait for him to broach the subject again when he was ready. Now apparently was the time.

"If it's important we had best hear about it now," she said, encouraging him to start.

"Was it difficult for you when you told your father that you were going to marry Dad?" Her son looked at her, reading her response in her eyes.

Maria thought before replying. Her father had not liked the fact that Harris seemed to be a man without a past or a family to support him. "It was difficult. My father was against our marriage but I didn't understand the reasons and thought it was because he had got used to having me around and was reluctant to give me up. His was a lonely life in the foreign service, always travelling and moving from country to country. He agreed in the end. We came from a different country and knew nothing of Dad's past. I still don't if it comes to that," she added quietly.

Her son's preoccupation with his own worries stopped him from noticing her last comment and he started, "Well you see, you know I told you that my fiancee wouldn't understand Dad and his ways? Well the reason is that she has a different background from us. Her parents are from India. They are proud of their heritage and after last week at the hospital I'm worried about Dad's reaction as well as their's. I'm not sure how they'll respond to Dad's views on me marrying their daughter."

"What's her name?" Maria asked her son.

"Surinder. Surinder Nehru." He listened while the kitchen tap dripped into the sink, marking time in the silence. He had gone over the family complications of his engagement in his mind many times in the past few weeks. His mother's support was important to him as he loved her dearly. He had never been close to his father and had anticipated his fathers negative reaction to his engagement. He was however surprised at the overwhelming response that had resulted when he broached the subject a week previously in the hospital.

The tap still dripped. There was no other sound until Maria spoke. "She must be a very special person and I am looking forward to meeting her."

"She is." John leaned over and kissed his mother.

"What does she do?"

"She's a nurse. Didn't you know that doctors always marry nurses?" He was feeling lighter, less anxious but knew that his father had to know. "Will you tell him? He's likely to have another heart attack if I do."

Ten minutes later Maria came from the room where Harris had shut himself in for the past week. She looked puzzled rather than unhappy or flushed. She looked at John and told him, almost incredulously, "I don't understand it. This time he seemed to be quite happy that you're getting engaged. After last weeks events I was almost too frightened to tell him. In fact he seems to be really pleased. He was interested in the connection with India and says he wants to visit there some time."

Harris had not sufficiently regained his composure after his week of anxiety concerning the potential risk to his secret to be able to cover up his relief that the threat no longer existed. He was delighted with the news.

4

...Wenten forth in hire wey with many wise tales,
And hadden leve to lyen al hire lif after.
The vision of Piers Ploughman

A reminder of past misdeeds and help with some more, an accident treated and an accident prevented, more lies and an unpleasant surprise.

"Mr. Harris, there's a gentleman waiting to see you." Natalie's voice on the office intercom, with its hesitant inflexion over the word 'gentleman', should have given Harris a sufficient hint to make himself unavailable. However, a voice audible from the visitor himself in the next room disallowed that possibility. "He says he knew you from before the war," Natalie continued.

Harris' apparent response of jovial welcome to an old friend hid his anxiety when he said, "Send him right in." As years had passed he had become increasingly suspicious of strangers or of people who had been where he had professed to be in the past and even of people and acquaintances he had known well in recent years. His move to Bishop Falls had been for practical business reasons, to oversee the construction of a dam and bridge his firm had designed, but he had also gained, in moving away from Vancouver, the advantage of a temporary equanimity of mind. Each time he moved, he distanced himself from the risk of a hidden threat to his secret that would become greater as he increased his circle of business associates and family friends.

The door opened. Natalie introduced, "Mr. Kitchener," her expression matching her previous vocal inflexion as she left in the room the visitor, a short angular man about fifty years old who was notable particularly for the fact that his face was reminiscent of a greyhound. His eyes, bright and large in relation to his small pointed face, moved continually around, absorbing as much information as possible about the room, and also, without looking directly at him, about its only other occupant, Richard Harris.

The eyes rested finally on Harris' certificate of engineering, framed on the wall above his desk. The small mouth allowed its thin lips to turn up a little at the corners in what was evidently its version of a smile as its owner said, "Aha! Still go' i' oi see." His eyes didn't confirm his smile as he spoke, missing the letter t in a Cockney accent which required a glottal stop between vowels. He turned to Harris, the greyhound eyes directed somewhere below his chin and remaining there.

Harris reached up and touched his chin without thinking before offering his hand to the visitor. He couldn't remember where it was that he had seen him before.

"It's good to see you again." His greeting allowed time for further hints to be made about this old acquaintance's identity while he affected an exaggerated air of relaxation to hide his level of anxiety, now much increased since the forged certificate had been brought to his attention.

The unconfirmed smile returned as the visitor chided Harris, "You don't remember me now without my beard do you?" The voice lowered to a whisper before completing the sentence, "Mister Plunkett?"

Harris started violently from his assumed air of relaxation, his underlying anxiety now reflected in his uncontrolled reaction to the name he had not been called for well over thirty years. In his confusion he looked around the room wildly to ensure that there was no one there who might have heard it.

The visitor spoke. "I'm Scratchy Stubbs." He held his elbows flexed, palms towards Harris, as might an actor awaiting rapturous recognition on stage at the end of a play. Such was not forthcoming so he changed his stance, leaned forward and tapped the side of his nose in a conspiratorial manner and added, "We all need to change our names sometimes, don't we?"

"What do you want?" Harris manner was brusque. He was angry at having lost control, at having shown weakness and he was worried about Scratchy's presence in his life again and the threat this might be to the secret of his past. He had not seen him since he bought his passport from him all those years ago in Camberwell Green, since further 'professional' arrangements had been effected by mail. This unexpected confrontation with the past was disquieting and its implications potentially far-reaching.

"Well, for now oi wan' a be'ah place to stay Thought you might be able to 'elp knowin' the ropes locally as they say. Oi'm stayin' on the Del'a Queen an' it's no', 'ow can oi pu' it, congenial for a gen'leman like me. There's a lo' of undeesirable people stayin' there." One might argue that the actor's acclamation that Scratchy had failed to elicit earlier from Harris was in fact now his due, for the depth and breadth of meaning he was able to portray in the last adjective. He had paused momentarily before the word 'undesirable', to give it importance. The letter e was pronounced soft but given an accentuation which projected critical judgement on the people he described. At the same time he was able to exclude himself from their company by looking around the office to confirm, what he already knew, that no one was listening who might feel cause for offence.

"An' oi ge' seasick," Stubbs added, forgetting that the Delta Queen had been beached before its conversion from a Mississippi paddle steamer to a dormitory for the construction workers.

Scratchy Stubbs, or Kitchener, as he now called himself, did not look like a gentleman. There was something, in fact almost everything, missing. That his shoes were covered with mud, as were his trousers, was not unusual in Bishop Falls at that time of year. The town seemed to have been built on a pool of mud and as the roads were still unpaved, it was not possible to walk without getting spattered half way to the knees.

It was however his manner of social intercourse that best described his real self. He was a Uriah Heep with the added dimension of a sublimated aggression that energised a determination to get what he wanted from anyone else. His personality was offensive to most people. He wheedled and whined and ingratiated himself with those from whom he thought he might gain something and he claimed close friendship and understanding with the same people as they recoiled and tried to distance themselves from him. People were known to see him coming in the street and to change direction to avoid him. If they were unsuccessful in doing so, they expected to be misinformed, misquoted and generally manipulated themselves, and then later to be accused of being the instigator of whatever untruths had been shared.

As a result Scratchy Stubbs, now known as Kitchener, was a lonely man and there was little possibility of a resolution of this difficulty in his life. The condition was self-perpetuating and it brought about the very insecurities that exacerbated his unsocial behaviour. He was long resigned to other people's reaction toward him and came to look on them simply as a means of providing himself with a living. He always came out ahead. He was a survivor.

"It was a good job that," the forger said pointing his face at his handiwork on the certificate on the wall with a self-congratulatory nod.

"Yes it was, Kitchener." Harris thought it was time to distance himself from his old 'friend' by using his surname but couldn't carry it off as it had been changed and didn't seem to suit him anyway. "I'll ask around and see what I can do for you; about your accommodation that is," he added.

The conspiratorial tone of shared secrets returned, "That's right, you're 'Arris an' oi'm Kitchener. We'll keep i' that way won't we?" The question, although posed as rhetorical, was left hanging uncertainly. Harris realised that he would be expected to provide something for his old friend if they were to 'keep it that way'.

"Thing is, oi can't go back there. To that boat oi mean." He paused. The silence demanded an explanation. "Well, we was playin' cards an' they go' upset abou' somethin'. Don't know wha' all the fuss was abou'." Scratchy had always cheated at cards but was not as good at it as he was at forgery. If he had had friends they would have advised him to stick to his day job. Now he had nowhere to go.

"I'll arrange for you to stay at our work site." Harris felt obliged to help although his motives were not entirely altruistic. "There's a watchman's building with a kitchen. You can stay there."

"An' 'ow much will oi be paid as a watchman?" he asked to show that any payment would be for work done and not to obviate the possibility that he might denounce Harris.

The cards had been played. Harris had no immediate alternative. An arrangement was agreed.

"So now oi 'ave a job wiv 'Arris-McQuaid Engineers." Scratchy spoke with mock pride. "An' now oi am reminded that oi 'ave a message for you from no less than Mr. Larry McQuaid."

Harris blinked but his face remained impassive.

"We 'ad a long chat. 'E's comin' to see you." The greyhound eyes darted to Harris' face to see what might be his reaction. The news of McQuaid's possible visit was a further blow to Harris' composure. He had virtually taken over McQuaid's business by encouraging his alcoholism and buying him out with a nominal payment, oiled with a few bottles of whisky. The last he had heard of him was that he was on the street drinking methylated spirit and vanilla essence. Harris had assumed that he was dead and this suggested reincarnation was a great surprise to him.

"How is the old rascal? I haven't seen him for years." Harris again affected a friendly interest in an old colleague.

"'E's on the waggin. Cured. 'Oly. 'E's Reverind McQuaid now. Dog collar an' all. The Sally Ann." Scratchy seemed to be enjoying himself. Or perhaps he was just pleased for McQuaid.

Harris felt uneasy. He could deal with McQuaid as an alcoholic and Scratchy Stubbs as a forger, but with McQuaid recovered and with Scratchy's new-found, if undeclared, occupation as a blackmailer, there was likely to be trouble. The first shoe had dropped. He was going to have to wait for the second.

—

"Go away." The effort to shout out the words was not proportionate to the muted gargling sounds which broke through his disturbed sleep that night as Harris dreamed of confused disassociated images and illogical thoughts. They didn't convey any certain concept of direct harm, but rather a sensation of danger, hidden and unrecognised which resulted in a black mood of horror overall. In his deep sleep, his rate of breathing increased, sweat appeared on his brow, his tongue dried, sticking to the roof of his mouth and his eyes rolled beneath closed lids as he found himself sharing a table with a black dog eating food smelling of burned apples. The dog changed into a black bear, snarling, clamping its teeth, making regular sounds like a hammer pounding in his ears or like a train increasing in speed. An irregularity was then interposed giving a sensation of imminent disaster and the bear now appeared as a man in black with white band around his belly. He pointed at Harris accusingly from the road where he lay, a bottle in his hand which he shared with a crowd of others like himself. These all had bright dog-like eyes which were directed accusingly at him, angrily rejecting and pointing in his direction. The pounding sound, now faster and louder in his head eventually awoke him with the increasing irregularity of his own heart beat on which his mind focused allowing the dream to fade. He was left then only with the feeling of horror and a sensation of impending disaster, as the remaining images and memories of them, seemed to dissolve as if in a fluid vortex, penetrating again beyond recall, the subconsciousness of their birth.

Harris got up from his bed. Maria slept soundly. He felt disturbed and anxious when he recalled the visit he had received the previous day and poured himself a glass of cognac. As discretion was of paramount importance for him, Harris normally drank only occasionally and then in moderation. However this night was to be the exception to prove the rule. A second, third and then a fourth cognac tested both the rule and also his ability to think logically about his new worrying circumstances.

It was not for himself, Harris decided, that he would have to take decisive action, but for the others who relied on him; his family, his employees and, although she was not aware of it, Anna Plunkett. It would be his responsibility to ensure that Scratchy Stubbs, or Kitchener as he now called himself, and McQuaid too were sent far away somewhere. It might be unpleasant, but it was necessary. They would have to go. It certainly wasn't his fault he thought, watching the light from a reading light on his desk reflected through the amber liquid in his crystal glass. In fact he realized, his thinking processes made less critical by that same amber fluid, it was the fault of the very people he was planning to protect. He would not tell them this however, and any action he might take was therefore righteous, moral and good. He would thereby be an anonymous benefactor. This conclusion, reinforced by the last measure of cognac in the bottle gave him a warm feeling of self-righteousness which finally purged the last sensation of fear remaining after his dream.

Harris slept well and late the following morning. Maria looked questioningly at him as she handed him the Alka Seltzer but knew intuitively that she shouldn't ask about it. When she stole a sideways glance she saw that look of aggressive truculence which he often had in the early years, not now directed at her, but at the outside world. She pretended not to notice. She had learned that a long time ago.

When Harris made a decision, he no longer questioned its wisdom, but focused singlemindedly on how it might be put into effect. This applied to the practical aspects of engineering problems, to family problems and even to problems related to making people 'go away'. Maria soon forgot about Harris' disturbed night and certainly no one else noted anything different in his behaviour over the next few months. McQuaid was apparently not in any hurry to visit Bishop Falls, his failure to arrive there increasing rather than decreasing his old partner's uncertainty about his motive for coming at all. As well, it caused Harris greater anxiety the longer he waited, about the content of any discussion that might have occurred between McQuaid and Scratchy Stubbs the forger, who was now known, at least in Bishop Falls, as Kitchener.

—

"How are you Kitchener?" Scratchy was surprised to see Harris appear one day after hours at the watchman's quarters. He enjoyed his work, which involved minimal effort for a regular wage that enabled him to develop other nefarious occupations for which recompense was less certain. He was concerned that their arrangement might be questioned but was reassured on that score by Harris' affable manner, while realising that something was going to be expected of him, perhaps something he might turn to his advantage. He shrugged in reply non-committally.

"How's your artistry these days? Not getting rusty I hope." Harris was holding a sheet of paper in his hands. He rolled and unrolled it hesitantly.

"You want me to copy something for you don't you? Be a pleasure to 'elp an ol' friend. So wha' is it? Don' be shy." Scratchy briefly held the upper hand and played it to its limit. He would certainly be immune to Harrisisms, even though he had not heard of the word, since his street- smart thinking would see through it all right away.

Harris knew this and didn't even try. Feeling irritated, he passed over the piece of paper which Scratchy read carefully. He was a professional.

"Wha' the 'ell d'you wan' wiv this? You aint no bloody pilot. You're jokin'." It was a certificate of medical examination for fitness to fly an aircraft and was issued by the Department of Transport.

"You failed your bloody medical exam. You 'ad a 'eart attack and so you failed it. Oi don' believe it. That's the trouble these days they don' have no sympathy for the sick... It's all the same...". His voice trailed off and then, a somewhat incredulous, "an' now you wanna fly a 'elicopter?"

"Yes, yes, I can't fly unless I get a medical certificate with a few changes on it to make it acceptable." Harris nodded toward the certificate. "I need you to make me a new one with no mention of the electrocardiogram changes which show my old heart attack. We'll need another cardiogram from someone else and you can add my name as certified fit to fly."

Scratchy hadn't felt so good in weeks; in fact not since he had found a wallet in someone's pocket on the worksite two months before. His thin lips smiled and this time his eyes followed suit. He almost looked happy for a moment before the eyes stopped smiling and the dealing had to start.

"Na. Too risky. If oi'm caught they'll send me back to the Big Smoke. Its jail for me back there..." He hesitated. In his enthusiasm he had given Harris a lever to use later if he needed it. They both realised that at the same time. The cost could therefore be reduced.

"Three hundred dollars should cover it." Harris' voice regained its authority.

"For a ol' friend oi 'll do it for five." The conspiratorial look returned as the professional again tapped the side of his nose as he spoke, "This is a difficult job this is."

"Four hundred."

"Oi'll need 'quipment. It's hexpensive."

"Four hundred and fifty."

"Done."

"Thanks Kitchener."

"Dr. Kitchener to you if you don' mind." Scratchy's humour had returned. "Only doctors can sign these you know." He tapped the right breast pocket of his jacket where he had secreted the certificate and then again the side of his nose. He was his old self again. Secrets such as these would have to be torn from him by anyone else. Or at least they would have to paid for.

—

5

There are dragons in my heart...
They sleep so softly, yet not the sound of the lamplight wakes them...

Lucy Ditters

A love story and a love child, a misunderstanding and a mountain odyssey, a father who knows he is and one who does not.

"Mr. Kitchener, the doctor will see you now." The receptionist's voice woke Scratchy Stubbs from his day-dreaming in the doctor's waiting room.

Scratchy, his concentration focused on the possibility of forging some Canada Savings Bonds, rose with a start from his seat and walked through a door where the name 'Doctor Anna Plunkett' was printed in black capitals across the frosted glass of its window panel. The printing, spacing and background of these he noticed as he passed; he was a consummate professional. But it was only with an afterthought that he registered the name itself and the look of surprise resulting from that observation caused the pleasant auburn-haired woman sitting at her desk to smile in order to put him at ease.

"Good morning Mr. Kitchener. You don't mind seeing a woman doctor do you?" She smiled again and added, "Don't worry, I don't bite."

Scratchy had heard that there was a Doctor Anna in town but had not had cause to hear her surname until then.

"No' a' all. Pleased to meet you. Oi was just noticin' your 'andle, your name that is. Plunkett. Seen it somewhere before". Scratchy started fishing for details. 'Perhaps there's a connection with Harris' he thought and said aloud, "You English?"

"Yes I'm from Gloucester. Now, what can I do for you today?"

It was time to get on with the matters in hand. Anna's days were always busy and this one was no exception. There were two of her patients in labour in the maternity ward and a man with a broken leg would soon be back from X-ray and would need attention. She had an afternoon list of three patients needing anaesthetics for surgery and those others waiting to see her now would have to be seen within the morning time she allotted herself for that purpose or be put off until evening. Then she would have to give up the time she always tried to keep clear for personal matters at home.

"Nuffink much. Oi need an electrocardiogram." Scratchy answered and as Anna looked at him enquiringly he added, "Please," thinking that the direct request must have sounded rude and that therefore a little ingratiation was in order.

"Oh, do you have heart trouble then?" Anna looked concerned and reassuring.

"Well, it 'urts 'ere." Scratchy pointed at the centre of his chest over his breastbone, beneath which he was certain that he had a heart.

"Is it sharp or is it like a heavy weight; the pain I mean?"

she followed, seeing his incomprehension.

"Both." He would cover all bases. "Oi need a electrocardiogram." A change in approach was needed and he looked more assertive making eye contact for a moment.

"Well I need to examine you first and then we'll see what we need to do." Anna realised that outright refusal of the unnecessary test would not help her to resolve what was really wrong with him. If he had pain she knew it was unlikely to be coming from his heart. He looked unkempt and undernourished. 'Perhaps he's depressed,' she thought as she started her examination.

Later she left him to get dressed while she made some notes and completed some requisitions for tests.

"Well," she said, "your heart sounds pretty good to me." Scratchy tried a mildly truculent look and said aloud, "Oi still need a electrocardiogram," and to himself, 'of course oi do. 'ow else can oi do your Dad's cistificate.' He smiled to himself then at the secret within a secret he had uncovered.

"The thing is," Anna Plunkett looked serious, "you do have a bit of a lump in your stomach which shouldn't be there. We'll need to look into it."

"You're no' lookin' into moi stummick. Oi just wan' a electrocardiogram." This was an unexpected turn of events for him and Scratchy looked worried.

"Look, you really do have to be checked for that lump. It might be serious. We'll worry about the ECG later, OK?"

The telephone rang. Mrs. Clyde the multiparous patient, well practised at giving birth and now doing it for the fifth time, was pushing hard and would deliver her baby at any moment.

"I have to go. Get these tests done and see me after." Anna left the room as quickly as she could.

Scratchy picked up his requisitions and added to them an electrocardiogram he had noticed on Anna's desk. It had someone else's name attached, together with a report which he read with satisfaction. It said, 'Normal E.C.G.' and was signed, 'J. Carter'.

He placed the form in between the other requisitions which he then waved to the receptionist as he left the room.

"She says oi'm okay. Fancy a date?" She responded appropriately.

—

Mrs Clyde presented her husband that day with a nine-pound baby girl who helped to increase the population of Bishop Falls above the twelve thousand mark. Later that night, around two in the morning, Anna returned to deliver the next patient who, being less practiced at the process, was taking much longer about it all and so she was kept waiting.

As the clock moved slowly on towards three in the morning, her thoughts lingering on the past, she thought again about her 'precious memories' from times gone by. As often happened to her in such a night-time soliloquy, she could see these events pictured in her mind as if she were an observer watching and re-living them. That night as she waited for her patient to deliver, she recalled a time ten years before when her life had changed direction.

—

"I'm sorry I couldn't get an earlier train George." Anna Plunkett, then in her early twenties, carried a small suitcase onto the platform at Oxford Station. "Are we late? It'll only take me five minutes to change."

"No we're okay for time. Glad you could come. We've got a minute or two. I've booked you in at the Randolph. I'm staying with Harry." George Mandleson had met her at the station.

George's brother Harry had bought four tickets for the May Ball at Oxford for himself and George, George's fiancee Ellen and his own partner Eve, but as appendicitis had taken priority two days earlier over Ellen's spare time, it was she herself who had suggested that George should ask Anna to go in her place.

"After all," she had said, "you all know one another well enough and Harry and Eve have often gone down to London to stay in the flat and they both get on really well with Anna." Ellen was George's childhood sweetheart. They had arranged their wedding date for July that year, as soon as George finished his final examinations. George Mandleson, Anna and two others had shared the flat for nearly five years. They were all of a like mind in their determination to qualify in Medicine and as a result a teamwork developed between them, with some degree of unspoken rivalry between Anna and George on the one hand and Wendy and Alan on the other. It was this friendly rivalry which both ensured their eventual success and also brought Anna and George closer to each other.

Anna loved George. She couldn't help it. Perhaps it was because he was the first man who seemed to really care about her in a practical way; helped her with repairs to her bicycle, bought cough medicine when he saw she was ill and things like that. Her mother had not married after the train crash. There had never been a man in the house and when she had died Anna had gone to live with a maiden aunt.

George didn't know that Anna loved him. To him they were friends who made a great team together and both knew that he and Ellen would marry some day. Perhaps his lack of recognition of her feelings showed a degree of insensitivity in his own, but if so, and this is a not unusual state of affairs for many people, it was not seen to be so by Anna because of the love she felt for him. He did know that Anna was very attractive. He could scarcely not have noticed over the years they had shared the flat together, but perhaps it was not until that evening that he noticed that she was in fact beautiful. No other word was appropriate to describe her that night.

In her hotel room Anna said, “Just wait there a second. I’ll change in the loo,” and it was less than five minutes later when she emerged with an intentionally overacted flourish. “Ta-ta-ta How’s this then?”

There were a few moments of silence while George looked at the light green gown she had borrowed for the occasion. It was set off perfectly by a gold and emerald necklace, a gift from her Aunt. He found himself lost for words and simply stared at her in a state of confusion.

“Oh, are we late?” She was not sure what was wrong with him.

“Yes. Well no. Well it’s alright but we should go soon though. I had no idea…” His voice trailed off into silence.

“Well lets go then.” A pause, then, “No idea about what?” she asked.

He hesitated, embarrassed, unsure whether he should say it but after knowing her for five years, he thought, ‘Why not?’

“No idea that you were…,” he shrugged his shoulders, “well… beautiful,” and then he added, “I’m sorry.” He was still confused; afraid that he might have caused offence by not noticing before.

She smiled at him, blushing lightly and covered her own confusion with a toss of her head to reprove the curls which had wandered forward as if to listen to their talk. George saw that familiar habit of hers and was himself again.

That Anna was extraordinarily beautiful was an obvious truth. She had reached a stage in her life where her physical appearance, personality and self-confidence complemented by her considerable intelligence made her incomparably attractive.

Her hair, auburn and recently cut short with curls unrestrained by comb or styling, accentuated the animated and spontaneous expressions of her face. She had large brown eyes, alive and interested and ready to respond with a smile for anyone she chose to receive one. Her whole bearing displayed the infectious exuberance of youth in such expressions. Her lips were full and for this occasion she had used lipstick and George was now mesmerised by the movement of her mouth as she spoke.

To regain his composure he lowered his eyes, only to find his attention drawn to the movement of the emerald necklace she was wearing. Anna had practiced ballet as a child and her earlier career aspirations along these lines had taught her the graceful flowing movements of her limbs which had now become second nature to her. He looked at her then directly as only a long time friend might do. "I mean, you really are beautiful," he repeated unnecessarily.

"You're not so bad yourself," Anna looked back at him, her own confusion redirecting attention away from herself. "I haven't seen you in a black tie for years and years." She mimed an exaggerated curtsey, gesturing outward toward him with her one hand, the other held gracefully across her breast. "What an occasion this must be!"

As she turned to straighten herself he noticed, flowing through her body that liquidity of movement which he knew so well. It moved inwardly from her fingers, her hands, arms and chest until, just as a wave might expend itself in pebbles on a sandy beach, he saw finally a tremor in the emeralds which followed the rounded contours of the white skin above the neckline of her gown.

He didn't hear the knock at the door and it was Anna who opened it to admit Harry and his girlfriend, Eve.

Harry slapped his brother on the shoulder, waved to Anna and then after a second look in her direction turned to George again. "We are indeed most fortunate to have with us tonight Aphrodite, Helen of Troy, Venus de Milo, Anna Karenina, Madame Curie, Jane Austin and Madame Bovary. (Well at least her beauty but definitely not her guile.) There are all of these with us tonight in these two ladies." Harry's pompous loquacity was helped by that half of the champagne which no longer remained in the bottle he held in his hand. He gestured grandly with the second half as he continued, taking the attitude of a master of ceremonies. "A repast has been prepared fit for guests such as these," A sweeping bow spilled some champagne from the bottle, "and nectars from Babylon are ready," he eyed the bottle in his hand, "and luxury cruising on the waterways of the world await our ladies' pleasure." Harry had rented two punts to take on the river after dinner. As they were late they left to eat.

Looking back, as she often did when she was alone, Anna could remember every detail of that evening; what they all wore; the menu; the dancing. These were some of her special memories which she kept for herself, not to be shared with others who weren't there. That the lettuce was limp and the potatoes unsalted and the chicken perhaps a little long around the farmyard before its presentation on the night, were not remembered however. Only the good things deserved that.

After the meal, and there were some speeches inevitably, they took with them whatever comfort they might to the punts on the river. A punt allowed one or two people to sit in front while it was propelled from the stern by a third using a pole pushed into the shallow river bed from its unsteady platform. There being many others out that night, the two boats kept close together until a view of an open riverside field seen through some trees along the bank, showed a marquee where a band was playing and people danced. As the evening was calm and warm, the sides of the tent had been removed and light flooded the field illuminating couples and larger groups walking outside and throwing long shadows across the field. They could hear the sound of people laughing, talking, dancing and shouting; the sound of happiness.

"A fair field full of folk". Harry quoted William Langland. "Come on Eve lets go and join them!" He looked at George and Anna who had both decided to stay on the river and waved as the current allowed them to drift slowly away.

What had made the occasion so memorable was the unusual warmth that day in May. The punt drifted with the stream for fifteen minutes until it stopped against a tree root and they looked up to the starlit sky. George pushed off with the pole and sat down next to Anna drifting, his arm around her shoulders. They passed some gardens. The Spring blooms were past but a yellow azalea wafted its scent across the water. Ahead was a low bridge, its rounded tunnel darkened, its walls covered with moss. The stream carried them through slowly toward the other side and the opening beyond. It seemed as if the unseen beyond the opening was a reminder that their lives were about to change for ever. Anna realised that she might not see George again and took his hand in hers.

"Thank you George; for tonight of course, but also for the last five years. I shall always remember you." She raised his hand to her lips and kissed it.

He in turn kissed her on her cheek. "Thank you too. We

made a great team didn't we?"

The punt moved on through to the river beyond the bridge. It was the same river but Anna felt as if she had changed in some way but was unable to explain how that might be. George looked introspective. They were drifting onward but time seemed to intrude. It was three in the morning.

"I think I should go back soon. I have to be in London after lunch." It was Anna who gave in to the inevitable return to living a life which would make its demands on her and not allow her to drift lazily on a river. They left the punt and walked back through the almost deserted streets to her hotel.

"George. Come and talk a little longer." Anna knew that this would probably be for the last time. He would be married soon and it was unlikely that their paths would cross very often.

Inside her room she opened the window. A half-moon lit dimly a courtyard below. Some footsteps crunched there on the gravel, out of sight. It would be either a late-night reveller returning home or an early riser going to work. George stood behind her, his hand on her shoulder, listening to the footsteps receding into the distance. She turned to look at him and with one of her flowing movements gently pulled his face to her lips. There was no resistance on his part then, or when she sat back, leaning on the bed head and held out her arms toward him inviting his head to lie where the gently undulating line of emeralds lay across the white skin above her gown.

"George, just then in that tunnel under the bridge, everything seemed to be just right, the way things should be and then I felt as if a change were happening. Tell me what you felt then. I'm so tired I think I'll be asleep before I can count down from ten but I want to know what it was like for you out there. So tell me soon. Tell me before you go." Anna moved down so that her head lay on the pillows while his remained on her breast. She closed her eyes.

"It was soft and still," he began, his voice quietly resonating through her body as his head moved almost imperceptibly with her breathing, first up and then down. He spoke slowly from tiredness, his sentences abbreviated by the sensation of her skin rising to his lips with each breath she took.

'Ten.' She was counting time with the same breathing.

"There was music. Far away." Its memory now faded into a soft silence.

"Gershwin I think." He could hear the air flow in, and then out from her body, slowly and rhythmically, in concert with his own breathing.

'Nine.' A small voice spoke within her.

"Warm air. Slowly flowing." Her heart's pulsation increased as air flowed in and slowed as she breathed out again, caressing his hair with a soft warmth.

"Scented flowers." Her perfume's aroma recalled the memory.

"Softly streaming." They were drifting, near sleep, in gentle waves.

'Eight.'

"Sitting by you. Floating." His words transported her in her mind back to the stream.

"A bridge. A dark tunnel." She seemed to float again through it's enveloping darkness. Sleep came closer with each breath.

'Seven.'

"Soft moss on stone walls." In their minds they could feel its cool softness.

"Stars reflected on water." A small light in the blackness.

'Six,' her mind still counting.

"You held my hand."

Softness and warmth.

"Kissed. A light sensation." Lips gently caressing.

"Floating. Weightless".

'Four.'

"Lips on soft skin."

'Three.'

"Light, floating, weightless."

'Two.'

"Dreaming. Timeless."

'One.'

"Out into open space."

Their hands, gently held, then floated upwards as one, brushing lightly his forehead and her face at the same time. Together they felt an overwhelming sense of peace and relaxation, each through their whole being. It was a hypnotic sensation which assured them that all was well and as it should be and for Anna, at least as she now looked back on the memory of it, there was a clarity of perception and a recognition of the possibility of an unconstrained fulfillment of her destiny. She held him close to her, gently touching, feeling and giving as he responded.

There were many footsteps on the gravel below when they next looked out of the window. They couldn't account for the time that had passed but there appeared to be no reason to try to do so.

It was George who spoke first. "Anna, I'm..." His words were stopped by her forefinger pressed against his lips. She looked at him. Her expression told him that there was nothing that needed to be said then, or ever would be for that matter.

George soon joined his footsteps with those of all the others in the courtyard and she had not seen him after that.

Voices in the next room interrupted her memories.

"Deep breath in and hold. Push. One two three four five. Quick breath. Push. Six seven eight nine ten. Now relax."

"Doctor Anna, she's ready. Can you come?"

"Oh...Yes. I'll be there."

—

So now he was coming. She would see him again as she always knew she would one day. The depth of hopeless, empty longing she had felt in the early years, which time had later softened with a mantle of healing acceptance, was now tinged with anxiety at this prospect. Anna hadn't seen George since their meeting in Oxford ten years previously and neither had made contact with the other during that time. It was not, in Anna's case, that she had not thought about George. In fact she had done so every day. She had a reason. Her name was Georgina and she was born a few months short of a year after Anna had sat her final examinations.

"Those in favour?" Jim Sanders, chairman of the Medical Staff Committee at the Bishop Falls Hospital, counted votes of support to invite a Doctor George Mandleson to visit on a monthly basis to provide orthopaedic services for the hospital.

"How about you Anna?" he asked, interrupting her memories, now recalled the more vividly at the possibility of seeing him again. "Not in favour? You'll have to find time to do some more anaesthesia for him if he comes. Do you think you can?"

Anna awoke from her day dreams. "Oh no, I mean yes, I'm in favour."

The motion was carried.

Later that night, unable to sleep, Anna looked out of the window into the darkness of the northern forest and saw herself reflected, in her own mind as an insubstantial image hovering above the snow and against the forest edge, alone. She felt then an overwhelming need for someone; a companion, a friend, someone to love. She thought of George and wondered how he would feel about her when they met and thought about how he might feel about Georgi when he found out about her. The anxious feelings returned.

It had been one year after Georgi was born that she had decided to move to Canada when she received an offer of an intern post at Vancouver General Hospital. There were no facilities for an unmarried mother to work as an intern or house officer in the British hospital service. Anna was met with rejection, usually polite but occasionally otherwise, when she revealed her marital status on an application to work there. In the nineteen fifties an unmarried physician with a baby was definitely considered 'persona non grata' by the rest of the profession, particularly in the heirarchical career structure which existed at that time. In Canada she was judged on her performance as a physician and was not found wanting and so she had stayed and worked in Vancouver and then moved to Bishop Falls when the new town was under construction.

She twice visited England with Georgi to see her remaining distant relations and to show her daughter where she had come from. She herself felt a need to belong, to have roots, family, stability and people who knew and accepted her, and she knew that it was important for Georgi, growing up without a father and in a still-judgemental society, to have the same. There had been another reason she went to England, which she hardly had admitted to herself; she hoped to see George when she was there. Perhaps she thought, she might see him on a train, a bus or in the street or in a shop. The meeting would have to be by chance for she would not be able to arrange to see him directly. She had never told him about Georgi since it would have such a complicating effect on their separate lives and yet, on another level, perhaps more selfish or perhaps more self-fulfilling, she now wanted him to know, so that she could imagine his support when she needed it. When she was alone she often talked to George as if he were there to hear.

The chance meeting never happened. The years went by and it seemed to Anna that she loved him all the more. Georgi was growing, was pretty and had Anna's auburn hair and bright brown eyes.

"How are they all doing?" Anna asked Alan Cawthorpe at a medical meeting in London. Alan had shared the flat with them in their student years and had now married Wendy, the fourth of their group. She really meant, "How is George doing?" and as he listed the whereabouts of everyone he could remember and had not mentioned George she had to ask him.

"And George? What about George?" she asked, her tone affecting only minimal interest so as not to declare her feelings.

"Oh, I thought you would know about that yourself. He moved to Canada last year. Works in Vancouver. Orthopaedics."

"And his wife, Ellen?" Anna had to ask, her eyes searching his for the answer.

"Yes they are both there," she heard and her eyes looked downwards for a moment.

Anna no longer looked at other passengers on planes, trains or buses in the hope of finding George there in England. She showed the countryside to Georgi and was happy when she had to return to her home in Canada.

It was less than a year later when she learned that

George was to visit Bishop Falls every month and only one month after that when he arrived.

On that day her mind was in a state of turmoil. She would have to meet him at lunch time when it had been arranged that he should meet all the medical staff. She knew he was probably unaware that she was in Canada. She had to refer a patient to him and having signed the referral letter thought that he would realize that she was there when he saw it. There were not many Anna Plunketts in the medical field, she felt sure. But George hadn't noticed her name and his surprise was evident when they met and their greeting muted by the social milieu in which the meeting took place, as well as by their memories of their last time together, an occasion they hadn't ratified between themselves by subsequent discussion and acceptance.

"How did Georgi's show at school go yesterday then?" Brian Philpott asked Anna who replied that it had been a success.

"So you have children then?" George asked. "I see you have kept your maiden name."

"Just one, Georgina. And yes I'm still Anna Plunkett."

Brian Philpott had arrived in Bishop Falls only a few months previously and had already taken on an unspoken role as Anna's protector. He signalled to George that the topic was sensitive and later whispered that Anna was an unmarried mother. The pressure of their work schedules ended the meeting after only thirty minutes but during the afternoon Anna's thoughts rarely left the subject of the meeting as she tried to interpret everything that had been said which might have a bearing on the matter which had such hidden significance for her. George was not the same relaxed man she had known as a student, but he was ten years older now and had been up since five o'clock that morning so that he could catch the morning flight from Vancouver. She explained to herself the reasons she could imagine for his cool greeting.

It was not until later in the evening when she was able to speak with him alone. His last patient had left the room. He was dictating a note and signalled to her to take a seat opposite him while he finished. She watched him. He was tired, looked older and there were even a few grey hairs scattered in the black, but he looked well. His shirt collar was pressed and he had gained a little weight. Ellen was still with him she deduced and immediately felt guilty for considering the matter. Her face flushed as it always did when she was unsure about circumstances of importance to herself. She had yet to decide whether or not to tell him that Georgi was his daughter but George failed to notice her uncertainty and with her tacit agreement, finished his dictation before turning his attention to her.

"Well, we're both a little older and wiser than we were ten years ago. I suppose ten years of this sort of business is bound to teach us a thing or two." He pointed to the pile of twenty charts of the patients he had seen during the day. They were records of people who were hoping that he would be able to resolve some of there major life's problems for them and he was referring to the responsibilities they had both taken on in their professional lives.

Anna was aware of this meaning but also sensitive to the line that his conversation was taking in not referring to their previous relationship. She found herself seeking alternative interpretation to the words she had waited ten years to hear. At the end of the day he was feeling tired and stifled a yawn. As he did so Anna, noticing it, felt an emptiness replacing the anxious excitement of a few moments before.

"Well, what have you been up to all these years?" he

asked, realising that his yawn had been noticed and then, even as he said it, that his enquiry, although genuine, sounded distant and disinterested when considered in the context of their past together. Anna's smile faded and he noticed.

"Oh this and that. Up here mainly." She replied in like vein and the distance between them seemed further than at any time in the past ten years. She had wanted to talk about London and Oxford and to tell him about Georgi. She had hoped to be able to know that he was there for her; not to make any call on his time or to compromise him in any way. She felt like crying as her emotional world of the past years, built on hope and an imagined fantasy which appeared to her to be based on reality, now crumbled before her.

George didn't notice. He was wondering why she hadn't married the father of her child but felt that he couldn't ask as they seemed to have drifted too far apart. The possibility that he might be Georgi's father didn't present itself to him as he would have expected to have heard from Anna before if that had been so.

"How's Ellen?" she was able to ask. "I heard you two were married."

"She's fine. Busy as usual." Anna heard the irrelevant small talk excluding her further from his life.

"Well, it's been nice to see you again. Perhaps I'll see you next month if you come again. I must get back to Georgi." Anna was able to make it out of the door without showing her new feelings. She cried when she arrived home. Nothing had been said. Everything had been misunderstood

"Have you hurt yourself?" It was Georgi who noticed the tears when Alison, the sitter, had gone home.

"Yes."

"Where?"

“In my heart.”

“Will it get better?”

“Soon.”

“Good. Will you read me that story? There’s a dragon in it. Ali started it before you came back.”

“Alright, but only if you promise to go straight to bed afterwards and if you get into your pajamas first and wash your face and brush your teeth.”

“Are you better yet?” Georgi asked anxiously a few minutes later.

“Not quite.”

“What’s wrong with your heart?”

“I think it’s got dragons in it. That’s how it feels.”

“Don’t be silly Mummy. Dragons are only in stories. They’re not true.” She kissed Anna and sat close to her, by her heart, to listen.

—

“Doctor Anna. Emergency. Stat.” The paging system demanded immediate assistance in the emergency room. The Latin abbreviation stat on occasions like this, implied urgency and Anna was expected to stop whatever she was doing and to deal with the matter immediately. She knew that life threatening problems were involved and that she would be expected to resolve them and always felt a surge of anxiety when summoned in this way; the more so on this occasion as it was followed by a second call over the paging system of “Code 246". A critical situation had already developed before she could arrive.

A small industrial town like Bishop Falls, where a major construction programme was under way and where the forest industry was involved in active logging, would be expected to provide the emergency staff with much cause for anxiety in situations such as this. Anna had fewer resources to call on in difficult cases than might be available in bigger hospitals and certainly fewer of the specialists that she might need to help her. At times like this one she felt that she was practicing at the limits of her technical ability, through necessity rather than choice.

She felt the anxiety, the adrenaline surge, the responsibility of an expectation of being right every time while knowing that such was impossible and then, on arriving at the patient's side, the redirection of focus into an intense concentration of mind needed to assess the many aspects of care needing to be confronted in the next few critical seconds.

She simplified communication to single words or phrases of medical jargon interspersed with ongoing assessment and as she walked through the door the emergency nurse who had put up an intravenous fluid line and tipped the stretcher head down a few degrees said to her, "Pressure's unrecordable. No pulse. Apex 150 on the monitor." Anna saw the cyanosis, blueness from poor circulation and obstructed breathing, before she reached the stretcher.

"I'll intubate. Size nine. He's a big man. Care with neck while I do it. Can't wait for cervical spine X-ray. Blood in airway. Chest and skull films. Second fluid line on other arm. Cross match eight units. Aspirate pharynx and down tube. Positive pressure breathing. Catheterise and record urine output. Call Operating room staff and Jim Sanders. What's under that pressure dressing? Look. No, stop. Bleeding too much. Do it in the O. R. after chest skull and spine films and check right humerus, radius, ulna and clavicle. Any cardiac tamponade?. Check abdomen. Soft? Increasing in size? Measure it. Check ears and nose for C.S.F. Basal skull fracture? How much I. V. in now?"

"Two litres in and the third up now. Blood will be ready

in forty minutes. Here's the chest and cervical spine films."

"Not good I'm afraid", the X-ray technician spoke, "the films or what they show. Couldn't get a good odontoid view. I could try again, perhaps in the O. R".

"There's a pulmonary contusion and a pneumothorax on the right. and fractures of the clavicle, eighth to tenth ribs, humerus and the right zygoma. Better get a swimmer's view and some facial bone films. Get me an ophthalmoscope. A small hyphaema".

"His pressure's up to eighty. Rate is one twenty. Pupils still equal and reacting."

"There has to be some good news."

"He's still not reacting to his tube. May have had a brain injury. Colour's better now. Keep up IPPR with oxygen. I'll put him on a ventilator in the O. R. We can move him as soon as the O. R.'s ready for us. Are there relatives? What's his name?"

"Dave Wilson. Single. Relatives on the way."

"Ah, Jim, he's as you see him." Jim Sanders, the surgeon arrived. "Pressure's up a bit but he's still unconscious. Oxygen saturation better now. We haven't explored the wound. That's yours to do. He's had three litres of fluid and his blood's started. The O. R.'s ready." Anna was grateful for Jim Sanders' help. It seemed to her that he was always there when she needed him.

"What happened to him?"

"A tree fell on him. There's still earth and tree bark in the wound. We couldn't get it out. That's yours too and the laceration. It goes from his neck below the clavicle, up past his right eye and to the back of the scalp. It's still bleeding through the dressing now his pressure's up. He's had tetanus vaccine."

Three hours later Anna brought the patient back to the ward. He was 'stable'. He hadn't regained consciousness but his pupils and other reflexes were the same on each side making major bleeding in the skull less likely. His breathing was still kept going with a mechanical ventilator and a tube had been put through his chest wall into the pleural cavity. This allowed air from the cavity to be squeezed out through the tube and underwater seal each time the ventilator pumped allowing his lung to re-expand.

Anna and Jim talked to Henry and Martha Wilson, Dave's grandparents and explained what had happened to him.

"He's had a major injury to his chest and head. We don't know how it will all go but we should have some idea by the morning," she told them when Jim Sanders had explained what he had had to do to repair the injuries.

"We'll stay with him tonight." Henry and Martha, his grandparents, would watch over him until he regained consciousness. Anna was always impressed by the care that the Haisla people gave to their relatives and fellow villagers as a stream of well-wishers visited during the evening. She would not be back home until late that evening. There were more emergency patients to be seen as well as the work put off earlier by the emergency, the routine work, arthritis, sore throats, ear infections, depression and all the rest of the ailments that can afflict humankind.

Six hours later, the night well under way, Anna sat in a chair by Dave's bedside, tiredness, both physical and mental, taking its toll. She checked his chart, fluid intake, output, blood pressure and all the rest that she had to do in ongoing assessment. The light caught one side of his face, away from the dressings and she remembered only then when she had seen him before. The face was unmistakable, now that it had been repaired. She had not found out who he was that day, a year ago, in Foch Lagoon, but she had had good reason to be glad that he was there.

Anna had taken Georgi twenty miles down the Douglas Channel in their twenty- two foot boat. They headed for Foch Lagoon and hoped to go in on one high tide and to leave twelve hours later on the next low water slack tide, when the rush of water in and out of the narrow inlet was temporarily calmed due to the tide levels being the same inside and outside the entrance. She didn't know that the high tide inside the inlet was delayed by over an hour compared with the channel outside because of the time it took for the water pouring through the narrow entrance to flood in sufficiently to fill the five miles of inlet which was otherwise landlocked and so it was a surprise to her to find that their boat literally ran downhill in a current that took control of their direction.

It left them safely inside after a short journey of terror caused by their loss of control of direction as they swirled around in whirlpools close to the rocky outcrops protecting the entrance. The water appearing to be boiling and flowing in all directions after the initial ride down the cascading cataract into the lagoon and then, suddenly, peace and tranquillity surrounded them as their boat took them into the now still waters away from the surging falls, still heard only in the distance behind them.

The lagoon, landlocked by three to four thousand foot mountains, some rising vertically from the water's edge, others sloping sufficiently to allow the growth of a cover of cedar and spruce trees, ended five miles further on at a river, navigable only by small boats which could manoeuvre around the rocks protruding along its path. There, along this highway for salmon returning from their migrations, seals waited to interrupt their passage, lying on rocky rests, fat and complacent in a land of easy living now warmed by the sun, their movements sluggish and ponderous until intruders encouraged them to return to their own element, the water that brought them sustenance.

A narrow valley carrying the river to the salt lagoon was the home of black bears living in the tall grasses and willow herb, the fireweed which paints all of the surrounding valleys pink in the summer months. Georgi saw for the first time, sitting in the grass a black bear cub playing with the fireweed and reaching for the white sunlit seeds as they floated off the stems when they were disturbed. Below their dinghy which they took up the river, chinook salmon which had escaped the attention of the seals that were probably already satiated, now continued their nearly completed journey to the spawning grounds in the fresh water higher up the river.

The lagoon itself, calm, its surface on that day unruffled and protected by the encasing mountains was a fishing ground for halibut, red snapper, rock cod and crab as well as the spring or chinook and coho salmon. In their season chum salmon would make the water look black when seen from above, as they teamed in their thousands toward the spawning grounds. On one cliffside leading to a mountain, rough hewn rock and derelict wooden steps told of the past years when gold mining took place there, as it had been also outside the lagoon. There old pilings remained standing gaunt from the mud of a bay. The walkway leading to them was now defunct and the trail in to the mine through the now overgrown bush obscured from view. The track, now almost obliterated, led to a crumbling hole in the mountainside, a signature of someone's past hopes.

Georgi looked back at the black bear cub, now joined by its mother. It was a moment for both of them to remember always from that beautiful place. It was a magical place there, where the delicate rhythms of wilderness life were yet in balance with the magnificent physical surroundings of which they were an integral part.

Anna's timing of the low water slack tide when they left was again one hour out, since the tide tables she used referred only to the main inlet from the Pacific ocean, the Douglas Channel. Water was still pouring into the lagoon when she started and fear of losing control in the whirlpools if she attempted to return to the calm water of the lagoon encouraged her to try to keep going against the cataract of water flowing against them. The tide then took control, throwing them toward the rocks at the edge where a drowned tree snagged the boat, the current pushing it against the trunk and threatening to pull it underneath. Anna wished then that she hadn't attempted this type of expedition without help and feared for Georgi's life in the dangerous predicament in which she had placed them both.

"Rope! Here!" It was this man in the ward next to her who had helped her that day. Dave had been fishing outside the lagoon in his skiff and had seen her mistake but was too late to stop it, even if she could have heard him above the roaring water. He appeared unexpectedly beside her boat having made his way through slack eddies in the maelstrom surrounding them and towed her bow around and clear of the log so that they were able to make their way back into the lagoon.

"Wait. One more hour. I'll show you when." He let go of her bowline as she waved her thanks and later shouted that she should follow him outside. The water was then level and the current reduced to a confused seething flow, sending flotsam darting this way and that without controlled direction. Dave had started fishing again when she waved. She noticed his lack of facial expression but felt an unspoken understanding with him. She hadn't been able to ask his name.

So it was this man who had in fact saved their lives that

day. Anna made up her mind that she would repay the debt and remained close to his ward throughout the night watching his progress closely then and in the coming painful days of recovery, setback and eventual discharge. As consciousness returned to him she noticed again the return also of an unspoken understanding between them. Anna found that she could be with him yet know that she didn't need to speak unless a communication was needed on some matter concerning his care. She had noticed that when any two people share a space together they usually feel a need to speak of some trivia or other to generate conversation to accept each other's presence. She wondered if being present with someone and not to feel this need possibly suggested a communication on a subconscious level, although having never heard of such a thing before she dismissed the possibility from her mind.

Dave Wilson had a long road to travel before recovery, which included severe pneumonia and complications which almost ended his life. During this time Anna could have been thought to have repaid her debt although neither of them would have seen it in those terms.

—

"It's Maria Harris here." The voice on the telephone accented and somewhat hesitant and apologetic continued, "I wondered if I might talk to you about something. It's not a professional matter or I'd call in to your office. Could you drop in to our house for a few minutes on your way home this evening?"

It was an unexpected turn of events, Anna having met only once or twice, and then only briefly since her arrival in Bishop Falls, the woman who neither of them were then aware might be considered to be her step-mother. Maria's invitation was pressing however and Anna told her she would be there at six o' clock.

"I'll see you at six then. Richard will be home but we can have a short chat anyway," she heard.

'Why might we not?' Anna thought, remembering the irascible man in the ward in Vancouver General Hospital five years earlier and glad on this recollection that it was not she who shared a home with him. But there was something about a letter, she recalled and remembered that he had then seemed familiar to her, although she had never met him before. She put down the telephone and thought no more on the matter.

Perhaps she subconsciously recognised her own inborn physical similarities with this strange, angry man, through his facial structure, body language or pheromones. On the other hand it was possible that the familiarity she had perceived was subliminally recognised through eye contact with Harris, particularly after he had realised that she must be his daughter. Anna herself had noticed that messages sent by a momentary glance between two people at even a most transitory meeting are often laden with subconscious transfer of information; instantaneous and bidirectional. Considerations of attractiveness, intellectual standing and sexual appeal and its reciprocation or rejection, recognition of social position and of belonging or not to the group were all capable of being transmitted unwittingly in this way, as were feelings of hostility, liking, happiness and sadness. All this information can pass in that first 'bat' of an eyelid, that 'coup d'oeil'.

'It's only surprising,' she thought to herself, 'that people don't make mistakes of interpretation more often when you think of their often subliminal origins.' This insight however didn't help her in the next possible step in her thought processes; that of recognising that Harris was her father.

The dark-haired Portuguese woman in her late fifties who opened the door for Anna when she arrived that evening smiled a welcome into her home, but ushered her into a room without calling out to her husband that a visitor had arrived.

"I was always grateful for your help with Richard when he had his heart attack in Vancouver and never had the opportunity to tell you so," she began. "But there's something I want to tell you about, which is another matter and I hope you won't mind my intrusion." Anna half inclined her head to one side and raised that shoulder slightly, waiting for her to continue.

"I know quite a few people here already, through the Church," Maria said and Anna remembered seeing her there; devout, wearing black clothes always, as well as a black hat; alone usually; her husband never with her.

"Last week I was talking to the woman whose twins you delivered. She's very upset about the way her husband treated you and says that he has complained to the hospital board and may have a lawyer involved. I was wondering if I might help by having a word with Richard. As you know I'm sure, he's chairman of the hospital board and they seem to do everything he tells them." She nodded as she said this, understanding why it was so.

Anna's heart sank. She was not really concerned about the hospital board but the possibility of a legal action against her was a serious blow to her self-esteem both professionally and in her private life, even though it had no grounds based on any fault in her management. She was already vulnerable after George's apparent rejection and her mood had become depressed lately as a result of this so that she began to accept any criticism as justly applied.

"Well as you know, I can't discuss professional matters with anyone else, but if you think that you can help I'd be grateful." Anna thanked her and made as if to go but footsteps on the stairs indicated that Harris was about to join them.

When he came into the room Maria noticed an expression on his face which she had not often seen before. Usually with visitors he was reserved, in control, more like an actor in a role which was not naturally his own. On this occasion however Harris smiled, welcoming Anna to their home, appearing indulgent and solicitous for her well-being almost to a fault. At the very least Maria thought, he was pleased to see the doctor who had cared for him so well when he had been ill. 'Perhaps that's why,' was the only conclusion she could reach.

"The Jamison problem I suppose," he said, sensing the nature of the discussion which had taken place before his arrival and recalling the letter of complaint he had received.

"Yes." Anna said simply. She remembered the details of the circumstances which she couldn't discuss. The Jamisons had requested termination of a pregnancy by abortion.

Anna had been unable to help them as there were no legal grounds to do this and in any case her religious convictions prevented her from helping them. They had left her office, the husband angry and she had assumed that they had obtained care elsewhere. She was surprised when the patient returned at the thirty second week stage of her pregnancy, in premature labour. The denial which she must have used to deal with her husbands anger at having another child in middle age, was now confronted with reality and twins were delivered uneventfully, with Anna giving her usual verbal commentary of her actions from which others were able to learn. On this occasion her description had the advantage of confirming for anyone who might ask, that everything had been done properly. The problem had arisen later when one of the twins was shown to have a mild cerebral palsy; a brain injury or congenital problem often thought erroneously, to be due to obstetric mismanagement. Anna had become the focus of the family's frustration which the husband vented with complaint.

"Well I can tell you that as far as I'm concerned, and I shall represent it strongly to the Board, you are an asset to this community. Your reputation is of the highest standing and as chairman of the board I am proud to have you working here." Harris nodded abruptly as he said this, giving emphasis to his words and implying that no one would be likely to dare to contradict them.

Anna looked relieved and was thankful for his support. She thought about that letter from five years back but couldn't recall its content.

"I'll still have to find a lawyer to act for me if I get a summons," she said anxiously.

"Don't you worry about that until and unless you get one. Let me see now, Jamison? I think he works for me. There was something about his job being taken over. Or was there? I'll have to be seeing him about that soon. Perhaps I might mention this business at the same time." Harris seemed to be talking to himself but Anna interjected, "Oh, please don't involve yourself on my behalf in your business affairs."

"Of course not," Harris replied properly.

Maria was surprised as well as pleased at the degree of involvement which her husband was prepared to take on Anna's behalf. Harris had not spoken more than a few words to his daughter in her lifetime and this unguarded warmth, and affection even, began to elicit unspoken questioning from his wife.

"I must get back to Georgi." Anna rose to leave. "I don't see enough of her you know."

Harris had not yet finished with surprises for Maria. "Why don't you bring her over on Sunday for lunch? We'd like to see her." Harris meant that he would like to see his granddaughter but Maria also was pleased to hear the invitation. They rarely had visitors.

"That's very kind of you…," Anna started to say.

"Then that's settled." Harris was for moving on with the next matter for consideration so Maria found it necessary to add, "We really would like you to come if you can."

—

On the face of it they were an oddly assorted group assembled for lunch on that Sunday. Harris was the only one of them who knew that Anna and Georgi were related to him. Maria knew nothing of her husband's past before nineteen twenty nine. There was every possibility for confusion and misunderstanding but despite this the day was a great success. Maria rarely entertained because of Harris' fear of letting his secret be known when meetings were on an informal basis and Anna was usually too busy to do so, so the day lightened her spirits and Georgi noticed and was therefore happy as well. As often happens when adults uncertainly investigate their relationships with new groups of acquaintances, the focus remained on the child present and Georgi basked in the attention offered and rose to the occasion.

"She's been sad," she told the Harrises, nodding towards Anna as she said it. "She's got dragons in her heart." Anna gestured to her to stop, but smiled as she did so, not expecting her to listen.

"Oh, I expect I've been a bit tired recently," she covered up.

"Well if she's only got dragons that's no real problem. She can treat that herself," Harris told Georgi.

"She's got a red spot behind her ear." This time Anna's smile was omitted when Georgi spoke and the gesture was repeated.

"Now there's a coincidence; our son has one too. They must be quite common," Maria said as her husband recognised the significance of this particular 'coincidence'.

Georgi now felt at home with the Harrises. "My grandfather died in a train crash."

Harris' expression was unchanged although his soul must have been pierced by the arrow fired from this child's innocence as he asked her, "What else do you know of your grandfather?"

"He liked jellied eels. Mummy told me that Granny told her. Granny's dead now."

"Well there's another coincidence Richard. You once told me that you liked jellied eels," Maria recalled.

"Ughh", was Georgi's reaction to this news.

Harris became more guarded and said benevolently to her, "No, I expect it was something else I said that I liked. I agree they do sound horrible."

"My Daddy went away, so if you see him will you let us know?" Georgi addressed the request to Harris who seemed to be the authority who might be able to help. Anna shrugged, opening her palms as she did so, as if to say 'what can I say about it all' and not therefore needing the embarrassment of speech to colour her gesture.

Harris said, "I expect you'll find your Daddy one day."

A second arrow surely must have followed the first when Georgi told him, "Girls need Daddies, you know," as she agreed with Harris' suggestion and smiled at him as he was remembering waving from a second class railway carriage at Gloucester station in nineteen twenty- nine.

There was a silence until Maria said, "If ever you need to talk to a Daddy, if your mother agrees, you could always come and talk to me."

Georgi looked at her quizzically, a half-smile on her face, perhaps waiting to join in with her joke if that was what it was, and seeing that it was not, she got up and kissed her on her cheek and smiled at her with her mother's smile so that a warmth seemed to pervade the room.

Anna and Georgi often visited Maria in the months that followed but Anna unconsciously avoided times when Harris might be there. However she may have had cause to be grateful to him and no summons was received, which surprised her but not Harris, who did not seem to expect her to get one. Maria's friendship helped her to overcome the depressed mood she had developed and there were other factors which helped as well. One of these was exercise.

—

There are few things that exercise the mind, as well as the body, more than physical activity, as long as it's hard enough to make the pulse increase and the blood vessels open up to accommodate the needs of muscular exercise and to release endorphin chemicals from the brain. Together these induce a state of well-being, a lifting of depressed moods, a clarity of thought, a more positive cognition with increased cerebral action and the possibility of increased social contact and friendship. These rewards for this relatively harmless yet under-utilised activity are nowhere more commensurate with the effort involved than in hiking up a mountain trail on a clear morning.

A climber who leaves a comfortable bed for an early

dawn start after a rush of detailed preparation, may have no conception of what will follow. The first steps up a steep slope using muscles unaccustomed to such tyrannical treatment in the early hours will be painfully difficult, at least for most people, and even encourage refusal on their part to complete the project before it has been fairly started.

However the climber who hears the bird song of the dawn chorus, who sees the sun rise over an eastern ridge, bathing the trees with shafts of yellow light glinting through them as the ground is traversed, who feels the coolness of the morning where dew covers the ground and shines on the leaves, doesn't listen to those messages from a complaining body and presses onward to see more. There, a squirrel may be seen running up a tree and jumping to the branch of another while making a repetitive call, coarse like that of a jay, or an eagle similarly vocally challenged and sounding more like a farmyard hen, may spread its magnificent wings and soar from an old burned cedar perch where it has spent the night, its white head now moving from side to side, searching for movement in the river below or an unguarded crows nest with speckled eggs inviting.

Yet the birdsong of the morning now welcoming a climber comes from the smaller species; a continuous chorus from such as the pine siskin, the cedar waxwing, robins and wrens, many unseen but heard in passing, while a yellow flash of a goldfinch against the dark green of the cedars can be missed only by the most unobservant or introspective traveller. And in the background always, the sound of water falling over rock, clear and fresh, the essence of nature.

All such things may be seen as the climb progresses through trails in northern forests used only occasionally by humankind but kept open the year round by bears, moose, perhaps some deer or wolverine, any of which remain shyly hidden nearby, wary of the intrusion by strangers. Now a spider's web, dew-covered, hangs across a dark stump, a rare symmetry presenting a myriad of reflected lights, each with its minute spectrum of colour glowing within, illuminated by the sun now rising higher and warming the air. Clothing can then be loosened and layers removed without feeling the cold and with the heart pounding hard from the upward climb a rest may be sought. A glance at a fellow climber, is sufficient to tell that it's needed, and is a recognition of personal limitation and perhaps the need for a drink from a stream, clear, cold and fresh at two thousand feet above the start of the morning's climb.

Onward, the slopes steeper, a break in the tree cover from a past winter's avalanche allows views of rivers and of mountain ranges, blue in the distance and perhaps of the town, where all day-to-day anxieties have been left as if in a void, to await the climber's return. Then a levelling of the ascent may present an open area of water meadows; an unexpected change with gems of wild flowers of alpine varieties growing in grassy edges of pools of water. The pools, naturally landscaped, may run quietly from one to the other at different heights in a gently sloping terrain. Marsh marigolds, anenomes, the one leafed orchis, water crowfoot and lady's bed slipper grow here in summer where in winter all is frozen hard. At one pool's edge, sundew, its succulent leaves with their inviting tentacles awaiting their next meal of the insects already circling above them, grows close to where a harmless garter snake may lie hidden in the grass.

The sound of water falling high above the meadows may be pierced by the whistle of a marmot, standing sentry above, erect, keen-eyed and attentive. There, above three and a half thousand feet, the trees become shorter, stunted in their growth by past harsh winters' cold and now sparsely dispersed in patches where the topography gives shelter from the northern wind. Willow, growing in the water meadows below, the food of moose and deer in winter, is replaced at these altitudes by heather growing over the next one thousand feet towards the summit. There, bare rock predominates, its monotony broken by some tufts of hardy grasses and a few annual flowers, their seeds blown there by the strong autumnal winds of the previous year.

It was in one of these patches of sheltered trees on a southern slope of Clay Mountain that on one summer's day two climbers could be seen walking in the shade, close to a rocky outcrop, a thousand feet from the summit.

The branches of the trees reached over and almost touched the rocky walls of the mountain on the upper side of the trail so as to form a dark tunnel. At the end of this a rock, ten feet high and standing like a sentinel, obscured the view of an open space beyond.

Anna and a friend Sandy, saw all these things as they climbed that day and left the shade of the tunnel of trees to pass the rock into the open space. There, a clear pool a hundred feet wide and several feet deep down to its rocky floor, was fed by snows melting above and running into it at its far end. At this point the views were outstandingly beautiful and instilled in them a sense of freedom from the problems of their lives far below. Anna felt at one there with the immensity of the land and its beauty, as if her own self were magnified to become included in its sphere while at the same time diminishing her anxieties and concerns about everyday life in the town below, where people behave as people do.

"It's cold but I'm going to. There's no one around." Anna felt the water cool against her skin, now sweating from the exertion of their climb. She turned to Sandy and saw that she had already undressed and they both raced to see who would be the first to dive in. The stimulating cold brought shouts of delight as they swam and dived in the frigid clear water and as her friend swam a last time to the other end of the pool, Anna, now feeling the cold, climbed out into the sunlight and stood at the pool's edge. She was still beautiful. Ten years had added to her figure at least as many pounds in weight which only increased the rounded femininity of her form and gave her now, beside the water, the appearance of a classical Grecian statue. However in her case, far from looking inanimate, her eyes sparkled with life, making her look the epitome of well-being.

She stood straight, drying her hair and looking out towards the snow-covered mountain peaks to the south. She was overcome by a sense of the freedom induced by the solitude and natural beauty around and she watched as Sandy, about to leave the water, stopped suddenly with a look of horror frozen on her face.

"What's the matter? Are you alright?" She turned, still drying her hair, her arms held high above her naked body as her friend pointed toward the sentinel rock as George Mandleson stumbled from the trees to the open space beside her. He stopped in his tracks, staring at her with the same look on his face that he had had ten years earlier before the May Ball.

This time however, the green ball gown which had long ago been returned to its owner and the emerald necklace which was not really needed for climbing mountains, were replaced only by rivulets and beads of crystal water, glistening as they ran down her body, accentuating the sinuously rounded lines of her breasts, waist and hips.

At first seemingly unable to move, George's right hand then seemed to float up towards his forehead, touching it lightly. He didn't know why.

"I'm sorry." He was able to speak finally. "I didn't know…," he began and then stopped, gesturing toward the swimmers.

Anna heard herself saying, "Didn't know what?" before she understood his meaning just as a sense of *déjà vu* occurred to them both with dreamlike unreality. There were images from the past appearing in their minds; memories of long ago flowing through time and obtruding on present social necessity.

It was George now who moved first. "Oh, Brian's with me, a few hundred yards back. I'll stop him while you…" He noticed Anna's clothes, left by the rock close by his hand, picked them up and handed them to her gingerly, as if they might be delicate or might compromise him in some way. Anna smiled her thanks and held them across her body, unconsciously crouching forward a little. Her moment in this particular garden of Eden in the mountains was over.

—

Their plans for the day had been made the previous evening at work.

"Georgi's going to a sleep-over at a friend's house tonight and then's staying on for a birthday party. She's going to be exhausted when she gets home. They seem to grow up so quickly nowadays; much too quickly for my liking," Anna complained to Sandy, the operating room nurse.

"You shouldn't complain. You should make the most of it while you have a chance," Sandy had told her and suggested that a climb up Clay Mountain would be an ideal way to occupy Anna's rare free time. "I wouldn't mind going if you want to go too," she added.

Anna weighed up her responsibilities. She had long ago decided to take any opportunity like this when it presented itself. The pressure of her work schedule might not ease again for a long time to enable her to take a day off when the weather was fine and when Georgi was otherwise occupied.

"Why not?" she said. "Let's go then."

"You could come too if you like." Sandy turned to George Mandleson who had just walked in. He was on his monthly visit to Bishop Falls.

"Come where?" he asked. Anna thought he looked as if he would be interested.

"Up Clay Mountain tomorrow."

"Not possible unfortunately. I've got a case booked in the operating room tomorrow. It's a hip. It'll take me till after twelve to finish, so no chance I'm afraid." He seemed to look wistfully at Anna; or perhaps she imagined it.

She felt relieved. She had come to terms with new and more rational feelings about George and his presence would have been a complicating factor that she would have to think through more clearly. So that although she was glad in one way that he was unable to come, she was sorry when she saw that he still had that wistful expression when he wished them well for the day.

"Another day perhaps?" It was Anna's turn for unintentional platitudes. The opportunity would be unlikely to present itself again. George knew that.

Now an unexpected meeting had taken place high on the mountain. For Anna there was a momentary embarrassment and the opportunity for discussion about the matters which she and George had to resolve, for Sandy a swim to remember for the rest of her life and for George, an unforgettable memory. There was also an unspoken agreement of silence made simply by the three of them, signed by each with a finger to their lips.

Brian, anxious to make the summit before midday,

encouraged them all to keep moving and Sandy got up to join him, leaving Anna who said that she was too tired to go further.

"I'll stay too. To tell the truth I am not as fit as I thought I was." It was George who saw the opportunity that Anna had offered. "I could do with a rest as well. We'll wait here until you two get back." Brian wished that it were he who was staying with Anna. He liked to be with her.

George had been released from his morning in the operating room because the patient was too unwell to undergo the procedure they had planned and needed a blood transfusion first. It had been Brian who had suggested that they should follow Anna and Sandy up the mountain as he knew the trail and wanted to make sure they were safe.

Anna and George sat in the open space looking at each other, wondering how to start, searching for meanings and trying to understand them.

"Why did you come?" It was Anna who spoke first after Sandy and Brian had left.

"We couldn't do the case. She wasn't fit enough," George prevaricated.

"No. Why did you come?" Anna repeated and added, to encourage him, "I'm glad you did."

"To talk to you. We need to talk about things."

"Why?" a pause then, "Well, I know of course." Anna had wanted to stand back, not to allow herself to be hurt again, but knew that they both had to be honest with each other now. Otherwise they would remain antagonists in a distant relationship with indeterminate boundaries. "How's Ellen?" The question was as much a test to see if George was ready to discuss matters seriously as it was a polite enquiry.

George thought for a while and sighed. "She's Ellen," he said, his reply inviting further questions.

"What does that mean? It's not my business of course." Anna needed permission to intrude further and waited.

"Well, you are involved to a certain extent," she heard.

"Me? How?"

There was a further pause in their conversation. A marmot whistled further up the mountain warning of the arrival of strangers in its territory. The sun passed the meridian and a soft breeze ruffled the surface of the water in the pool.

"It hasn't all been the way it might have turned out, down there." By 'down there' George meant in Vancouver, with Ellen. He stopped, hesitated, and then, the topic being too difficult, said "But you. What about you?"

"I'll tell you later. I want to know why I was involved 'to a certain extent' before I tell you my news."

"The truth is," he started, "I have found Ellen very difficult to understand. I suppose, not being medical herself she has difficulty accepting my working hours, having to cancel arrangement we have made and so on. She thinks other people are taking advantage of us and takes a superior attitude with them which tends to isolate us."

"You don't have children?" Anna enquired.

"We don't try. Well she doesn't like the idea," George looked away as he spoke "and she's very reserved and distant…emotionally."

"Why?"

"I don't know."

"Why am I involved 'to a certain extent' then?" Anna was determined to follow this up, to find out how she might be having an effect on George's marriage without knowing.

"Well, I just remember us at Oxford that night whenever we quarrel. It seems to help."

"Does she know about that night?"

"No. It probably wouldn't matter anyway. She would

only worry about it if she thought that other people might know or might find out."

"She should talk to someone about it. Someone professional."

"Not a hope. She denies that she has any problems and even if there were she would blame someone else. She says that psychologists and psychiatrists are all incompetent anyway. I think she's afraid that they might find out something about her which she has suppressed, something from her past, but I can't get through to her to allow her to discuss it."

"What do you think it's about?"

"I don't know."

A minute passed with no further words spoken by either of them. A fleecy cirrus cloud took some of the sun's warmth and the breeze on the pool increased. Anna shivered involuntarily. Perhaps her swim after the exertion of the climb had made her feel the cold.

"By the way, that time I came up to Bishop Falls for the first time and met you again; I know everything seemed to be wrong between us, but it was after Ellen and I had had one of our quarrels. The night before I hadn't slept because of that. She didn't want me to go and I suppose she felt rejected when I went ahead with the plans I had already made. I'm sorry if I seemed distant. I couldn't talk about it then." George knew he had to explain.

Anna thought about that day when her world had seemed to collapse around her. It seemed so unimportant now up on the mountain, talking to him again. The dragons in her heart must have gone to sleep. "Poor George. What will you do?"

"Wait and hope I suppose. Perhaps she'll change." It was time to change the direction of their talk. "So what's your news?"

"Well..." Anna thought for a long time, weighing in her mind the possible outcomes if George heard that Georgi was his daughter. "I have to tell you that I missed you when you went away to get married." She struggled with herself and decided that this was not the time to tell him. "After knowing you for five years in London that's not surprising is it? I loved you, you know?" She found herself using a past tense; uncertainly, but a past tense nevertheless. It seemed that it would lay less demand for a commitment from him if she were to tell him about their daughter later.

George smiled. "You can't have thought about me all the time though." He emphasised 'all' to suggest that someone must have vied for her affections at least once. He was intrigued to know about Georgi's father.

"No not all of the time," and after a pause, "but most of the time."

"Did he...? Did he just go away?"

"Yes. You can't blame him really. It was probably my fault. I knew he probably would. He didn't know about Georgi." Anna knew that if she told him now that he was Georgi's father it would lead to a break-up of his marriage with Ellen. She wasn't certain now that she wanted him to know, to feel committed to her and to act out a major life crisis on her behalf. 'Did he love her?' she wondered and realised that he couldn't say so if he did, without making a commitment. 'What about Georgi?' she asked herself. 'She needs a father and her natural father would be the best choice surely?' She answered herself uncertainly, 'Perhaps.'

George was unable to make a rational decision about anything at that time. The physical effort of the climb and the discussion of his feelings with Anna were part of the reason for this. The main reason however was an image, burned into his memory, of Anna standing in the sun by the pool with glistening beads of crystal water coalescing into tiny streams, caressing her body as they explored its beautifully moulded configuration. He touched his forehead lightly at the recollection. He didn't know why.

Anna looked directly at him, her expression not reflecting any feelings she might have towards him. George said nothing, but returned her gaze, making eye contact for several seconds, not obtrusively but gently searching for meaning. And there was understanding for both.

George looked away. "Let's go on up," he said. "We're almost there anyway. Twenty minutes or so should do it and we'll catch up with the others." Then with Anna following he led the way past the open space of the pool to a rock gully leading upwards, with one last glance as he did so at the pool's edge by the sentinel rock. A marmot whistled again, the high cloud dispersed and the sun was hot over the last thousand feet of their ascent.

At the summit Sandy and Brian had just finished eating a packed lunch with a vista around them of snow-covered peaks in every direction and in the distance, to the west, the Pacific Ocean melded into a blue haze at the horizon.

"We couldn't miss out on the view after all that effort," Anna told them. "But next time I'm going to get fitter before I start." She explained their delayed arrival at the top. She shared her packed lunch with George who had been unprepared for their day's outing and from the bottom of the bag brought out an apple.

"I've had enough. Anyone?" She held it up, smooth and firm, red against the white of the snow. "Quis?" It was George who was first with the schoolboy's Latin answer; "Ego." He reached for it first although Brian would have liked to have had it.

The descent was uneventful apart from some sore knees and a minor loss of direction when they reached the tree line, all irrelevant in the context of the overall experience of the day. In the 'Alpine' meadows George threw the apple core into one of the small pools where it floated slowly around attracting small flies, gnats and mosquitoes as it moved ever closer to the grass at the edge. There, next to a flowering sundew, a garter snake watched, coiled, smooth and delicately patterned in natural colours, its two black eyes willing the objects of its desire to come closer.

That evening George operated, inserting a metallic nail into the femur of the elderly patient who, having been given a blood transfusion was fit enough to undergo the procedure. The nail, attached by a metal plate to the bone below, gave it stability while the broken part regenerated. The operation finished at midnight and the following evening he left for Vancouver taking with him his thoughts and memories that would stay with him for a long time.

6

"I am the Lord God who brought you out of the land of Egypt and out of slavery and these are My ten commandments;

Exodus 20

Some advice given and some requested, some orders given and some received, a perceived threat removed and an unseen one unknown.

After her day's mountain hike there followed for Anna a lengthy period of reflection, her feelings vacillating from one moment to the next as she brought more factors into the emotional equation which held the balance of her equanimity. The discussion with George had made her realize that she still loved him, as she had for nearly fifteen years of her life and that now the matter was more complicated since they had discussed their relationship, albeit superficially. No declaration of feelings had been made by either of them. Neither could it be, without taking the next step; that of living out the meaning of their love for each other, precipitating the crisis of a marriage breakdown for George and Ellen and inviting social condemnation on both of their personal and professional lives. Anna found that the difficulty inherent in the resolution of this problem and the magnitude of the significance it held for all of them left her feeling exhausted and irritable. She lost weight, developed headaches and couldn't sleep.

All of these symptoms were cured by the simple expedient of deciding to put off any decision on the matter to a later date. That a decision one way or the other on her part would impact their lives to a considerable extent was evident. What was not so, was that a delay in making that same decision would do likewise. Anna then went on with her working life, immersing herself in her patients problems and needs and forgot her own. As she worked long hours she was glad that Georgi went to see Maria once or twice a week after school. She liked Maria, as did Georgi and was happy to have her as a substitute for the family which they didn't have otherwise.

"Ali doesn't need to come today. I'm going to see Dad after school if it's okay with you." Georgi spoke with the pressure of speech, common in an eleven year old, which seemed to deny in advance any possible refusal of the subject matter by its temporal immediacy; even though the request was made at breakfast-time that morning. "She said I can if you agree."

"You can't call Maria 'Dad'!" Anna said, considering her request.

"Why not? She said I could." For Georgi this was an open and shut case. Anna knew that there would be times in the future when she would be too tired to make the right decision on matters much more important than this one. She needed someone to help. The figure at the back of her mind as she thought vaguely about this future need of hers looked very much like George Mandleson. She smiled at the incongruity of her daughter calling a middle aged woman 'Dad' and again when Georgi referred to Harris, in conversation, as 'Him'. "I'm going to Dad and Him's tomorrow," she said one day. However she never referred to Harris in his presence other than by his surname, with a prefixed 'Mister'.

Maria was glad to have Georgi visiting and was surprised and pleased to see that the indulgence afforded Anna Plunkett by her husband was also directed to Georgi. She noticed however that school activities or homework usually curtailed her visits to a period just prior to Harris' arrival home from work. It would have been untrue to say that Georgi disliked Harris. It was simply that her child's intuition recognized dissemblance at an unconscious level and maintained a protective distance from him for herself.

"He just isn't 'true'. He pretends things and he doesn't want to play or joke around about anything," was the only way she was able to verbalize her dicomfort about him for Anna, "but I like Dad, she's really funny."

Anna also felt that 'distance' with Harris which resulted from his suspicious reactions to questioning or discussion on anything affecting his personal life, but in her case, she felt at the same time a paradoxical closeness and familiarity in his presence which she couldn't explain and was made to feel uncomfortable by it. She therefore avoided him as much as was possible while seeing Maria often and it was on one of these occasions that following a long period of reflective silence, Maria ventured, "A penny for your thoughts. I think that's what the English would say isn't it? If you want to tell me, I may be able to help you."

"I'm sorry, I'm guilty of day-dreaming a lot recently. I expect I'm tired, need a holiday or something," Anna excused herself and added the last word as an opening for Maria to continue.

"What sort of something? I don't want to intrude, but you are a bit introspective these days."

Anna thought for a few moments before replying. "Well,

there is something; something really important and I don't know where to begin to sort it all out. It just goes round and round and occupies my mind for any part of the day or night when I'm not working. I thought of going to ask the priest about it but I know his answer even before I ask the question." Anna thought of another hike up a mountain many years in the past, when the rules were written down in stone to answer questions such as the ones she was wrestling with since her own more recent day's climb on Clay Mountain.

"I would appreciate your advice on it." As soon as she said this, Anna felt relieved.

"I'm here. Go on." Maria encouraged her to continue. Anna looked at her directly.

"I have seen Georgi's father. He doesn't know he's her father. Also he's married." Anna told Maria the circumstances of her story without mentioning George's name.

"And you have loved him for all these years, this father of your child?"

"Yes."

"And this child who calls me 'Dad', this child who wants a father so much that she calls me 'Dad', this child of yours who has no other father except the one you keep from her; what do you think she would think about you if you decide to let him go back to the woman who doesn't love him?" There were tears welling up in Maria's eyes as she took Anna's hand in hers. She pictured Anna's years of loneliness and thought of her own life with Harris, staying because it was the right thing to do and suffering because the rules said she should stay.

"I just hope she would forgive me if she were able to understand." Anna's voice quavered as she expressed the uncertainty in her words.

"And this man loves you?"

"I think he might do." Her heart told her that he did.

"Then you must tell him he has a daughter. You owe that to him as well as to her. If he comes and if he stays it's up to him. That's what I would do and that's my advice to you." Maria spoke assertively and then softened as she added, "I really hope that you do tell him. I know it's all against the rules but rules can be broken. This can be an exception to prove the rule."

"I want to believe you, but I have to think about it a little longer before I do anything. Thankyou for listening and thankyou for your advice. I will always value it and will remember your help." Anna felt some sense of relief after their conversation and knew that when she finally decided on what action she would take, she would find it much easier as a result of Maria's support. She realized that George was waiting for her to send some kind of signal that she wanted him, but knew at the same time that she was still not yet ready to decide about it, even though Maria's advice had somehow shifted the emphasis of the morality issue a little further away from her.

—

A new complication then arose in George's life; one which drew him back closer to Ellen than he had been for many years. The signal which he had hoped to hear from Anna had not been sent and the planning of a new direction for his life away from Ellen, was therefore pre-empted by this change.

"George, feel this will you? On the left side just above my nipple. What is it do you think?" Ellen had noticed a lump in her breast that morning during her shower. She felt at the same time a sinking feeling in her stomach and a surge of fear inside her, which frightened her with the immediate thought that this was cancer and that she would probably die from it. "What do you think?"

"Go and see John Jackman right away." George spoke imperatively after feeling it. He was as concerned as she was about the thickened tissue, firm against the surrounding softness and worried that she would refuse further investigation if he didn't stress its importance.

"Is it bad then?" She asked hesitantly, showing her fear so that he wished he had been less forthright.

"There's nothing to be done until we have it checked out. Phone him tomorrow. It could be nothing, but it definitely has to be investigated. There's no point in worrying until we know one way or the other." George knew that she would worry anyway and so would he.

"What will have to be done?" She had to know, to prepare herself in advance.

"Well, you will have to have an operation, a small one to find out if it is malignant, and if it is, if it is a cancer, it will involve a much bigger procedure afterwards." George stumbled over his words as he spoke them, unable to describe for her the details of a radical mastectomy, the total removal of the breast, the tissues underneath and the axillary lymphatic nodes, a procedure at which he had assisted on several occasions when he had been an intern and resident.

"And the bigger procedure? Removal of my left breast? Will that be all? Will I be cured?" Ellen already assumed the worst would be her fate. "Will there be a big scar? What about if it comes back again?" Tears filled her eyes as she pictured herself after the operation, her self-image cringing at the picture of the now expected mutilation presented in her mind.

"You might have radiotherapy afterwards if it's bad. We must wait till we know. Don't torture yourself worrying now." He reached for her and held her close to him as she sobbed.

That night she was unable to sleep until the early hours of the morning, her fear turning to anger directed at the thing lying inside her breast, hard and entrenched there like a parasite, evil, frightening and lethal. Sleep, when it came to her, didn't rest her mind as pictures of threatening violence occurred over and over again, directed at her self, her being, her ego, which was already injured in her past, a past of memories not given entry to consciousness or even to her dreams. She awoke when George touched her hand and held it in his. She was pale, exhausted, and anxious but she had a look which George had not seen in her face before, a look of angry determination.

"Your chest X-ray and bone films don't show any evidence of anything bad so that's a good sign." The next day after an examination John Jackman realised that he had assumed the unconfirmed worst and added, "Look now, it may be all nothing to worry about but if it is a cancer we are dealing with, this is what we'll have to do. You will need an operation. We'll make a small incision, about two inches long so that we can remove the tissue we have to check. It will heal without much of a scar. While you are still anaesthetised we will have it frozen and checked by the pathologist and if it is benign; if it is not a cancer, we will simply repair the wound and send you off home."

"And if…,?" Ellen began.

"If it is a cancer; if it is malignant and would spread to other parts of your body, then we will have to go ahead with a radical mastectomy." He outlined the procedure which George had described for her, but in greater detail so that she would understand the risks and complications which could arise. George wondered if she might refuse the operation and deny the existence of the lump until it was too late.

He was surprised therefore when he heard her say, with that newfound look of anger and determination still on her face, "John, get it out will you. As soon as possible. Just get it out please." The tears returned but the look remained.

The lump and its potential, hidden and as yet unknown, now became an agent for healing in their lives as well as a cause of fear. Ellen and George became closer and developed a facility for understanding which had eluded them for years, Ellen being driven by a need for support through a frightening illness and George through an empathy with her needs, perhaps assisted by feelings of guilt concerning the action he had proposed to take if Anna had encouraged him. The operation was scheduled for three days time and this was the period when understanding was going to be achieved between them if it could be at all.

"George, there's something I want to talk about but I don't know what to say or how to say it." Ellen started tentatively, her eyes weighing his reaction as she spoke.

"Just say it anyway it comes. I'll understand." A start had been agreed.

"We haven't been 'together' much in the recent past." She still had difficulty talking about sex, "and I know it's been difficult for you and I don't really know though why it is I feel this way. It's not your fault. There's something holding me back, something I've been afraid of facing up to, but the strange thing is that now this lump has come in my breast I feel that I will be able to deal with it all afterwards. A new perspective I suppose. But..." and there was a pause as she thought through all the implications involved, "we'll have to be patient longer until I can understand it all. And then again you might not want me afterwards, if my breast has gone." The last, a statement as much as a question was answered by George's denial that it would make any difference for him. She knew that it would, if only because her own self image was affected. She knew that George would feel differently about her but was happy about his denial and smiled.

"I will want you afterwards. Just as much as now. I know it hasn't been right for us recently as well as you do, but I may be to blame as well." George had not told Ellen that Anna was in Bishop Falls and only then realised the unconscious reason for not doing so, a reason which Ellen perceived immediately when he told her. He knew that they were at a crossroads, that they had been heading in different directions and that only open discussion would redirect them.

"And did you talk to her? Do you like her?" Ellen asked, already guessing the answers but not wanting to ask more specific details then.

"Yes and yes. But I don't go there to see her. I go there to work."

"And if I weren't here..."

"Don't say that. You are here and I love you."

"Come to me now then and make love to me." She felt an urgency to make things right, a threat from Anna in the north, a threat from the growth in her breast and also because of the way she had treated George in the past, the reasons for which were still unknown to her.

—

She remembered then another time when she had been in hospital, years previously.

"The pain is here on the right side but it was in the middle yesterday. Now it just hurts and I feel sick." She had had appendicitis. It was ten years earlier, just at the time of the May Ball in Oxford and she and George were going to go with George's brother and his partner, who had made the arrangements. Then, with the operation over and recovery not sufficient to allow her out of hospital, she had several days of enforced rest to allow her time to contemplate what was happening in her life.

She had been glad that Anna had been able to go with George. She thought it would have been a shame to let an inflamed appendix spoil it all for the other two and it was the logical thing for Anna to go with George because they knew each other so well. 'But was that all?' she wondered as she looked back on that time these ten years later, 'or was there another reason; something else which had made me suggest that Anna might like to go?' She knew that men all found Anna attractive but her mind refused to deliberate further on this. She remembered watching a nurse approaching with a meal trolley.

"No, Miss Calshot, you're n.p.o." The nurse responded to her enquiring glance. "As far as food is concerned that means no and that," she pointed to the intravenous fluid dripping into the tube beside her arm, "is all you get until the doctor says 'yes'."

Ellen was not hungry and with the help of the morphine she had been given earlier she lapsed into a dream-like state and imagined that she saw George and herself at their wedding. Her dress was a green gown, simple and tied with ties behind her. George was at a sink scrubbing his hands as if he were going into the operating room. There was no one else there except that a voice read the service and asked questions.

The doctor had replied "No." and the wedding was cancelled. She felt a feeling of relief which she couldn't explain and then awoke, realising that it had all been a dream and dismissing it as such, she only remained uncertain why she had felt relief rather than disappointment, shame and rejection.

She remembered another time when she had felt those last two sensations so strongly. It must have been when she was nine years old since it was before they had moved from Rotherham to Canterbury. She remembered her parents. They were angry and worried when she had refused to go to stay with someone who had invited her. She couldn't remember his name. There was a blank when she thought about him and she called him Mister Blank although that was not his name.

"Of course you'll go. Why ever not? Mr. Blank will be really upset if you don't go. He's made all the arrangements. You liked going to his country cottage last time didn't you?" Her father was worried about not wanting to upset his employer who had invited Ellen to go there with him to accompany his own daughter.

"No. No I didn't." Her reply had been emphatic.

"Why didn't you say? I can't tell him you're not going now."

"Because." She could only picture Mr. Blank with a blank face, both then and when she looked back in later years. There were no eyes, nose, mouth or ears in her memory which she could apply to that face. It was blank. She didn't go. And later when they moved, when her father lost his job, she felt that she had been to blame but couldn't think what she had done wrong.

'Because. Why because? Why?' Ellen wondered again those many years later whenever she thought about that time which was now repressed in her memory and not healed with the passing of the years. As their wedding day approached she felt a vague feeling of unease and yet she knew she should be happy. She loved George and had never loved anyone else. He loved her and they had made their marriage plans over eight years before. But there was something she was afraid of; something she needed to talk about yet feared doing so. She felt different, thought that other people saw the difference and rejected her because of it. To protect herself she developed a cool disdain for those people who did so. After the wedding, after the doctor had said "yes," these people sometimes included George.

Ellen found it difficult to get close to anyone emotionally. She lived with her mind on a different plane where she was seeing her life from the outside, living happily married to a man who loved her, surrounded by admiring friends who all lived on that same plane, never having to confront reality in life.

And in bed that time she struggled with herself as she always did, the fear of close contact being stronger than her will to please him so that she had to move in her mind to that different plane, imagining as she now looked down on herself from outside, that she was enjoying the passion, love and orgasmic experience which, in reality, would not come to her.

—

Before the operation there were blood tests, forms to be completed, arrangements to be made at home and then the waking up on the final morning; the day of reckoning. There was some anxiety before preparing to go to the hospital and there was a time of closeness just in case it would not be the same in the future.

At the hospital there was the depersonalisation of a hospital gown, the wrist band with her name and diagnosis and then the forms to be completed which resulted in a simplification of her life to its lowest common denominator listed for others to see.

Then premedication. A dreamy feeling followed and in the operating room, pentothal and sleep.

—

“It was just a fibroadenoma. Benign. You’re fine. you can go home tonight.” John Jackman tried to get the news through Ellen’s still partially anaesthetised mind in the recovery room. The lump would not end her life. In fact it might have saved her marriage and given her happiness and the strength to confront her past if only she were able to do so.

7

Monday's child is fair of face,
Tuesday's child is full of grace,.

A child's poem

An old acquaintance dies and a new one lives, deviance and innocence, selfishness and selflessness

---

McQuaid arrived in Bishop Falls two weeks after Scratchy's medical examination. He was travelling around the northern communities visiting people who, like himself in the past, had fallen so far off the wayside from alcoholism that they were unlikely to find there own way back to sobriety without help. He understood, had empathy and they listened to him.

As a younger man he had had a successful career and had worked up his engineering business prior to Harris' arrival in Vancouver. When alcohol took control of his life and his marriage failed as a result, he sold his share of the business to Harris, who was able to take advantage of the situation with a nominal payment only. As he continued his descent into alcoholism he looked older than his forty three years and although his figure remained upright, his face told of the depths of despair which he had suffered. He was saved from an early death by a worker with the Salvation Army. He owed everything he became later to the man who found him on the street and to his finding his God as a result.

McQuaid didn't blame Harris for taking advantage of him. In fact he was grateful to him for being the directing force which resulted in his eventually finding the path which led to cure. Harris didn't know this and felt threatened by his arrival, certain that he had come to Bishop Falls for a confrontation with him and that his previous contact with Scratchy had been part of a plan to denounce him. He concluded that the combination of these two past contacts, now both staying together in town, was doubly threatening to his new life in the north.

The first time Harris saw him in Bishop Falls was in the town's coffee shop and he happened to be there to witness McQuaid's meeting with Scratchy Stubbs, the man he only knew as Kitchener. Harris was by chance hidden from view behind a counter. The only other daytime meeting place was the Gordon Hotel which McQuaid never visited unless 'on business'. Harris watched their meeting from across the room, unseen. Scratchy and McQuaid unaware of being observed were deep in a conversation which was obviously private and personal. Scratchy looked awkward and worried. McQuaid was obviously encouraging him to undertake something which he was reluctant to do.

Harris was sure they were planning to denounce him. He remembered his conclusion some months earlier. He knew he would have to act soon, very soon. They would have to go.

McQuaid's voice rose and was heard across the room, "No Kitchener, don't forget it. Do something about it soon, before it's too late."

Scratchy looked around and then said quietly, "You

think oi should? Would you?"

"Yes I would. In fact I've already done it myself." McQuaids voice was just loud enough for Harris to hear.

"All right, I will." Scratchy had found a friend. He would do the X-ray tests that Anna had ordered now that he was persuaded to do them, but first he had to finish the medical certificate for Harris before he could go to Prince Rupert to get them done. "Oi've got some work for, ah someone, so oi'll go when oi've done it." This time his voice could be heard across the room in a lull in the conversation.

Harris, thinking that Scratchy was intending to collect his four hundred and fifty dollars before denouncing him, remained hidden until the two conspirators had gone and later left Bishop Falls for the month of October without paying Scratchy the money he was owed, hoping to delay his next move while he waited to receive it.

—

During the time that Harris was away the leaves of the birch and alder trees changed to bright yellow and showed patches of brightness on the mountainsides contrasting starkly with the darker evergreens of the native cedars, fir, pine, and spruce. By the time he returned however the yellow leaves had fallen prey to the early frost. The early snows on the mountains, at first sprinkled lightly over the peaks, were then covering them deeply as far down as the tree line and encroaching already on the lower slopes, warning that winter was near.

Harris' return was notable in that he came back flying his own helicopter. He flew it through the mountain passes from Prince George, where he had gained sufficient hours of experience to obtain his pilot's licence, which was now provided since he had a clean bill of health recorded on his medical certificate. The change in his life that this new experience gave him was beneficial. He admired the views of the mountains and rivers as he flew over them, saw snow covered slopes giving way to deep valleys beneath his feet as he flew over them, a glistening brilliant whiteness offset by the blue skies and the tall trees piercing the snow below him like black stitches on a tapestry of white silk.

The change had indeed done him some good. He decided he would talk to McQuaid and Scratchy and would buy them off if necessary. Money was not a problem for Harris. It seemed to come his way easily.

His arrival back in Bishop Falls however, brought back his old anxieties and the need he felt to protect his family and himself from imagined harm returned and exacerbated his concerns that his two old associates were planning to do him harm. He couldn't sleep. He lost weight. He affected an exaggerated air of relaxation which fooled everyone, except Maria who knew him better and worried about what might have caused him to act differently.

—

One November afternoon a high pressure area of cold arctic air had pushed into the Coast Mountains from the north. It brought with it both low temperatures and clear weather which together presented for any who might be there to see, unlimited views of natural beauty, yet almost untouched by humankind. The arc of the sun, low in that northern latitude and now near its end for the day being close to the horizon, sent beams of light transversely from the west so that the mountains, ridges and valleys were all accentuated in a clarity born from the etching of surrounding shadows on the snow covered slopes. The overall effect was made the more remarkable by the colour of the light itself as it reflected off the surrounding glaciers and snow. It presented a suffused orange to pink luminescence reflected from the eastern mountains which contrasted dramatically with the deep blue of the sky just above them while to the north and south, shadows in the ridges and valleys between the sunlit areas gave depth overall to the scenic grandure it created.

An observer would be moved to take in a deep breath as if perhaps to take in a small part of this beauty into his or her being. However visitors to the valley were rare at any time, unless they came to service a hydro-electric transmission line in the summer along an uncertain track, now covered in snow, or to do the same by a helicopter approach in winter.

The valley lay half way between the hydro-electric generating plant at Keemanu and the town of Bishop Falls fifty miles to the north, to which it was connected by an electricity transmission line taking power to the aluminum plant which was the reason for the town's existence.

On this particular day there were in fact at least three observers who marvelled at the beauty which nature demonstrated there and it was from the vantage point of a helicopter that Scratchy Kitchener and McQuaid saw it and it was Harris who was the pilot who had brought them.

"Down there. Look!" Harris shouted into McQuaid's ear to try to overcome the noise of the engine, but to no avail. McQuaid shrugged, pointed to his ears and looked down to the area that Harris had seemed to indicate. He saw only that the transmission line was doubled and that one line went on either side of the valley, high up on the slopes.

Scratchy remembered hearing about the valley where, to avoid the risk of a power failure brought about by an avalanche toppling the towers, the transmission lines were doubled with one line on the one side and the other, as a reserve, ran the other side of the valley on the mountains opposite. A platform was suspended across the valley between four of the towers. This was used to land a helicopter if servicing of the insulators became necessary due to snow build-up or other failure. The towers were accessible by narrow walkways from the platform, since access from below was hazardous or impossible in winter.

Harris banked the machine and started a descent towards the suspended platform, apparently to show his passengers what he had been unable to tell them due to the engine's noise.

The day had started uneventfully apart from Harris' increasing anxiety concerning the proximity of both Scratchy and McQuaid to his life and work in Bishop Falls. He had slept poorly having awoken at three o' clock and being unable to sleep again while calculating the risk to his secret of their presence and while formulating a plan to rid himself of them. It was later in the day when he saw both of them walking out deep in conversation toward the bush and past the landing area where he had a small hangar for his helicopter. Harris hurried in order to be there when they returned from their afternoon walk and having prepared for a test flight invited them to accompany him. It was all too easy.

Scratchy had said, touching the side of his nose as he spoke, "Oi 'ope you'r fi' enuff to fly this thing." Harris saw that McQuaid was not party to the implication when he glanced at him sideways to assess any reaction he might have.

"I'll last ten minutes I'm sure if you want to risk it," he answered lightly.

It was closer to twenty minutes later though when a listener in the trees below the hanging platform might have heard the distant pulsation of a helicopter's rotor blades beginning to encroach on the only other audible sound in the valley at that time; the continuous hum of electric power in the transmission lines. The machine was at first visible only as a black spot against the white snow and then, with the sound of the helicopter's engine and pulsing rotor blades increasing slowly with the closer proximity of the machine to the valley, it finally approached the platform, banked and descended with a roar of its engine which shattered the peace which had existed there before. Such a listener would now have to cover his ears to protect them from the unaccustomed sound, but would have been able to see two people climbing out onto the platform while a third remained at the controls.

Harris pointed to the edge of the platform gesturing that they should look down and also, solicitous that they should avoid the rotor blades, he pointed to them and indicated that he would stay in the cockpit for safety's sake.

It was close to a thousand feet to the valley floor from the suspended platform and the view was made the more fascinating by the light and shadow cast by the lowering sun; orange light on one side and a shadow of semi-blackness on the other, which even as they watched, moved slowly to engulf more and more of the valley floor.

McQuaid felt the cold. It was now twenty degrees below zero and falling. 'The valley of the shadow of death.' The words from the psalms seemed to come into his mind from nowhere. He looked at the shadow and shuddered involuntarily at the blackness while still marvelling at the light above.

It was Scratchy who realised first, in a small fraction of a second when the power increased in the helicopter's engine. They had been outmanoeuvred. He grabbed for the skid on the machine but missed as it took off and headed up the valley leaving the two of them on the suspended platform in the impending darkness and bone chilling temperatures.

McQuaid, non-plussed, saw Harris looking straight ahead as he flew off. Harris had solved the problem of his secret being found out and his mind was already rationalising his action. His enemies would quickly freeze to death and his work could now continue. It was an unpleasant fact of life, and death too. He smiled at his apt variation on the figure of speech, already distancing himself from his actions in doing so and thinking of all those who would benefit now that he would not be denounced.

"He'd better be back soon. I'm cold." McQuaid looked puzzled as he saw Scratchy's look of comprehension of what had happened to them when he watched the helicopter disappearing up the valley, the pulsations of the rotors fading into silence.

"'e's not comin' back," he heard. A pause followed while the significance of the statement registered in his mind and then Scratchy added, "Looks like oi won't be needin' no operation anyway. Never wanted my stummick out in the first place."

They looked at each other, McQuaid incredulous and Scratchy resigned now that he knew he had been outplayed, but looking for the way out as he had done all his life. It was therefore the forger who led the way.

"Come on, we'll freeze if we don't ge' down. Tha' way looks best." He pointed to one of the walkways leading to a tower whose base, two hundred and fifty feet beneath the insulators at the top where they would access it, looked to be the best for climbing down the steep valley walls to the bottom, another several hundred feet lower down.

McQuaid was nervous and said so.

"Say yer prayers Reverind and come on now or you'll be able to tell them to 'im yerself in person if you stay 'ere."

Scratchy's assessment of their situation was confirmed by the arrival of a light breeze which increased in strength as the sun went down making the cold that much more dangerous in their exposed situation. If they made it to the valley floor it was still another thirty miles through the bush to Bishop Falls. They were both aware of this but neither mentioned it as they started along the walkway.

It took them only five minutes to traverse the narrow suspended walkway despite its being covered with snow and ice. McQuaid was in front, Scratchy, the survivor, behind. As the tower was approached, the hum of electricity in the lines took on a lifelike quality in the otherwise silent world about them. The sound seemed to take over McQuaid's mind, obliterating the fear which followed every step and even masking his appreciation of the numbing cold which was enveloping him. He looked down. The light was now fading in the shadow in the valley, but from the setting sun beyond the mountains to the west a last beam of orange light was reflected on the metal of the tower a step in front of him. He turned to the west and saw the glow of the same light from a glacier and was aware of a fleeting sense of its beauty as he reached out to take hold of the tower.

The humming sound grew louder. Cold reached through his clothing. He felt only the need to survive but his hands ached in the freezing air. He transferred a foot from the walkway to a metal strut on the tower. It was covered in ice. His foot slipped and his hand was not able to hold. His other hand grabbed at the tower as he fell but his weight dislocated his shoulder. He was falling. 'Why am I here?' There was simply incomprehension in his mind as his head struck the rock at the base of the tower, breaking his neck. He was not aware of his fall down the rest of the slope to a point three hundred feet lower down where his body ended wedged between two rocks. It made no movement afterwards.

The greyhound eyes followed McQuaid's fall to its end. Scratchy had lived the life of a petty criminal but had never seen a violent death before. The horror of this one was exacerbated by his own precarious position alone in the cold on the tower. He looked again into the shadow. He could just make out McQuaid in the darkness, lying still in the snow.

"Christ," he muttered and was aware of a greater meaning to life than he had contemplated before. His past life of criminal activity had not presented him with the ideal background for spiritual consideration but he was then mindful of something he had missed in the past, of another dimension of being. It was only momentary however. He had to survive.

The forger climbed down the tower towards the darkness in the valley, taking care to avoid looking in the direction of the shape between the two rocks. He was cold, his mind confused by fear, focused only on reaching the forest edge below as he scrambled and fell for half a mile down snow-covered scree and rock. At the tree line he stopped, panting for breath and holding onto a cedar branch for support. His mind, driven by anxiety, the cold making him feel nauseous and weak, he tried to plan his next move.

He looked around into the darkness and as he did so his greyhound's eyes opened wide in bewilderment and horror heightened by his confusion. A face, long and thin with unsmiling eyes stared back at him, a scar on one cheek livid in the cold air. Scratchy recoiled. He wanted to run but had nowhere to go. 'Was this the face of death?' He was afraid.

The man moved towards him. Scratchy fell backwards, terrified at the vision in front of him. His eyes looked down, his pulse racing as much from fear as from his exertion.

The face, for the rest of the man was not visible against

the dark forest, spoke to him; "You had better come with me. You'll die if you stay here." The man turned and walked off into the forest. Scratchy followed blindly, numb with cold and unable to do anything else. After about a mile through the snow they reached a cabin by a frozen creek.

—

Whether in the old nursery rhyme it was Monday's child who was fair of face and Tuesday's child who was full of grace, or whether it was something different had no relevance to young Dave Wilson. Suffice it to say that he evidently was born much later in the week when the remaining lists of attractive attributes were somewhat limited after the rush to acquire the more desirable ones earlier.

People visiting Dave's mother when she came home from the hospital would admire his knitted coat and hat but somehow didn't seem to notice him; or at least they didn't mention him. Their attention seemed to be directed to other matters.

Born after his father Tom had left home, he spent much of his time alone, his mother being busy with the family and going out every evening and meeting with her Russian friends. She had learned to speak Russian from her parents, immigrants who worked on the railways with the Swedes who taught her Christmas stories. She had started to drink before she met Tom and didn't stop after he left her.

Dave's brother Henry and his sister Eve, being older than him, showed no interest in him or were possibly embarrassed about their brother with his strange looks. There was nothing seriously wrong with him, mind you. It was true that his eyes were a little too close together and too narrow and that his mouth looked a little too small and low down on his face, which itself was too long to be attractive. Perhaps the accentuating fact about him was that he never seemed to smile. People love others who smile. It makes their own problems and adversities seem to be less when the smile includes themselves in its sphere of radiance and they love the source of it for its recognition that they truly deserve inclusion. Dave never smiled and was not included. This he accepted as a child and played outside by himself most of the time. He was no trouble.

But he was not really alone because Gordon was there. Why he called his imaginary friend Gordon, remained a mystery to his mother.

"Who do you know who's called Gordon?" she once asked him, perplexed at his certainty of the existence of his friend. "I've never met a Gordon."

"Gordon," he replied, with his child's logic.

However his play kept him occupied when she was busy and when he was outside she no longer felt that vague uncomfortable feeling which she had yet to recognise as guilt.

'It's true that I have a drink or two now and again,' she would admit to herself, 'but not that much,' her thoughts again directed to the cupboard in the corner, denial overcoming remorse.

Gordon never said anything. He was just there. Like Dave, he too never smiled, but he was like a reassuring presence who never made demands on him when playing, never pushed or shouted or tried to take control. He was a friend.

Gordon would only usually come to play when it was quiet so he didn't come at first when Dave started school. Dave, rejected as usual, felt lonely. One day, however when the wind blew the trees across the schoolyard so that they waved in front of the morning sun Dave, staring at them, went blank for a few seconds, and during that time Gordon came. It was definitely him. He had a badge with his name on it like Dave's and the other children's. He didn't stay long though and Dave was sorry. He looked again at the trees and when the light flashed, his mind went blank again and Gordon came back. He found that Gordon would come if he waved his fingers in front of the light and made it flash. He made Gordon come often.

"His name is David. We call him 'Dave' for short." His mother stated the obvious to the doctor in her apprehension, brought on by denied guilt. Dave had never heard himself called Dave-for- short before. He always wondered why he was shorter than his school-friends and now thought it must be something to do with his name. He thought of his name badge at school, and Gordon's too and then when the doctor wrote her notes Gordon stood next to her for a moment. The doctor had a name badge with her picture on it. She looked nice.

"The doctor says you have to take these pills for seizures," Dave's mother said. Dave thought he didn't want to have seizures, but if he had to, he would take the pills anyway if his mother asked him. He was no trouble.

Then as Gordon didn't come for a long time he stopped waving his hands in the air and his mother was pleased.

Seven years passed. Bill was visiting. He often came and stayed for a few days and Dave noticed that his mother was always happy then. Dave was growing up but not as quickly as his mother had hoped. He was not good at school work but he was no trouble. For a hobby he made models out of matchsticks and that day was finishing a model of a house. He was deftly applying the last part of the roof and was adding the chimney with delicate excitement when his mother made an expansive gesture in telling Bill one of her stories. In so doing she knocked over a tray with glasses and a bottle which fell slowly down, or so it seemed to Dave, toward the matchstick house.

He shouted out loud, "No!" Afterwards Gordon came and it didn't seem to matter so much. Bill gave him a quarter for candy but he didn't go out to get any.

Bill was sorry about the model house. He liked Dave and it was he who, ten years later after Dave's mother died in the accident, arranged for him to have a job as a faller in a logging camp. Dave had been with her in the car when the accident happened. He saw the truck coming but somehow she didn't seem to press the brakes on time. He could never understand why. Their car rolled down the embankment and his mother was killed right there. Dave was unhurt and Gordon came and it seemed to help.

He liked working in the forests and was good at what he did and was always a faller. He knew how to cut down a tree so that it would fall exactly where he needed it. The camps became his home. In the forests there always seemed to be the smell of diesel fumes and the sweet scent of fir and cedar in the heat of the sun and the stronger smell of sap bleeding from trees after bucking or cutting off the unwanted branches and skidding the tree trunk with a wire tow towards the loading pile. For some reason he didn't know, this smell reminded him of his mother and his home of years gone by. He never drank strong drink; couldn't explain why, but just didn't.

Dave had little need for money in the camps. His food and bed were provided and as he neither drank nor smoked it was three months after he started work when, as he needed some boots, he had to go to town to draw cash from the account set up at the bank where his weekly pay cheque was deposited for him.

He felt nervous about the process and waited to see what

other people did before going up to the teller himself. He felt uncomfortable, his hands sweating. He wished that Gordon was there and his eyes strayed to a poster on the wall where a starving Ethiopian child seemed to look directly at him, appealing desperately for help. Dave walked over to the poster trying to read its message, his fingers following each word as he mouthed them for his own understanding. He knew the child needed him to help and knew that it was all wrong that he was so thin. He wanted to help but didn't know how.

"Mr Thomas, there's a gentleman acting strangely in the front. Could you come and see?" A young teller had noticed Dave and was sure that he shouldn't be there so she had called the manager.

Rick Thomas looked round past the door of his office at the unusual-looking man who was obviously nervous and upset. "Leave this to me, I'll take care of it."

"Can I help you sir?" He approached Dave, his manner brusque, business-like, in control and correct.

"I need money." Dave felt more nervous and wished he hadn't come. Other clients in the bank looked at him.

"Do you have an account here?" The manager thought it unlikely until he saw a cheque book in Dave's hand and his manner changed when Dave nodded. Rick Thomas then changed the direction of his questions to disavow his previous suspicious manner and nodded toward the poster of the child.

"Tragic, isn't it. But what can you do?" The question, although rhetorical, was answered by Dave.

"Send him some money," he said simply.

"That's easier said than done. Whose money can we send?" As he spoke Dave's eyes glanced at the drawer at the teller's desk, but the manager continued, "There's not much around to spare these days."

"He can have mine. Will you send it to him for me?" Dave meant it. He wanted to help.

Rick Thomas realised that here was a client who needed help with his financial affairs and asked him into his office. As Dave went in, the other waiting clients looked at him suspiciously, one looking out for the police car he assumed must have been called by the teller who watched from her station at the desk.

"Come over here. Now let's see. Sandra would you bring an account statement for Mr. Uh...?" Dave didn't know that he was expected to tell them his name since he hadn't been asked directly, so the manager held out his hand for the cheque book. "For Mr. David Wilson. Number 8023-6479."

Dave sat looking at his boots. The sole was coming off one of them and he had tied it on with some wire. He tried to hide it by covering it with his other boot but the laces had broken in that one and his sock showed through at the top, where a large hole framed an area of skin totally impregnated with forest material.

"Here it is Mr. Thomas." Sandra brought the account.

"You haven't taken anything out of the account yet. How much do you want today?"

"A hundred dollars." Dave felt nervous asking for so much money but he needed it for new boots.

"And how much do you want to send to...to him?" The manager nodded toward the outer room with the poster.

"He can have the rest." Dave remained resolute on the matter despite the manager's hinted advice that he may need to keep some. "He can have everything I don't need from my pay- cheques."

"That's very generous of you. Very generous indeed." Rick Thomas now felt a responsibility about such an arrangement. "Sandra, come here will you. Mr Wilson wants to send half of everything he earns to Famine Relief.

Would you arrange this for him?" The amount was the manager's idea. He couldn't conceive that anyone would be able to send more than that. "This will continue as long as Mr Wilson wishes. You understand that you can stop the arrangement at any time you want, don't you?" He made sure that Dave understood.

"Yes," Dave said. As he went out he looked at the poster again. He thought that the child looked happier than before. In fact he thought he looked a little like Gordon, but much thinner.

When the boots were bought it was nearly a year before he had to leave the camp again and then because of a shut-down of the forest industry due to fire risk after a long dry summer.

At other times the camps were closed during the spring melt when equipment became bogged down in mud and at times such as these Dave often went to stay with his grandparents Henry and Martha in Kitamaat. They told him stories of the old days, of their journeys by canoe to Vancouver over five hundred miles to the south and up to Port Simpson and Metlakatla. They told him the legends of the native peoples, the Cowichan stories of the flood, and the migration of the early Haisla people up to Kitamaat. They told him also about the arrival of the white nations, of the benefits of the new technologies, of the uncertainties that these engendered when the changed life-styles of the people made them turn away from the old ways and also of the residential schools which had seemed such a benefit at first, but had had a high price to be paid for in terms of cultural repression.

When age stopped Henry Wilson from making use of his trapline and as his son Tom Wilson rarely came north except for the occasional visit at Christmas and once for the oolichan run, Dave took it over. He used it to get furs whenever he was away from the logging camps.

He rarely thought of Gordon in those days as the forests and trees somehow gave him that same feeling of security he used to have from his imaginary friend. He often left the camp to sit alone. The other forestry workers were used to him being different and not smiling and being alone so much. In fact, with the few exceptions of people who rarely seemed to be the one's who stayed long in the camps, he was liked by the others. They admired his self-sufficiency and lack of materialism and envied his acceptance of whatever difficulties life put in his way. Dave never complained and seemed to be immune to the effects of adversity.

His last day in the camps was a hot one in mid-summer. Dave sat on a log having his lunch alone. The noise of trucks, skids, generators, chain saws, and cranes had all stopped as their operators took a break. A bird sang close by. Men talked and smoked at a canteen. It was hot. Dave watched some wood ants working around a rotting cedar log as he ate. The old fallen cedar had splintered into matchstick-like fragments and the ants seemed to him to be like forest workers amongst the logs. The heat from the sun made the cedars smell stronger and he thought of home and his mother and the Russians. As he did so Gordon was there beside him. It was the first time for many years, but this time was different from those others when he had come as a reassuring presence. This time he came with a purpose. Gordon pointed to the forest floor by the rotting cedar. Dave's eyes followed and the cedar fragments seemed to build up into a matchstick house which then even as he watched, collapsed onto the ants working beneath it. He looked up and saw a driver climbing into a truck and starting the engine. He saw a loose branch jammed into the chassis behind as the truck backed towards a log-pile waiting for loading. Two men and Gordon stood below the pile. Dave knew the branch would make it roll.

"No!" Dave shouted but his voice was drowned in the sound of a generator starting up. He ran down the hill to the pile and saw that Gordon was no longer there and as the logs fell he pushed the two men away but was unable to get clear himself.

In hospital he remained apparently unconscious, but within himself he recalled images of the past; of his mother, matches, badges with names and happy faces drawn on them, school, trying to read, the car crash, the forest, the sea, Henry and Martha, the trapline and Gordon.

Then he heard the Nurse tell his foreman that pneumonia had set in. He couldn't see past his bandages but he pictured the foreman with his name on his shirt standing there at the bedside. He wanted to tell him something but was unable to speak.

Then in his mind he was back in the forest. It was dark and cool there and he felt that he had to move on to a brightness in the distance. It was like the sun breaking through the trees to a forest glade; something familiar and he then no longer felt alone. The light dazzled him coming from the darkness and although he was aware of someone's presence he couldn't make out who was there.

He screwed his eyes to see, although the light wasn't painful, but this enabled him to see a name written across the other's chest and on seeing it Dave Wilson actually smiled.

"Hey Gordon. They spelled your name wrong. They missed out the the R, the O, and the N." He paused and then added, hesitantly, "It is you isn't it, Gordon?"

And Gordon, if indeed that was who it was, smiled too.

Dave knew then that he had to go back. He didn't really want to but he went as he knew he had to. He was no trouble; not to anyone.

—

Dave saw the forest glade recede into the distance at lightning speed and then from high up in a room in which he next found himself, he could look down and see his body lying on a hospital bed, his head bandaged almost completely. He was aware of the extent of the injuries beneath the dressings, yet he felt no pain. He watched as the doctor attempted to revive his body with heart massage. It was Anna who removed some of the dressings to enable her to insert a breathing tube into his throat so that she could force air into his lungs. He was aware of her anxiety, her caring and the intensity of the emotion she was feeling for him as she worked to keep him alive and he saw too the nurses adding medication to his intravenous fluid line and setting up a respirator. Their faces told of a degree of concern and caring which he had never experienced before, never thought was his due, and yet now he realised that love had been surrounding him all his life, though he had been unable to grasp it.

Anna glanced at the clock to see the length of time he was being deprived of oxygen. It was twenty five seconds past two fifteen in the morning. She needed help to assess the situation and called for the on-call doctor for help, but knew it would be ten to fifteen minutes before he could arrive. Her mind, computing all the facets of the proper management of his condition then seemed to go blank for a fraction of time as a white flash blocked out all thought and then replaced it with a feeling of intense relief. His condition appeared to be unchanged. It was still twenty five seconds past two fifteen. The flash had come from within her but it seemed to have been directed by an outside force.

Dave felt the same will driving him to return to his body

on the bed, yet he seemed to have no control over it. His disembodied vision of what was happening to himself below, soothing rather than frightening; dreamlike, yet with an intensity superseding reality appearing to reach a climactic level when a brilliant white light obscured everything he saw.

The second hand on the clock stopped moving.

The light seemed to be an experience rather than a physical entity. It encompassed everything in time, space and thought and was incomprehensible. Dave knew eternity then; both past and future. In it he saw his mother, people he didn't know but who he knew loved him and others he had never seen before. He saw a fairground with a girl dancing in front of brightly clothed musicians. He saw trains, apples and an attache case in the midst of smoke. It contained a blue package. He saw a river, old brick buildings, a small boat, a stone bridge, stars and a tunnel and he felt a warm softness, an almost orgasmic sensation of intense love and then loss, as it was replaced by loneliness.This fragmentary lens-eye vision, from worldly near-reality through the structure of time and space into the totality of all being, showed him a glimpse of the interconnection between all living things created by an ultimate being.

The electric clock began to move again at its accustomed rate. Dave now neither saw nor recalled anything. The vision had gone and time had returned.

A voice; it was Shirley the registered nurse who said, "We have a pulse. It's fairly strong."

"Check his blood pressure would you and we'll raise the bed head a little." Anna slowed the intravenous rate as she spoke. "Can you get us some mannitol?"

Anna moved to the desk to write some notes. She was exhausted and looked white, her pallor exaggerated by contrast with her auburn hair.

"Are you all right Anna?" It was Shirley who noticed.

"I expect I'm a bit tired, and yes that offer of a cup of tea sounds really good to me." She looked introspective; worrying and wondering about what had happened. She couldn't tell anyone that her mind had gone blank in the middle of a resuscitation, even though it was for less than a second. 'It was nothing,' she thought to herself, but lacking the propensity for denial which she might well have inherited, her mind continued to dwell on it.

'There were forests and trees and children wearing badges. There were model houses, fish, eagles, bears and children at school in an African country. And there was loneliness,' she recalled. 'What does it all mean?' she wondered. Tiredness however denied her any possibility of an explanation then. Later she decided that that same tiredness must have created the images which were so foreign to her and that she should make sure that she got more rest in the future in case it happened again.

—

For over an hour Scratchy Kitchener sat huddled in a corner of the wooden cabin beside a woodstove. Not a word was spoken during this time. The cabin, made from logs stuffed in between with mud and willow, was not built for comfort and cold air seemed to circulate at will, despite the frequent refuelling of the stove by its owner. There was no furniture other than the stove which smoked continuously, making the view across the small space in the one room to be shrouded from view at times as draughts of cold air circulated. The other man seemed to disappear in the smoke and then to reappear as if at will, his expressionless face making the scene the more frightening for Scratchy who shivered and watched continually with his eyes never leaving his rescuer. The latter had a livid healing scar on one cheek stretching from just below his left eye to a point two inches beneath the angle of his jaw and another on the right side of his scalp at the back where the hair had now grown partly over it. The yellow light from the stove accentuated the scar and the swirling smoke sometimes partly hid it. It looked as if it had been caused by some massive crushing injury.

"Who are you?" The man gave him a mug of hot water and Scratchy was able to stop shivering for long enough to ask the question.

"Dave Wilson."

"An 'ow did you know oi was there?"

"Saw you. Up there." Dave Wilson gestured upward using a skewer he held in his hand and nodded in the direction of the transmission line.

"An did you see...?"

"Yes he's gone." Scratchy was uncertain whether Dave was referring to Harris or to McQuaid but guessed that he had not seen the latter's fall from the tower since he would expect him to have been more animated in his reply if he had done so. He decided to leave the subject for the time being.

"An what was you doin' 'ere anyways?"

"Hunting. Trapline.I got a fish, chinook." Dave Wilson brought in a salmon he had caught and gutted earlier, cut some pieces and cooked them on the skewer. He offered some to Scratchy who ate a little but was still too far from recovering from his ordeal to have any sort of an appetite.

"Ow do we get back to town from 'ere?"

"I got a boat at Kildala. Three miles. Then three or four hours if the weather's good."

Scratchy was beginning to get warm. The shivering

became more intermittent and his level of anxiety which had kept him speechless for so long earlier was now being replaced with a brooding anger directed at Harris. He decided that he would tell all and would start with Dave Wilson right then and there.

“That was ’Arris.” He pointed up in the direction of the platform."Only ’e’s not ’Arris, ’e’s Plunkett, an’ ’e’s a bigamist, a cheat, a thief an’ ’e’s no’ a engineer like ’e sez. An’ ’is daughter is that Anna Plunkett only she don’t know it ’erself. An’ now e’s a murderer an’ ’e left me to die out there an’ that’s what I’d a’ done if you ’adn’t come along nifty like. Me’ oo never did any ’arm to no one."

It was at this point that he looked at Dave to see what his response might be. He could see the left side of his face but it showed no change. He could see that his eye was open or else he might have been sleeping for all the interest he showed. He didn’t know that since the accident Dave’s eye never closed properly. Before going to sleep Dave remembered his grandfather telling him not to believe everything a whitey might tell him. “Some of them just talk too much,” he had said. It seemed that he was right and it wasn’t Dave’s business that he talked about anyway.

It was just then that Scratchy realized that it was not in his interest to complain too much about the treatment he had received from Harris, despite his only very narrow escape from death as a result of it. To complain would necessitate him declaring his illegal alien status in the country and suffering an ignominious return to England where a jail sentence awaited him; a result of services rendered to others who had found themselves in similar circumstances to those that Harris had experienced twenty years or so earlier.

As the night went on he also realised that his deliverance by the unlikely looking guardian angel who slept on the other side of the cold and smoky cabin now gave him a final opportunity to blackmail Harris for a large part of his worth. He was glad that he hadn't mentioned to Dave about McQuaig's untimely end and realised that the necessary law enforcement involvement in that occurrence would not help his cause at all.

"'the hell's that?" A rolling vibration of the cabin and the ground beneath was preceded by a loud cracking sound and a metallic crash as the one drinking mug they had shared earlier, fell from the top of the stove to a grate beneath. Scratchy's level of anxiety after the previous day's events made him jump to his feet almost as soon as the mug landed on the floor.

"Earthquake." Dave too sat up in surprise at the sound, waking him from a deep sleep. "There was one yesterday. Not as big as this one." Dave turned as if to go back to sleep. He had seen an otter acting strangely the day before and at the same time some ducks had taken flight in a panic and he had felt that tremor himself when sitting on a log cleaning the salmon he had caught. Earthquakes were a part of the history of the coastal people. Henry and Martha had told him of the tremors they had felt many years before when the big quake had hit Alaska. They didn't know about the Pacific plate, part of the earth's crust which was pushing eastwards at a few centimeters every year against the North American plate, building up immense pressures deep under the surface. They just knew that eventually a big earthquake would return. It had happened before and their ancestors had told them that it would happen again. So they knew it would.

The morning brought some relief from the sub-zero temperatures overnight. The sky was clouded and snow was falling when they left to find the skiff with the outboard motor which would take them back to Kitamaat from

Kildala Beach. The snow increased as the day wore on and visibility in front of the boat was severely limited so that Scratchy was unable to understand how Dave was able to find his way. However his longstanding knowledge of the area enabled him to get back before his passenger succumbed from the cold. On the way some landmarks could be identified and these were named in response to Scratchy's enquiries. Coste Island with the logging operation was just visible when they passed Gobeil Island on the left. The waves, now increasing in the early afternoon, hit the skiff sideways making a zig-zag course necessary to avoid being swamped.

"Gobeil Island." Dave gave an evasive shrug of the shoulders when asked about it. The ancient burial island of the Haisla's was no longer used for the above-ground burials of past years but was their property and of no significance to anyone else.

They passed the sawmill at Clio Bay. It was named after H.M.S.Clio which had anchored there as a threat to the people of the village to encourage them to trade with the Hudson's Bay Company and no one else. There were only two more miles then with a following sea before they reached Kitamaat village.

8

Diseases desperate grown by desperate
appliance are relieved.
Or not at all.

Shakespeare – Hamlet

Skills piscatorial and chirurgical, threats and arrangements, holidays at home and abroad.

The earthquake awoke Harris as well in Bishop Falls at five o'clock that morning. He heard a loud crack followed by a vibration lasting about three seconds, which had stopped before he was fully awake leaving no evidence within his room of its passing. 'It was probably around a four on the Richter scale,' he surmised, allowing only a brief consideration of the possibility of it causing any damage to his dam or to the access bridge he had also designed over a nearby creek. They were built to standard specifications and would withstand a much greater shock than the one that had woken him.

Now awake, Harris remembered a day four years back. He had gone fishing in the Kitamaat River near to where a bridge had been built by another firm. Downstream, pools of deeper water were known to attract salmon as they made their way up to the spawning grounds and he had made an early start to be there first, hoping for the best position. He was thwarted in this respect by a man with a rather unusual appearance and fixed facial expression, who had arrived earlier and was already fishing.

"How's the fishing," he asked him. The man gave only a non-committal shrug and continued fishing.

Harris sat on the bank, fifty yards upstream, preparing his line and watching the other, whose considerable skill at casting and placing his lure was belied, prior to the newcomer observing it, by the rather basic quality of his fishing equipment. He was using a spoon-shaped Kitamaat lure, red on one side, silver on the other and the whole given only the smallest extra weighting with a piece of lead. He stood on a rock in mid-stream, balanced on its sloping surface, his feet already wet from wading to it but safe from the numbing cold of the snow-melt waters hurrying past in the shallows. The focus of his attention was in the dark pools of deeper water across the stream. The lure glinted in the sun as he cast just beyond the place where salmon rested before their onward odyssey. The smallest of splashes hidden in the faster running stream beyond the pool would not be noticed by the fish in that Chinook run. He took up the slack in the light line, drops of water falling from it closer to his rod and glistening in the morning sun as he did so. But the rest of the line, across the river in the pool remained a hidden tether for the lure, writhing and twisting like an injured fish as it crossed the deeper, still waters.

Now standing in hip-waders upstream as he fished another pool, it was half an hour before Harris heard a splash as his neighbour stepped off the rock into the water for the first time to play a Chinook salmon he had hooked. It was not a big one by local standards, about twenty five pounds Harris guessed, as he noticed that the man had no landing net and called out asking if he needed to borrow his. The man shook his head, let the fish run, hauled it closer and let it run again, sensing the time to do so to keep the line from parting and then reeling it closer before letting it run yet again. This was continued for about fifteen minutes, a run for the shelter of a drowned tree being steered back to the pool, a run over the shallows to loosen the lure dealt with likewise, until the fish, exhausted, lay in the shallow water, its journey now ended. Harris' patience, always limited, had already run out and he walked down the river to watch the fish being finally landed.

"You staying?" he asked the fisherman, hoping to be able to take over his fishing spot.

"No. One fish is all I want," he replied as he looked up toward the bridge, checking the distance he would have to carry his fish as he gutted it there on the river bank. Harris followed his eyes to the bridge as the fish's bloody entrails washed back into the river, watched from nearby trees by a crow and two eagles, awaiting their chances.

For conversation's sake Harris, following the fisherman's line of vision said, "Good bridge that." The bright red newly painted supports and struts contrasted attractively with the natural deep greens of the forest surrounding them and his 'professional' interest was genuine.

The fisherman simply said, "No, it will move," and made to carry away his catch.

"Why?" Harris was amused.

"Water will wash it out underneath."

Harris saw that the plinths supporting the columns and the roadway above were surrounded by the standard quarter ton angular rocks, or rip wrap, required to prevent the scouring effect of the heavy water flows of the spring melt, when the snows higher up warmed into the swollen streams and creeks in the mountains. The construction appeared to be sound.

"No, don't you worry, that bridge won't move." Harris sounded confident.

"No, it will move," Dave Wilson said, for that was his name he told Harris when he was asked.

"Why will it move?" Harris was intrigued by Dave's certainty.

In answer Dave bent over where an eddy in the river washed over some sand and placed a small stick on end in the middle and supported it with small rocks around its base. The flowing eddy washed sand from under rocks until they moved and the stick fell. Dave had made models of bridges and buildings all his life and he knew it would.

"Needs more rock underneath or it will move."

Harris learned from observation and advice rather than the theory he had never studied and when he designed the Falls bridge on the way to the second dam, he put rock deep underneath as well as around the plinths. He remembered Dave just then, four years later, after the tremor.

Denial and a channeling of all of his attention on future matters were so much a part of Harris' life that it was several minutes that morning before he even thought about the two passengers he had left in the cold the previous day. It had been thirty degrees below zero during the early part of the night and a light snow had fallen later, now blowing in wild seething patterns across the roads and level open spaces seeking some obstruction to order them into drifts. He was sure that McQuaid and Stubbs would be dead and now he had to remove them from the platform so that they could be found closer to the townsite as if they had been lost overnight and frozen there. The weather allowed him to take off in his helicopter when the snow stopped at nine o' clock in the morning and it was soon after then that Harris discovered that both of them had disappeared from the platform above the valley. He became understandably anxious. McQuaid's body, now covered with snow, was not visible and the same snow now covered any tracks that Scratchy might have left before getting on to the forest trail leading down to the cabin by the creek.

On his return to town Harris was unable to work but sat nevertheless at his desk in his office at the worksite. It was Sunday and fewer interruptions were likely than might occur on other days and he stayed there to avoid having to talk to anyone while he thought through the various actions he might take. He had some brandy and then some more as it seemed to help. The day progressed. He didn't feel hungry and sat much of the time, his head in his hands, thinking over the circumstances which had brought him to his present predicament; explaining, blaming and denying until he confirmed his own innocence to his mind's satisfaction.

Another brandy and then another followed. He dozed fitfully remembering the past at times, between sleep, and thought of his daughter who had so inexplicably ended up in the same town as he and his wife Maria. He remembered his first wife and being unable to see himself as innocent in that situation, he fell asleep.

The train accident recurred in his dream and he recalled the fire. He was burning. A man carrying a pink newspaper ran towards him crying and thrust it in his face. He turned away and some curtains were placed around him while doctors pushed tubes into his throat. He was dying and had not admitted his guilt. His head nodded forward onto the desk and he lay there bent over until he was awoken suddenly when the door opened and Scratchy Stubbs walked in.

"Well, what are we goin' to do abou' i' all now?" The

greyhound eyes looked directly at Harris, who averted his gaze.

—

"So, 'ow can we come to some kind of a friendly agreement on all of this?" Scratchy, or Aloisius Stubbs, or Kitchener, the forger and neophyte blackmailer, looked across the desk at Jim Plunkett or Richard Harris, the clerk, thief, bigamist, would-be engineer and now, as yet unknown to himself, the murderer of Lawrence McQuaid.

Harris tested a light tone to see what response it might elicit. "Well, we could go into business together, share our talents and retire with a fortune. We could ask McQuaid to join us too." He wondered why McQuaid had not come in with Scratchy and hoped for enlightenment on that score.

"'E wouldn't want to."

"Why not? Everyone has his price surely?" Harris' assumption, based on his own philosophy would have been wide of the mark for McQuaid.

"Because 'e wouldn't." Scratchy realised that Harris was not yet aware of McQuaid's death and decided to withold the information until its impact would have the greatest effect to gain maximum benefit in their 'friendly agreement' negotiation.

Harris opened with, "What would our friendly agreement cost me and what would I get in return so as not to let anyone know that my friend Scratchy Stubbs is in Bishop Falls?" He felt reasonably confident of his position knowing that Scratchy was needed in London to discuss some matters of joint interest between himself and Scotland Yard.

"Well, le' us see," Scratchy decided to play cat and mouse for a while. "the last time oi was able to be of service to you, it cost you four hundred and fifty dollars. You was quite satisfied with that oi 'ope?"

"Yes. An excellent job it was too. We do work well together don't we?" Harris was relieved to think that he could deal with the problem for a relatively small sum of money.

"But for this agreement it 'as to be a bit more though." The look he gave Harris implied that he expected this to be turned down although he knew it could not be.

Harris relaxed seeing it. "I think we could accommodate some further understanding for say, five hundred dollars?" He affected an air of magnanimity.

"The figure of five 'undred sounds reasonable all right, if you add three noughts to it and pay it into moi bank account in Zurich. Oi'll give you the number. It doesn't 'ave a name. Oi wouldn't know which one to give them anyways." He couldn't help giving his conspiratorial gesture as he said this.

"Don't be bloody silly. I can't find money like that. I'll get you back to London pretty damned quick if you don't start to be reasonable." Harris was angry now and just a little worried about Scratchy's confidence when he asked for half a million dollars. "And anyway, once I've made an agreement with you I expect McQuaid will want the same and I just don't have it, so get out and damn you and your friendly agreement."

"No 'e won't."

Scratchy decided that now was the time to tell Harris.

"Who won't what?" Harris asked apprehensively.

"McQuaid won't want money, not where 'e's gone."

"How do you know he won't?"

"'e's dead, that's why, and you killed 'im."

Harris sat still looking cornered for a moment. Then calculating the odds and planning the means by which he could make Scratchy 'go away' as well as McQuaid before any damage was done, asked, "Where is he? McQuaid, I mean."

"That's just a little secret of mine oi'm afraid and will stay like that until we reach our friendly agreement and, oh by the way, oi told a few people that oi was comin' 'ere to see you just in case oi was 'indered or delayed in moi return, if you know what oi mean." Harris did know what he meant and had already considered such a hindrance as an attractive possibility for a resolution to his present difficulties and lacked only the means readily at hand to effect it. And so Harris, again at checkmate, where denial, projection and the possibility of violence all failed him, was left with no alternative. "How do I know that you won't come back for more if I give you money?"

"You don't. But oi won't. Wiv 'alf a million oi won't 'ave to. You'll just 'ave to believe me. You know oi'm trustworthy, never let you down 'n 'at which is more that oi can say for you." Scratchy pictured the ultimate let-down from the helicopter onto the freezing landing pad but did not feel vindictive towards Harris. This was simply business.

"It'll take me two weeks to get the money together." It was Harris' turn to be business-like. He knew he would have to pay up now and would have to arrange for Scratchy to 'go away' later.

"That's all right. Oi 'ave to 'ave a operation tomorrow an' oi'll be restin' for a couple of weeks after so oi can look forward to a sort of 'oliday wiv pay, if you know wha' oi mean Mr Plunkett, ah, oi mean Mr 'Arris. It's a shame my friend Larry McQuaid can't be 'ere to visit me in my hadversity, wiv grapes 'n 'at instead of sittin' up there playin' 'is 'arp."

The reminders were unnecessary for Harris.

"Get out!"

"Oh, Oh yes, of course Mr Plunkett, right away Mr Plunkett." Scratchy effected a mockery of a fawning exit, turned at the door as he left and looked directly at Harris, pointing at him.

"Five hundred thousand. Two weeks."

—

The operating room list for Tuesday, November thirtieth at the Bishop Falls Hospital listed a partial gastrectomy as the first case. Jim Sanders was the surgeon and the anaesthetist, Anna Plunkett. The patient, Aloisius Kitchener, was to have a large part of his stomach removed and the upper end joined to the small intestine in a complex procedure lasting two hours, unless at operation the cancer was found to have spread already to surrounding tissues. If that had already happened the operation would be restricted to the internal examination only and then terminated with closure of the incision and would in that event, be literally an open and shut case. The prognosis for survival of the patient then would be limited at best to only a few months.

Jim Sanders was an experienced surgeon. Anna knew that she couldn't be experienced in every field in which she involved herself and was always anxious during procedures such as this, knowing the number of possible problems which might arise.

"He's had his atropine and demerol an hour and a bit ago," the nurse advised Anna, "so he seems to be sleepy." The greyhound eyes opened and moved nervously to show that he was not. He was told that the pre-medication was not expected to be an anaesthetic and was then quickly given sodium pentothal intravenously, which was one. He was then given some galamine to relax his muscles so that his breathing could be taken over by a ventilator through a tube inserted in his windpipe.

“We’ll keep him on a nitrous oxide and oxygen mixture, about three to two ratio, and some halothane in a closed circuit with a little intravenous meperidine.” Anna started her commentary on the treatment she was using; she always did. “Keep the dextrose and saline mixture going and make sure the blood’s ready in the lab in case we need it later. Could you check his pulse and blood pressure every five minutes while I squeeze the bag until I can set up the ventilator?” Anna talked to the anaesthetic nurse who knew the routine anyway. “And can you check that the air is going into both lungs?” The position of the endotracheal breathing tube was critical.

The incision through the abdominal wall revealed a cancerous growth restricted to the lower part of the stomach with no obvious spread to the liver or surrounding tissues. The chances for recovery from this serious condition were not good but were at least better than average as it had been detected early and had not metastasised or spread to other parts of the body. Despite this the procedure did not go uneventfully.

Scratchy had not lived well and there was little reserve in his body to cope with the stress of a major operation. His experience two days before mitigated against his recovery since he was left close to exhaustion, a fact that he had not imparted to anyone since he had made his ‘friendly agreement’ with Harris.

“His pulse is going up and his blood pressure is dropping. It can’t be the atropine. That’s wearing off and he’s had some more demerol so it can’t be breakthrough pain. Is he losing much blood?” Anna asked Jim Sanders who was preparing the anastomosis; the suture line between the upper and the lower ends of the gut now that the cancer bearing area had been removed.

“A bit. Not too bad though,” he answered, “perhaps if we

push the intravenous and add a little potassium it might help."

Ten minutes later the patients blood pressure was even lower and a blood transfusion was started, but it was not until after the operation was finished, the galamine had worn off and the halothane eliminated from his body, that the readings came back to normal.

"Dr Anna. Message for you. There's a patient in maternity and two in emergency waiting for you. Can you see them between cases?" Anna thought to herself, 'I'm going to be old soon; very soon. That took two weeks off the end of my life. Is it worth it?' and to the anaesthetic nurse she said, "Can you get the next patient in and start the intravenous line with glucose saline while I see what they all need?"

—

Two days later Scratchy looked surprisingly well. At least he looked almost as well as he normally did despite having no food in his stomach and being maintained on intravenous fluids. Anna had visited on a routine assessment and told him that a visitor was waiting to see him outside. She called him in. It was Harris. Scratchy looked from Anna to Harris and back to Anna as the two of them passed the time of day. They seemed to know one another well he thought as he recognised the familial likenesses they shared and was amazed that Anna had not realised exactly who Harris was.

Anna moved on and Harris attempted the role of hospital visitor. He had omitted to bring anything with him and sat at the bedside uncomfortably.

"Well?" Scratchy spoke with difficulty as he still had a tube in his nose to drain stomach secretions up from the operation site. A pump at his bedside gurgled them into a glass container.

"Well what?"

Harris eyed the jar with evident distaste. He had not come in a supportive role and made no attempt to pretend that he had.

"'Ave you go' the money yet?"

"No. I told you two weeks."

"Why did you come then?"

"To see an old business partner," Harris lied. In fact he had wanted to assess Scratchy's chances of survival from the operation before getting the half million dollars for him.There was a long period of silence. Scratchy put on some ear phones to listen to the radio. Harris rose to go.

"Two weeks then." Another unnecessary reminder from the patient.

Harris left the ward. He would not come back again. Scratchy released the intravenous fluid line which somehow had been kinked and blocked in the drawer of his bedside locker during the time that Harris had spent there. As he did so he thought to himself, 'Bloody amateur. Business partner? Not bloody likely.'

—

South of the river Thames the heavy rain earlier in the afternoon now settled into a grey drizzle as the light faded over Clapham Common and the noise of London's traffic increased to a heavy drone as the evening rush hour started. Horns sounded by drivers, confused further by the semidarkness and their rain-covered, misted windscreens, increased to a cacophony of sound mellowed only partially by the sounds of the vehicle engines of the thousands of fellow travellers, each seeking to escape from the city to the refuge of home.

Yet another red London Transport bus stopped outside Frank Watson's house, its throaty diesel motor ticking over quietly, resting before moving off towards Balham, Streatham and the outskirts of the Metropolitan area at the sound of the bell pushed by the bus conductor collecting fares inside. It was filled to capacity with tired people, some rubbing condensation from the windows in an attempt to see outside past the rain, while others attempted to read, isolated within their own worlds which ended at arm's length with the evening newspaper.

"I'll 'ave to be goin' soon.," Hector Stubbs smiled then as he added, "It's good to be able to say that and know you're free to do it too. Sorry I couldn't 'elp any more."

"No, Hector," it was Frank Watson who spoke, "it's me who's sorry that I couldn't find Aloisius for you. If I do hear I'll let you know right away though. You were a great help anyway, and now don't forget your carving and thanks for letting me borrow it."

Hector looked for a moment at the carved salmon with the abalone shell decoration. "I don't really want it. Who'd want a wooden fish anyway? It's not important is it?"

"It's part of the culture of the First Nations People of the Pacific Northwest."

"What's that to me?" Unlike his brother Scratchy Stubbs, Hector had not had the same opportunity to travel and broaden his mind.

"Probably nothing much," Frank Watson replied thoughtfully.

"You keep it."

"I'll look after it for you in case you ever change your mind."

"Cheers."

"Cheers."

The door closed as Hector Stubbs stepped out to catch the next bus already splashing into the stopside rain puddle, while Watson carefully considered the new information he had learned. He was no longer particularly interested in Scratchy Stubbs, the man he had in the past travelled six thousand miles to find. His interest now was focused on Richard Harris, who was the reason for Scratchy's choice of British Columbia for his new homeland now that his country of birth had pronounced him *persona non grata*. Hector didn't know who Harris was, but did know that 'Scratchy', his brother Aloisius, had 'helped' someone who had wanted to 'disappear' after escaping a train crash in Gloucestershire many years before. Scratchy had told him that he was going to visit the man when he left for Canada.

Watson dialled a number on the telephone. It was next to the model longhouse.

"Roberts, could you help me again with that West Coast affair; the Stubbs business?"

"Thought you were retired now sir."

"You're right I am, but I can't let this one go quite yet. I need to know the names of anyone reported missing, whose remains were not identified after a train crash in Gloucestershire in the late twenties or early thirties".

—

The barometer on the wall above the nineteen seventy-seven calendar had risen over the two days since Watson's phone call and a clear morning sun painted the trees over Clapham Common with a yellow-orange light suffused by the remnants of the last day's fog, still in the atmosphere. Owners walked their dogs across pathways, avoiding the heavy morning dew on the grass and greeting each other with a nod or a smile, more friendly and outgoing now that the weather had improved. Watson had been one of those out for a morning walk and arrived home in time to answer the call he was expecting.

"Oh, Roberts. Any news?"

"Oh, yes,... yes,... ah ha,...yes,...really? Well there's a surprise. Thank you. Thank you. Now could you find out if there is anyone with either of those names who got an engineering degree in the early nineteen thirties? Oh yes, and I'll need the date of birth of Doctor Anna Plunkett, born in Gloucestershire around that time." Watson put down the telephone and stared long and hard at the longhouse model, smiled and said aloud, 'Well Dave Wilson, you old son-of-a-bitch you knew all along didn't you?' and then, after a pause, 'and you told me and I didn't listen, did I?'

Roberts had reported his findings on the nineteen twenty-nine train crash. There had been three people reported missing whose remains couldn't be identified, Muriel Lonsdale, a fifty-five year old teacher, Jim Plunkett a twenty year old clerk, and Robert Blaydon a seventy-three year old man from Wales. Jim Plunkett was the only one of them who got on the train in Gloucester. He had a wife who died fourteen years later, leaving a daughter, Anna.

'So Richard Harris was Jim Plunkett. Is it possible that Anna still doesn't know that?' It seemed incredible but was possible Watson admitted to himself. 'I think I'll take that holiday I promised myself and go to see my friends Dave and Jonas again.'

—

One summer's day in nineteen seventy Dave Wilson stood again on the bank of the Kitamaat River casting to the deeper pools close to the opposite side. As usual he would catch just one fish for himself and call it a day, but this morning having caught one earlier in the cool, fresh early hours he stayed on until the day reached its best time at nine o' clock. The sun, still low in the sky then, painted the trees, rocks and wild flowers with a depth of shadow and contrast in their colours which would wane as it rose higher. Then, the water running over the shallows ran whiter against the blue reflection from the skies, later to turn to grey when lit from above.

The fisherman looked up as two canoes appeared upstream, separated from each other by about a quarter of a mile. In the first, a thirteen year old girl, pretty, with auburn hair and brown, bright eyes, paddled hard although less effectively than the man in his late twenties who sat in the rear, controlling their direction as they sped with the current downstream. Their canoe, painted bright yellow, contrasted in the sunlight with the darker greens of the vegetation of the bank opposite Dave Wilson as they approached. He reeled in his line for them to pass.

"Sorry," the girl shouted excitedly, "another one coming after us I'm afraid. It may be some time though," she joked as she looked back to see the slower progress of those behind.

"Which is the main channel?" The man spoke from the rear seat, seeing that the river apparently divided just ahead of them, lying as it did in a flood plain littered with trees, stumps, roots and tangled branches which altered its main course from year to year.

Dave pointed to the right side and stood waiting for the second canoe to pass. It took another fifteen minutes for them to reach him, the paddlers simply keeping their vessel headed with the stream, drifting more quickly over the shallows and slowly as they reached the deeper pools along the river's course. They were deep in conversation, making only an occasional righting manoeuvre to keep their heading.

A warm feeling accompanied Dave's recognition that it was Anna sitting in the bow of the canoe facing the stern where a dark-haired man he hadn't seen before, controlled their direction with his paddle. Anna had only occasional work to do fending off the trees threatening to interrupt their progress. They didn't notice Dave until they were level with him, when he straightened and raised a hand acknowledging Anna as she drifted past. He always remembered her care of his injury when the logs had rolled on him, but he remembered her also because of some recurring dreams which included her and which might have been the reason for her making him feel comfortable and happy in her presence, even when no words were spoken.

She watched him as they passed and smiled a smile with a warmth which should have lit up his soul, though if it did it was not betrayed by his expression which remained unchanged. He knew she was beautiful, but that morning in the valley of the Kitamaat River in the sunlight, she was more so. He stood still, watching, willing the moment to stay as the current took her away as he knew it would.

"Hi Dave," she called as his heart seemed to turn over inside him.

The canoe drifted on and followed the left hand branch of the river, covered from either bank by trees arching over to meet in the middle. There it was cooler, darker and the air infiltrated with the scent of the wild flowers around the willows on either side. These trees were separated along the banks by fireweed colouring the intervening spaces with a pink glow on a matrix of darker greenery and grey rock. The sound of water running over the rounded pebbles and rocks in the shallows outside, an effervescent musical accompaniment to the flow of the stream, was quietened in the backwater where the canoe had been taken by chance. A sun-warmed sandy bar ended the stream there and the trees obscured any view of the fisherman still standing on the bank upstream. The canoe drifted aimlessly, slowly revolving in its course as it moved beyond Dave's sight, its passengers facing each other in the tunnel formed by the willows, possibly in deep conversation still, although possibly not. He couldn't see from the river bank.

Dave, who had not put his line back in the water, now sat still on the bank, remembering those weeks a year before in hospital when she had come to see him every day, when they rarely spoke as there was no need. His feeling of happiness induced by Anna's smile of recognition remained with him but there was also now a sense of heightened excited anxiety. Since their first meeting in Foch Lagoon two years before, he had loved her with an unspoken love with no possibility of declaration or mutual recognition. Now as her canoe drifted on he felt a sensation of all encompassing love which enveloped his mind from outside itself, but which he knew was not for him. He could feel his heart beating faster with each breath he took. His arms were around his bent knees, his head moving imperceptibly up and down with each breath. The excited anxiety increased as he sat there, the sun now rising higher in the sky, until there followed some time later a sensation of relief and the canoe reappeared to take the true channel downstream.

The colours and shadows in the trees and wild flowers were now flattened by the angle of the sun's light, now almost approaching the meridian. Anna, in front, remained facing backwards towards George Mandleson as he steered their direction onwards. Any change now was up to him as she had relinquished control over it and was happy to do so.

"We were worried about you," Georgi shouted as they

arrived at the prearranged picnic site. "We've been here for hours. We've been fishing but haven't caught anything. Where have you been?"

"We were exploring,"Anna offered.

"Where?"

"Everywhere. And we found our way here."

As he climbed from the canoe George had some difficulty focusing as he looked at Georgi. His eyes seemed to be watering and he brushed them with the back of his hand as he spoke.

"Must have got something in my eyes. Hi Georgi. How'd you get here so fast?"

"Brian's a fast paddler. Look, we've lit a campfire to cook weiners. Come on." Georgi's enthusiasm, infectious for those around her, stimulated more and more activity as the day progressed. It seemed no time before they had to take the canoes home on the truck they had left previously for that reason at the downstream park.

"Are you really going back to Vancouver tomorrow George?" Georgi asked him. She had felt an instant liking for this mild-mannered man she hadn't met until that day. "Why don't you stay? We could go on the river again. I could come with you next time in your canoe. I bet you could go faster with me than with Mum."

George reached over and touched her head allowing her hair to caress his fingers for just a moment longer than he should have done, as if to help make up for the years that they could not do so. His eyes had a sorrowful look as if hiding an unexpressed emotion. She withdrew slightly, uncertainly looking to Anna for the explanation she couldn't give her.

"I've got to work.," George told her.

"Will you come back later?"

Georgi wanted him to come again.

"I don't know when. I think I will."

George seemed rather distracted.

Brian drove them all back to the start point and then took the canoes and Georgi home while George and Anna returned to the park to fetch a lost camera.

"Well, do we tell her?"

"Not yet,"Anna decided.

—

Back there at the river's bank, where they had been unable to do it for themselves, fate redirected their lives. Standing in front of a rock with George it was Anna who first saw the lost camera and bent to pick it up. In doing so she was aware of a sound like the crack of a whip sharply punctuating that of the background rush of water and realised that George had been jolted sideways as if struck by some heavy weight. She felt a wet warmth as blood spattered her clothes and heard a groan as George sank to his knees grasping at his right shoulder with his left hand. His right arm fell uselessly to his side and they both realised at the same time that he had been shot. Anna used her clothing to stem the flow of blood from a bullet wound in the front of his shoulder and also another behind it where the bullet had gone right through.

She shouted for help and it was Dave Wilson, now on his way home, who was first to arrive. He looked at the trail of blood running down the rock where George had been standing and saw it congealed on the ground beneath. He looked towards Anna before running for help.

She lay George's head on her lap trying to apply pressure to the wounds as she did so and the amount of blood loss, at first massive, then slowed as so much had drained from his body. His face, a deathly pallor now replacing its previously ruddy complexion of good health, looked up at Anna, his eyes looking into hers directly. He felt her body's warmth against his cheek, heard her heart racing with her anxiety as she tried to help him and felt a weakness overcoming him from a tiredness such as he had never known before. He seemed to be panting for breath as if he had been running and yet his legs felt leaden.

"Don't go. Please don't go." Her voice seemed distant but he saw the meaning in her eyes and knew that death was not far from him. She rested his head against her as she had done in another country years before. He felt the movement of her breathing and felt her heart beat which seemed to give him strength. He remembered the night long ago when he had heard her heart sounds before. His field of vision narrowed until it seemed to him that he was looking through a dark tunnel, the surrounding greenery blurred into an appearance like dark green moss. He tried to speak but was unable to do so as weakness prevented him. He looked up into her eyes and saw light reflecting through the darkness around him. His hand felt cold against the grey rock at his side.

"I don't know what to do." He formed the words with his lips and Anna gently pressed her finger against them and then against her own and remembering when she had done that before, she felt an intense love together with a desperate fear of further loss as George lapsed into unconsciousness.

The loud siren of an ambulance, which had been audible for several minutes as it approached, now stopped as it arrived at her side. Anna noticed it only then.

—

Dave Wilson felt Anna's pain yet could do nothing for her other than to go to fetch help for George Mandleson. He saw the blood running down the rock, saw Anna's fear of loss and felt the proximity of death. He had no fear of dying himself after his own past experiences but he knew the feeling of loss that it brought about and felt and shared Anna's anxiety. He was excluded from her world by cultural, social and intellectual differences and his world reciprocated this divide. Yet there was understanding.

He had to get away for a while being unable to wait there, feeling her need and knowing it was beyond his means to help her. He went to his home and after a return to the town-site went back to Kitamaat to fetch his skiff to leave for the night, spending his time where he was at his happiest, on the water, alone. But he was not always alone there, for Gordon often went too and he knew he would be there this time. At the town-site, on Anna's porch he had left a model of a canoe he had made several weeks before that day. There was a man in the stern and a woman sitting in the front facing him. There was no message and he didn't ring the door- bell for there was no need; the gift was the message and it would be understood.

By the morning he had either drifted or idled his outboard in or out of gear until he was twenty miles down the saltwater channel and there he stopped at the disused cannery at Butedale. He bought some oil and gasoline and some chocolate from the store which opened there in the summer months to supply passing boaters. He looked across to the route into Bishop Bay that Henry and Martha had paddled on their way back from first seeing him after he had been born in Vancouver forty-one years earlier. He wouldn't have remembered how long it was but Martha kept count for him. He followed their route back and was within five miles of home when he felt the skiff lift slowly upwards on a wave about six feet high. It stayed there for a few seconds before gently lowering him again.

The tsunami had passed all but unnoticed, its bulk hidden in the deep water beneath him as it sped towards the top of the inlet searching for some solidity on which to vent its huge potential energy. At the shoreline on either side he saw now a wave breaking with destructive power and ahead, closer to home, he saw the wave cresting and stirring up dead heads and their roots, crab pots, driftwood and even rocks from the cliff-side. Yet when the sun set an hour later, calm water reflected its glow and there was silence in the valley except for quiet voices calling to each other from the chaos.

"You can stay." Henry said when Dave stepped ashore. "Martha's gone." There were tears in his eyes. Henry was seventy-five years old and couldn't start again by himself.

Dave stayed. He never went back to the camps, to his cabin in the woods or even into the forests to hunt. He stayed with Henry. And after that, he stayed by himself.

9

Wise are the children in these dayes that know their owne fathers, especially if they be begotten in the dogge daies when their mothers are frantick with love.

Greene, 1589

Fathers lost and found, love found and lost, truth told and truth withheld.

At first it hadn't seemed to matter that she didn't have a father at home. As an infant and only child, Georgi had all the love and attention she needed from Anna. This was enough for her and she was happy. When her world became divided into two parts however, when she went to school, she was able to look at the one from the perspective of the other and noticed that there was a deficiency in her life. It was not a serious one but one more like having to deal with the way she spoke or with her warts and freckles and she had plenty of both of those. Her speech was tinged with an English accent, learned at home from her mother in her other world, and this difference was noticed and pointed out to her. She began to feel different from the others, who all felt their own differences and worried about them, and her child's sensitivity led her to see what she might do about it.

Her accent was easily changed but the freckles were not. However after the summer break there were many who couldn't point the finger of criticism on that matter and her main preoccupation became therefore to solve the problem of her missing a father. She soon learned that she wouldn't be able to enlist Anna's help in her search when she noticed that she became upset whenever the question was raised, but she did learn that her father was still alive and that he had married someone else a long time previously. Although in her mind this man, her father, was above any form of criticism, she allowed that he had in fact made a mistake in not seeing that Anna would have been the ideal wife for him.

When Maria had offered to be her 'Dad' she had thought it the best thing that anyone had ever done for her; better than when Abigail Spencer had given her her last stick of chewing gum and better even than Christmas. Admittedly her perspective of the latter from the viewpoint of a summer's day might have made it comparatively less desirable than that which the immediacy of mid-December might have presented.

Now, seven years later at the age of thirteen, her hope that her father would come home was no less on her mind than it had been in the intervening years. Georgi heard Anna's car arrive home and heard her go straight upstairs without the usual hug and kiss she expected.

"Mum, is that you? Did you find the camera? What took you so long?"

"I'll be down in a minute. I have to change." Anna's voice was strained and Georgi ran upstairs to see what was wrong to find that her mother was crying.

"Georgi, go downstairs and wait for me there. There's something I have to tell you; something important and I need to think about it for a minute first." Anna had changed already. Georgi noticed the discarded clothes with blood on them but said nothing.

When Anna came down Georgi was sitting at the empty table, her hands clasped. She looked frightened and knew that she was about to hear some bad news. Anna drew up a chair near to her and having regained her composure started to tell her the events that had happened after their day out on the river with George.

"George Mandleson" she started, "the man who went on the river with us today…," Anna paused and Georgi, seeing her hesitation nodded encouragement for her to continue, "is seriously ill in the hospital. I have to tell you that he may not live. He's having an operation at the moment. He was shot. It must have been an accident." Anna couldn't conceive any possible reason for George being shot and assumed that it must have been accidental.

Georgi's response, intuitively reading her mother's feelings, caught Anna off guard when she asked her. "Do you love him?"

"Yes," Anna told her, "yes, I do."

Georgi got up and bent over to give Anna a kiss on her cheek as she said, "He'll be all right. I know it. Don't worry." Then Anna remembered the infirmary at Gloucester when her mother was expected to die but didn't.

"What's that on your arm?" Georgi was referring to the bandage stuck on the front of Anna's elbow.

"Oh, I gave some blood for his operation. He has a rare blood group like me and they needed a lot of it." Anna remembered the thirteen people from the community who had all come when asked to give blood for George's operation. It was always like that in a small town; people helping people they don't even know. With that thought she was given strength to continue, strength to tell her daughter what she should perhaps have told her years before.

"There's something else I have to tell you. I don't know what you'll think; whether you'll hate me for not telling you before." Georgi stared fixedly at Anna's eyes, her head shaking slowly from side to side, denying that she could ever feel that way about her. Anna hesitated, seemed to take a deep breath and said simply, "George Mandleson is your father."

Georgi's expression changed from the fixed stare to one of incredulity and surprise for a few seconds and then, slowly, her lips widened into a broad smile as her mind registered the meaning of the words she had just heard.

"Can I give him some blood?" She was ready to help. She knew he would get better and that she would make it happen if she could. She got up to fetch her coat.

"No. Stop. They have enough now." Anna's tears returned, moved by the pathos behind Georgi's offer.

"I'll make some tea. Can I see him afterwards? Tonight?" She wanted to get on with this father business right away.

"No. He'll be in the operating room for a long time and will need rest afterwards. Perhaps you'll be able to go after school tomorrow." Anna spoke until she had explained everything that Georgi could assimilate about her new-found father, about the circumstances of her own birth and George's only recent knowledge of the fact that he had a daughter. When she stopped there was silence as Anna looked down to the floor uncertain about the emotions she might have released. She then felt a kiss on her forehead, a child's arms around her neck and an intense sensation of relief.

At six o'clock in the morning Anna was up and preparing to go to work. The telephone had rung several times during the night but that was not unusual and Georgi had eventually slept through until morning after a sleepless excitement had dominated her mind earlier. On waking her first thoughts were of George.

"Is he all right?'

"Yes. He's awake but very weak. I'll let you know later if you're allowed to see him after school. I'll ask Ali to make you some breakfast now. I have to go."

"No, it's all right. I'll do it. I'm okay." Georgi was used to being independent.

Immediately after Anna's departure from the house however, she left by the back door and followed the path into the forest where she would often walk with Anna. In the early dawn shafts of yellow light shone through the trees lighting her way and she walked for twenty minutes until she came to a clearing. She had worried about bears and saw one in the distance but it was busy pulling down a mountain ash tree to eat its red berries and didn't see her. A twig snapped nearby and made her start, but a squirrel jumping from one tree to the next chattered noisily to explain what had happened and she continued on into the clearing where she saw, lit by the morning sun the orange-red flowers of the Indian Paint Brush. She was already late for school when she arrived back and went on instead to the hospital.

"Hi Georgi. How're you? Not at school today?" someone called out.

"I'm fine." She waved as she walked on into the ward as if she were on a mission. She was. She knew her way. She had been there in the past with Anna and the staff knew her and were too busy to notice her when she saw George and walked up to his bed.

"George," she said, "I've brought you these." The wild flowers were now in a small jam jar which she put into his hand while she held his wrist, tightly as if to stop him from leaving. She sat in a chair at his side. George acknowledged her with a smile but was too weak to say anything. She was aware that a nurse was approaching.

"You can't stay here Georgi. It's not visiting time and Doctor Mandleson needs a rest. Why did you come anyway?" the nurse asked, wondering why she wasn't at school.

"He's my Dad." Georgi said proudly and looked as if she wouldn't allow anyone to make her leave. She didn't move.

A fair-haired woman then walked into the ward and approached the three of them. Ellen had arrived on the first morning flight from Vancouver carrying some red roses.

"How are you George?" She stood back and handed the roses to the nurse who put them on George's bedside locker together with the flowers from Georgi which were now hidden behind.

George managed only a non-committal look and Ellen turned her attention to Georgi, sitting at his side.

"Hello. Who are you?"

"I'm Georgina Plunkett." She remained seated, inclining her head sideways and nodding towards George as if to declare ownership over him she said again, "He's my Dad." She still held tightly to his wrist.

Ellen stared uncomprehendingly as Anna came into the ward and saw what must have taken place.

—

On that summer day in nineteen seventy, fate had not yet finished with them. Perhaps, Anna thought later, there is just so much joy and so much hardship to go around and as the first had been spent disproportionately this was simply the reckoning, the evening out of the ledger of life.

At seven thirty that evening the Pacific plate part of the earth's crust, which had been pushing eastward towards the North American plate for centuries, had again caused a level of pressure where a movement along a fault line would occur. These movements were frequent, usually small and only rarely significant. This one was an exception and occurring off the Queen Charlotte Islands under the sea, an immense shock wave, registering six point eight on the Richter scale, travelled at thousands of miles an hour towards Bishop Falls. It was followed more slowly by a tsunami, a giant wave created by the underwater movement upwards of the seabed at the epicentre of the earth movement.

—

That evening, after Georgi's enthusiastic declaration to Ellen of her newly-discovered relationship with George, Anna returned to her home unsure about the reaction she would receive from Ellen who had accepted her offer of a place to stay that night. Ellen had little alternative to Anna's offer and even less emotional drive to go out to find one. The earthquake earlier that evening had added to the emotional confusion surrounding them as well as shutting down power and water as well as the hotels.

"I'm really glad you decided to stay here tonight in the end. I wouldn't like to think of you staying at the hotel anyway by yourself and worrying there about .... things, even if they could take in guests after tonight's events." Anna's voice trailed off into uncertainty. She had told Ellen briefly earlier about herself and George and the circumstances of Georgi's birth and had left her to think it over during the day, knowing that they would need to talk about it again later.

Ellen looked away and shrugged one shoulder. The gesture expressing her unspoken resentment rather than disinterest, and they both knew that open discussion on her feelings would not be productive.

"How is he this evening?" Ellen was able to ask.

"His blood pressure's better and his kidneys are beginning to work again so he's through the worst as far as his survival's concerned but as Jim told you this morning, the injury to his arm is serious and he's unlikely to be able to use it well enough to continue in surgery as a career." Anna repeated Jim Sanders assessment of the gunshot wound that had damaged the nerves and the main blood vessel to George's arm as well as puncturing his lung. He had been lucky to survive.

"Do you feel hungry? We've no power but I can open a tin of something and cook it on the barbecue." Ellen didn't answer Anna's question. She looked lost and tired and turned towards her.

"Where do I stand in all of this?" She had moved on in her mind from George's injury to the hurtful feeling of rejection that welled up inside her. It was a feeling coloured by righteous indignation that however could not gain its full expression of aggrieved ill-treatment which her inner self expected her to show because it was tainted by an inexplicable feeling of relief. Where she had continued to present to herself and to others a picture of ecstatic happiness in her marriage, she had been unable until then to see that it was all an illusion and that her marriage had failed. The relief showed through the resentment on her face and enabled Anna to discuss the matter further.

"It's not really for me to say," she started. "I am obviously…an intruder in your life and know that what I've done appears to be wrong, yet for Georgi's sake I have to be here talking to you, trying to justify the unjustifiable. You know, I've waited so long I almost feel as if I've paid some kind of a penance for my wrong-doing, and now, if he were to ask me, I would have him gladly. At the same time I would have to live with the guilt of what I would have done to you; a guilt for which I would have no right to expect you to forgive me. Yet I would live with it because I can't bear the sorrow of living away from him any longer. Georgi needs her father and it would be partly for her that I would do it, but I have to tell you in honesty that I would also now be looking at my needs which I have ignored for almost fifteen years. So I can't play the part of the penitent because that I am not. I suppose I am simply self-interested and am therefore diminished by it in that respect, but I can do nothing else." Ellen said nothing and Anna continued, "Could we work together to help him regain his strength first? The rest would have to take its own course. And Ellen, I've always thought about you as a friend. I don't expect you to return that friendship now but I want you to know that I care about you."

Ellen raised her eyes from the floor and shrugged her one shoulder again perhaps acknowledging a resentful acceptance of fate's dictate, but then her stance seemed to straighten as her mind moved from thoughts of self- pity to another plane; that of emotional survival. In that she had had practice and had mastered it well.

"I'm delighted to stay with you Anna and appreciate the help you gave George when he was injured. He might not be here if it hadn't been for you." She paused for a moment searching for the most advantageous moral high ground. "My husband is a highly qualified doctor and you are our friend and have been so nearly as long as he and I have known each other. It was just after our engagement that he went to London I believe? We've had a successful marriage and I am sure that he'll be able to work it out for the best and I certainly don't intend to influence him, to persuade, cajole or get angry with him. I shall go back to our home in

Vancouver tomorrow and when he's well enough I am sure he'll go back there to join me. Everything will be as it was before for us and I expect he'll soon forget all about your daughter and her ideas. I am sure he'll write to keep in touch so that I can follow his progress in hospital."

On her self-pitying plane Ellen didn't believe what she was saying, but the positive thoughts about their relationship, even though it had never existed in the way she had imagined, enabled her to live through the rest of that evening with Anna and the rest of her life without George. She had emotional strength from her past that kept her on this different plane of existence and she relied on it always. To the outside world she was a competent self-confident woman. She was an asset as an employee, hardworking but somewhat distant and even rigid in her personal relationships and her criticism of others although frequent and judgmental in her own mind, was never outspoken or shared.

On this plane she expected George at some time to come back into her life as if he had never left it, but on her brief forays into reality she knew that he never would. Over the years she wrote to Anna, Georgi and George, her letters separating George from the other two both in content and in mailing. After all, George was her husband and always would be. The question of divorce was not therefore a consideration at any time.

Like Ellen, Anna too was a person of considerable independence but her personality differed. Her independence was grounded in reality. The support given by her mother before her death and her father's apparent death in a railway accident were factors in this development, so that she had learned early on to find strength from within when she needed it. She had a catholic understanding of right and wrong and a nineteen fifty's sense of morality. But just the earliest breath of a wind of change had sustained her life-style in its then socially questionable, but soon to be accepted form.

Nevertheless she still anguished over her role in George's marriage, while for Georgi, not looking 'through a glass darkly', there was no room for debate. George was her father, Anna her mother and they should live at home. There were inevitably some who raised their eyebrows in criticism and Anna tried hard to be friendly with them. Her work was above reproach and the criticism slowly diminished until there was only the occasional innuendo hinted by one of those seeking in so doing to raise his or her own self-image to one of righteous superiority from its self- perception of inadequacy. In short, their lives all returned to normal.

—

"What's the weather like at the Bishop Falls airport? Will we be able to land there today?" a harried mother asked the flight attendant of a Boeing 737 bound north out of Vancouver while her two boys fought over a dropped toy, fallen into the seat in front. She bent forwards to retrieve the boys and the errant toy and gave a sigh of relief when she heard that they could expect to land on time. The weather would not therefore force on them the three-hour drive from Prince Rupert, which would be the plane's alternate destination in bad weather. Across the aisle a burly older man heard the news with similar feelings. However from their vantage-point of twenty five thousand feet he had guessed already that there would be no difficulty, as the mountains of the Pacific Northwest up and down the coast could be seen, snow-covered and clear in the morning light. The rising sun threw shadows to the west giving depth to the view of the brightly-lit eastern slopes, accentuating the patterns of white and every shade of blue reaching westwards to the Pacific Ocean.

"It's a long way to come isn't it?" The man nodded to the woman when they received the advice. "You were on the same plane as me yesterday from London. You'll be glad to get to where you're going, I imagine."

"Oh, I didn't see…" she started to say.

"You were too busy with those young fella's." He pointed to the boys whose war had started again but who looked quite relieved when the toy was confiscated, despite their protestations of aggrieved unfair treatment. It's hard being a boy, especially after a long- haul flight with a brother.

"I'm going to Bishop Falls. I'll be glad to get there too," he said with evident relief at the prospect of arrival.

"We're going there as well. A short holiday with my aunt. She's a doctor there."

"Anna Plunkett?"

"Yes. Do you know her?"

"Met her once almost three years ago. I was hoping to see her on this visit as well. My name's Frank Watson."

"Sylvia James." She held out her hand across the seat, "I'll tell her we met and that you might call."

"So you're not a Plunkett."

"No, my aunt's the only one left now. My great uncle was killed in a train crash and his wife died a few years later. My aunt keeps her maiden name and her daughter's called Plunkett."

"So she didn't marry again?" Frank Watson knew that Anna had not been married previously but respectfully implied a denial of that knowledge in the question concerning her subsequent life.

"No. There was some talk though… but I'll leave that for her to tell you," she said, realising she didn't know this man herself and cutting short her words as a result. "What do you do?" She felt that it was not too intrusive to ask after the information shared so far.

"I'm retired. Worked all my life for the metropolitan police. I came here last time on business but this is simply a holiday; general interest. It's a fascinating place, fascinating people too. In fact that package I've carried as hand luggage all the way here is for someone I met here last time. It's a model of London Bridge." Watson sat back wondering what the effect would be on all these people when they learned that James Plunkett had lived for years in Bishop Falls, Vancouver and who knew where else, after his disappearance in nineteen twenty-nine.

The plane touched down an hour later under a blue sky and Watson, together with Sylvia James and her two combatants, transferred to the bus for Bishop Falls.

—

The next day Watson found the drive to Kitamaat Village along the winding coastal road was very different in summer than it had been in the snowstorm on his previous visit when he had carried the model longhouse back to town in a taxi. The estuary was mirror calm and the spring tide was now at its turn so that no movement could be seen on the surface of the water, or around the old tree stumps snagged on the bottom where some tide of long ago had stranded them. These now were the occasional perches for bald eagles, seagulls and for cormorants drying their wings in the sun after diving for small fish under water.

The dark convoluted skeletal patterns of the roots showing above the water and now reflected in its glassy surface by the bright morning light, appeared as might stark primeval images at the dawn of nature, until the eye saw above them, across the estuary, the smoke and gaseous discharges from the industrial processes of the aluminum plant and paper mill on the opposite side. Snow still melted from the distant mountain peaks but the morning was warm as Watson made his way past a log dump. There, log booms were being constructed from rafts of logs dumped into the water from logging trucks. They were being gathered for transport by stubby booming boats into wooden pens held by chained containing logs, before being pulled out to deeper water for loading onto a barge which dwarfed the tugboat waiting to tow it onward to the sea.

Ahead on the road a black bear squinted myopically at his approaching car before climbing up a steep bank at the roadside while an eagle watched it disappear into the forest from a burned fir tree which had survived still standing after a fire in years gone by.

'It's not like Clapham Common,' Watson thought to himself, smiling wryly at the odd comparison as he approached the village.

Dave Wilson was painting his skiff. It was inverted over two oil drums, its outboard engine removed. It was the same one which had carried Scratchy Stubbs back to Kitamaat one cold winter's day in the past, but now the sun dried the new coat of paint almost as soon as it was applied. Now the white snow flakes of that other time were replaced by black flies attracted by its pungent aromatic smell.

"Good to see you Dave."

"You too."

"How've you been?"

"Good. You?"

"Apart from age, fine."

"How's Jonas?"

"He's good."

"I'll go and see him later."

"He'd like that."

"Do you still make those models? I've still got the one you gave me. It had a close call though. A bottle fell off the shelf and broke one end but I was able to fix it so that it looks as good as new."

Dave said nothing. He was thinking of his childhood, of his mother and Bill and of Gordon. He didn't know why as he hadn't thought of them for a long time. Watson looked at him quizzically, unable as usual to read his expression. He looked much older now than when they had met before. Dave continued briefly to brush on the anti-fouling paint but the flies bothered his arms and he was glad of a reason to stop.

"They come in the first week of August every year. Only visitors we don't welcome," he spoke as he swatted at one with his brush, missing it and leaving a globule of red paint on one of the drums. It ran down like a trail of blood before congealing on the hot metal. The two men watched it until it stopped, an irrelevant visual focus for their unrelated thoughts, but one which stirred memories of past unpleasant images for at least one of them.

"I want to tell you about something Dave. Just between you and me if that's all right," Watson began. "I've retired now you know." The truth of this statement was evidenced by the absence of his tie and by the garish summer shirt he wore. It didn't suit him but it showed that he was at least trying to accept the enforced retirement dictated by age rather than competence.

"It's about that man Harris." Dave looked directly at Watson in reply and was apparently willing to help but when he added, "and about Anna Plunkett," the eyes were averted and his body movement became more guarded as he spoke.

"What about Harris?"

"Well, he wasn't. Wasn't called Harris at all. His real name was Plunkett. Same as Doctor Anna. Even where he and I come from it's not a common name." He paused to let the words develop their own significance and then added, "Anyway it seems that he was in a train crash years ago and survived it well enough to disappear for years until he came to Canada."

"Well?"

"He was her father."

"I know."

Watson had expected the information to surprise Dave but it was he himself who was startled by the response he heard. "How did you know Dave? It's taken me three years to find it out and you knew all along didn't you?"

"Yes. Kitchener told me."

"Who else knew?"

"I don't know. Maybe his wife, you, perhaps McQuaid."

"Where's McQuaid?"

"Disappeared. Never seen after the quake."

"And Anna Plunkett, did she know Harris was her father?"

"Don't know." Dave's eyes again averted, his manner guarded until he spoke again. "Coffee?"

Watson allowed the change of direction. He liked Dave and didn't want to put pressure on him, but he still needed to know and would get back on track later. "Thank you yes. I need one at this time of day to help with the jet lag." Dave didn't seem to understand him and he went on, "Did you say that you still make those match stick models?"

"Sometimes. Not often now."

"You should. They're good." Watson then asked quickly, "Have you seen Doctor Anna?"

"Yes."

"Have you told her about Harris?"

"No."

"Why didn't you?" Watson was intrigued.

"She wouldn't want to know. He wasn't a good man."

"Who told you he wasn't."

"No one. He tried to kill Kitchener so I know." Dave had never told the story about Scratchy's rescue from the frozen forest. There had been no reason to until then, and when Watson asked, there was no reason not to do so. The account of Harris' involvement painted him in a different light from that of an opportunistic embezzler and Watson's interest increased as the story unwound.

"So you don't think we should tell Doctor Anna about her father?" Watson knew the answer but wanted to see Dave's commitment to keeping it secret. Dave's reply was a non-committal shrug but his eye contact told him that it was something about which he had strong feelings. Dave had been protective about Anna for years now and this was simply part of a self- imposed mission. He lowered his eyes then as Watson looked away and said, after some lengthy period of consideration, "You're right. She wouldn't want to know. But is it right not to tell her what we know about him?" Watson saw that they were both becoming part of the deception that had started half a century before in a train disaster. "And what about his estate?"

"His what?"

"His money. He was wealthy wasn't he? If his wife dies Doctor Anna should get everything he owned and if we keep quiet it will all go to his son."

Dave Wilson shrugged again. Money had no relevance for him and he couldn't see why it would for anyone else. They sat on Dave's porch. It was on the same house where Henry and Martha had lived. The flies used to come every August then too, Dave remembered. Henry used to chase them around with a cedar batten and get angry with them while Martha laughed. He kept on until either they left or he was too tired to continue and he would then pretend to chase Martha while she laughed as he smacked the cedar against the woodwork. Dave missed those days with Henry and Martha. His father Tom never came up now and stayed in the city where he had worked most of his life. Dave was glad to have visitors.

"More coffee?"

"Thank you, yes. By the way, I've brought you something. Hope you like it."

Watson went back to the car and brought out a wooden model of London's Tower Bridge.

"Thanks. Did you make it?"

"Yes."

Dave nodded and tried the mechanism included in the central elevated roadway.

"Don't tell her."

"Perhaps not."

"No. Don't tell her." He held Watson's arm and looked at him directly and the latter didn't reply but thought to himself that he probably wouldn't do so. They sat not speaking for several minutes while two eagles circled overhead, the lift from a thermal current helping them to rise effortlessly higher. Two crows, which had been worrying them away from their nests, were left behind cackling and complaining at the earlier intrusion. Dave watched as they circled in opposite directions.

"It's going to stay hot," he said absently.

"How d'you know?" Watson was always intrigued by local knowledge and wondered how this new information about the weather was transmitted from the eagles. He watched them intently but could read no sign himself.

"It was on the weather forecast this morning." Dave couldn't understand why Watson seemed to be laughing at himself when he heard this.

"I'm going to talk to Maria Harris this afternoon. She must know something about him." Watson got up to go. "I'll be back later. I'll see Jonas then perhaps."

—

"Anna's out. She's at work." Watson was surprised by the change he saw in Maria Harris when he called round to see her at Anna's house the following morning. Knowing that Anna would be out he hadn't telephoned before going as he wanted to see Maria alone. He had heard that she was a permanent guest at Anna's ever since the earthquake had destroyed her own house.

"Yes, I know. I had hoped to have a word with you if that's possible. I could always come back later if it's not convenient but it's rather important that we are alone as I have some confidential news which is rather personal." Watson looked concerned and friendly as he said this. Years of interviewing every possible sort of person had enabled him to switch on the appropriate approach to succeed in gaining anyone's confidence and Maria responded by opening the door wider and standing back to allow him in.

He sat down in a chair with a view of the forest edge and distant mountains and looked out, avoiding facing her directly to put her at ease. He had already noticed that she was restrained and anxious, that she repeatedly looked away and then back to him as if there was something she wanted to tell him but which she was unable to confront in her own mind. After discussing the view, the weather and other matters of minor local interest, Watson opened with an enquiry about Harris' disappearance in the earthquake and seeing that her response was uncertain but not coloured with persisting grief he asked, "Do you know what your husband did before you met him?"

"He was an engineer." Her reply came easily but a slight elevation in tone on the last word suggested her own uncertainty on the matter.

"Did you meet his family? Did you know where he lived before you met him in London?" The questions followed quickly one after the other and seeing her guarded response as she replied in the negative, he returned to irrelevant matters to help her relax for a while before asking, "What did he do as a young man? Where was he born?"

She took a deep breath of resignation. "I don't know, but his passport which I didn't see until after he died, said the London Borough of Camberwell. We never went there, and as far as I know there were no relations there or anywhere else for that matter. Why are you asking these questions?"

"I promise you I am not simply intruding but I need to know what you know about him before I can tell you the news I have." Watson turned now to face her. Her sixty-seven years weighed heavily on her. Her shoulders stooped, not from the lower neck in the way that the soft bones of old age might make them, but from the upper trunk as if she was weighed down by some long-standing worry or some unbearable memory. A radio in the next room prattled irrelevantly while the two looked toward each other for what seemed to be half a minute.

"I think you've heard something about his past which I don't know. Please tell me," Maria said. "I know nothing about him from before the day I met him in nineteen thirty-two. He always refused to discuss his past. I thought it was because he had been unhappy, but in later years I suspected there might have been other reasons but didn't know what they might be."

"Why did you think that?"

"I haven't told anyone about this and need your help to advise what you think I should do. I am not well and may not have long to live." She was thinner than he remembered on his previous visit to Bishop Falls and her face was more lined. These were not the creases around the eyes and mouth which give some older people a permanent smile, but were those sloping in the direction of her drooping shoulders, matching them in an appearance of long-standing dejection. Her facial expression was flat while she spoke.

"It was seven years ago, the day before the earthquake. Richard had been getting irritable and tense for the previous few weeks. He said people were out to harm him and were following him and that Mr. Kitchener was trying to kill him. He started drinking a lot and became angry when I mentioned it. One time he looked around and spoke as if there were someone in the room beside the two of us and was angry when I told him it was just his imagination. At night he dreamt a lot and often spoke out in a strange voice so that I couldn't understand what he said, but one night he kept saying, 'Killed McQuaid. Stubbs next.' He often said the name 'Anna' but she visited us a lot then with Georgi so I wasn't surprised."

The lines on her face then eased into a weak smile as she said, "Did you know that Georgi calls me 'Dad'." Watson shook his head and nodded for her to continue.

Her voice became quieter, her brow furrowed again and her mouth was dry so that she fetched some water. She drank some, offered some to Watson and when he shook his head continued, "To tell you the truth, I think he had begun to lose his reason. I told him he should see the doctor but he said he had already seen Mr.Kitchener talking to a doctor that day and that that was enough for him. The next day, it was a Sunday, he went out and took his hunting rifle with him. He hadn't slept that night and refused food. He said he was going hunting. I was worried and followed him in our camper but had to keep a long way back in case he saw me. When I got to the river I heard a shot and his car went off afterwards in the opposite direction. That evening I heard that Doctor Mandleson had been shot. No one knew who had done it but I guessed it was Richard. He didn't come home and the next day was the earthquake and he was killed or so we believe. They could never find his body but his car was smashed to pieces by the logs along the water's edge when the tsunami wave came."

Watson said nothing for a minute or so and then asked, "And you said nothing in order to protect his memory?"

"No, not for that reason. I didn't want Anna to know that my husband had tried to kill Georgi's…"she stopped for a few seconds before finishing awkwardly, "…her friend."

Watson guessed the answer and didn't ask her what she had meant. He did the social arithmetic and balanced the equation for himself. So Maria's husband he surmised, who, unknown to herself was Anna's father, tried to kill his daughter's lover, George Mandleson, who was the father of her daughter, Georgina; a complex family association to grasp, even for Watson's experienced mind.

Nothing was said for a few minutes. "An angel passing do you think?" Maria asked with a smile, which was possible now that she had disposed of the feelings of the guilt caused by her years of silence.

Watson said he didn't know much about angels and started to tell her the story he had learned.

"Your husband, Richard Harris, was not called by that name from birth. He changed his name after surviving a train accident in nineteen twenty-nine. I have to tell you that he was married then but his wife died fourteen years after the accident. There was also a daughter. Maria counted the years from the accident until the time she had met him and realised the significance of the discrepancy.

"Did you know?" Watson needed confirmation.

"No, but I knew there was something he wouldn't tell me. What about his certificate though? That had his name on it from his engineering college."

"He was never a qualified engineer. He might have been a good one if he had been, but that certificate meant nothing. It was made for him by a man called Aloisius Stubbs who you knew as Kitchener. Your husband paid for it with money stolen from his employers. There is also the matter of his estate which rightfully belongs to his true heirs."

"What was his name at birth?"

"Plunkett. James Plunkett. He was born in Gloucester".

"And the baby? His only true heir?"

"Anna Plunkett."

Maria sucked in air through her teeth as she folded her arms across her chest and bent forward, rocking back and forth. She then looked up at Watson, her eyes beseeching.

"She must never know. It would be cruel. It's not necessary. Let her think he died in the train crash. Don't let her think that her father is a thief, a liar and a murderer." As she spoke the last word, she covered her face with her hands, her body began to shake and her shoulders twitched convulsively.

"Why do you call him a murderer?" Watson didn't know of McQuaid's death in the mountain pass and assumed he had died in the earthquake.

"He said so one night when he was delirious, or perhaps drunk or possibly both. Mr. McQuaid hadn't been seen for some time before the earthquake, so that may not have been the cause of his disappearance. Richard said that he had killed him and that it served him right." A minute passed, then another. Maria looked up. "I have told no one about this. Please keep it to yourself. It's been eating away at my soul and I am dying slowly from the knowledge of it and have been now for these past seven years. Soon it will be over."

Watson thought it through and then asked, "What about his money? Anna is his rightful heir."

Maria answered, "There is no money. Richard sent it all to a Swiss bank account belonging to someone else and our house, which was destroyed in the earthquake was uninsured as he wouldn't complete any application forms which asked about his past."

The radio in the next room gave out sports results in the background as she said again, "Soon it will be all over."

—

Watson met George Mandleson for the first time at Anna's house the day after he had talked to Maria. George and Anna had both been out then and he had been intrigued to meet the man at the centre of this particular convoluted human relationship which he had unearthed as a result of his earlier search for the whereabouts of Aloisius Stubbs. He went round the next evening at Anna's invitation and, as she was called out again to the hospital almost as soon as he arrived, he spent some time with George catching up on his story. He noticed the weakness in George's hand as he shook it on arrival and saw that the arm didn't move freely.

"Didn't they find out who did that to you then?" Watson needed confirmation of Maria's suspicions.

"No. It's still a complete mystery but we assume it was an accident and the person who did it was too frightened to admit his mistake. Anyway I didn't really know people here well enough for them to shoot me so it's unlikely that it was intentional." George was able to smile as he said it. "In one way, from my own point of view, I'm glad. I wouldn't want to go on reliving it all while the legal processes take their course. That's not usually something which leaves anyone in a happy frame of mind is it?" he asked Watson, who nodded agreement with the sentiment but doubted its wisdom.

"The gun?" he asked George.

"Never found. Probably some kid with his father's hunting rifle. We'll never know." Watson's knowledge on the matter left him feeling vaguely uncomfortable. He was becoming embroiled in the secret world that surrounded all of them yet couldn't discuss it. He was becoming part of their problem.

"It's only a small town of, what… about ten thousand people…," he began and George interrupted, "Well, I nearly kicked the bucket. It was a close call and if it wasn't for Anna…" His eyes softened when he said her name. "Anyway the earthquake came the next day and they were much too busy to worry about it all. I suppose it would have been different if I had been killed. I must have been the only person in Bishop Falls who slept through the earthquake so those medicines for post-operative pain must be quite effective. Every window in the ward shattered, cupboards fell over, door frames moved and beds crashed around the floor like fairground bumper cars. I was lucky that the underwater seal for my chest drain was hung from the bed and not on the floor or my lung would have collapsed again before they got to me. They thought I was dead, but there I was deep in the arms of Morpheus; the chemical one that is, not the Greek god's. I must be lucky to have had two close calls within twenty four hours and to be here to tell the tale." George reflected for a moment while

Watson agreed with him but interjected, "But you had quite a disappointment with all of that." He nodded towards George's shoulder. "I understand you had to give up your operating career because of it."

"Yes, but every cloud... as they say...;" He paused, then added, "Well, I quite enjoy medical journalism and there were some changes it all brought about in my life which I'm happy about and the hours I work are much better than they would have been in orthopaedics." He added the last comment to steer the discussion back away from his personal life. Men don't talk with each other about such things particularly with someone they have only just met. However he would have been surprised to learn that this stranger knew things about the background of those he loved which they didn't even know themselves.

"Only problem is, I have to travel away a lot; conferences and so on and I get into trouble with Georgi." His eyes smiled as he said this, "Well she gets upset when I go. She didn't used to want me to leave the house without her, let alone go out of town. Now it's Georgi who leaves town when she goes to university and I am the one who gets upset more than anyone. She phones every day so we do keep in touch."

This was all said in a matter-of-fact way but Watson had heard from Maria how Georgi had helped George through his difficult months of rehabilitation and knew the depth of feeling which they must have developed for each other even if it was unexpressed in George's words.

"Anna says that I spoil her but I don't think I do." Watson smiled as he shook his head as if agreeing with George that this was most unlikely. "Oh, by the way, Anna and I; we're not married you know. Ellen, my wife, has moved to Quebec. She can speak French very well and..." George's voice trailed off leaving the sentence unfinished, just as their relationship had been. He always felt it necessary to explain, to keep everything in the open as it were, even though most people simply reacted similarly to the way expressed by Watson's gesture; a single wave of his hand downward and to one side as if to deny any opinion on the matter which was not his concern.

"So Georgi spent her childhood without a Dad and now she has two. She calls Maria 'Dad' and me, 'My Dad'. She seems happy enough with the arrangement." Watson recognised, from George's expression, the role she must have played in the healing process for Maria, as well as for George, in the years following the earthquake, Maria's bereavement and George's injury.

"She's twenty now. At Queens. First year medicine. She's coming back this weekend. You'll be able to see her. Funny isn't it how they all know everything at that age. There's nothing complicated for them. Black or white, right or wrong." He stopped knowing that he had gone on for too long and Watson didn't need his policeman's mind to see that George was proud of his daughter.

"I'll look forward to meeting her then if it fits in with your plans. I'm here till Tuesday. Then I'm off for my Alaskan cruise."

Watson remembered about the time in his life when he thought he knew all the answers, when he was twenty and wanted to go to Alaska. He had seen the photographs of the Gold Rush taken in the eighteen hundreds and had wondered at the adventurous spirit that had driven the prospectors into the icy wilderness all those years in the past. He kept in his mind the photograph of a line of men, black against the white snow, climbing in an inhospitable climate to get over the Chilkoot pass to the Klondike gold fields. In nineteen twenty-eight however, a policeman couldn't afford to travel around the world and he had had to wait until his retirement to follow this youthful dream. It was due to be fulfilled the following week.

"When you're a child you do see things all in black and white and everyone says that when you are older you'll understand," Watson said. "What they really mean is that when you're older you'll interpret things in an adult way and then bend the truth to suit your own ideas. No you're right, children see things plainer than we do".

"You aren't the first person to realise that. Listen to this." George pulled a Bible from the shelf, turned to Corinthians and read, "When I was a child I spake as a child, I understood as a child, I thought as a child. But when I became a man I put away childish things, For now we see through a glass darkly; but then face to face; Now I know in part; but then shall I know even as I am known."

Watson said, somewhat to George's surprise, "We should try the new translation. Then perhaps we can find out what was really meant."

"And interpret it in our adult way as we choose between the two?" George was thinking as he said this about Georgi's opinion, perhaps partly self interested, on the possibility of his moving in to stay with them after the earthquake, when she was thirteen.

"Of course you have to stay here now. You're my Dad. Ellen can stay too if she wants to." For the child it was so simple, black and white, not 'through a glass darkly'. Ellen had not wanted to stay of course, but she saw the situation that had developed already and understood. There was for her even a slight sensation of relief blurring the disappointment of failure and rejection and her departure from their lives, although painful for all of them, had not been stained by malice.

—

George Mandleson was the only child of parents who worked in universities in England and had undoubted academic ability. There was an expectation that he would follow them into academia and they were surprised therefore when one day he announced his chosen career in orthopaedic surgery. He had always seemed to be somewhat indecisive and they were uncertain whether this might affect his competence in that particular field; one that required decisions followed by action. It was not that he didn't have opinions on important things. It was just that George eschewed the extremes, the polarised positions and he felt more comfortable in the middle ground. They approved of his engagement to Ellen whose parents were also in the academic arena. Her father was now a professor in an English department at a university in the north and they too had expected both Ellen and George to follow in their footsteps. Parents in general often assume that their children will follow them when they choose their own occupations. It is almost as if they are seeking reassurance that they have not been wasting their own lives with the knowledge that their own children are following them. The idea lacks logic but George could understand it.

"You should go into psychiatry George," Anna had said to him one day in their student years, "or perhaps family medicine. It suits your style."

However, George was determined to be an orthopaedic surgeon. His problem was that he was a moderate. He might hold a well-thought out opinion on something only to find that he agreed with the opposite when this was expressed well by someone else. Then, when someone supported his first approach, he would move to the middle ground and act as mediator between the two, usually successfully since polarised views often meet in the centre ground. He realised that the extremes were not for him but were simply a forum in which moderation could declare itself with authority.

In medicine, orthopaedic surgery is at the opposite pole from psychiatry, the home of the moderates where there is more room for deliberation and compromise. Anna had been right. Surgery was not ideally suited to George's philosophical ways and yet he was uncharacteristically determined not to change his mind. He overcame any deficiency his approach might cause with a strict adherence to protocol and a learning that he maintained up to date throughout his training and working life. Technically his work was good and his reputation unsurpassed.

At home, where protocol was not applicable, things were different. There too, moderation was not successful in overcoming his relationship difficulties with Ellen and the plane he found had worked so successfully in his professional life, couldn't be applied in their relationship. He and Ellen lived their lives on separate artificial planes that rarely intersected. Had he followed Anna's advice and become a psychiatrist or a family doctor he would have recognised sooner that his marriage couldn't succeed.

A week after the earthquake George lay in his hospital bed. His pain medication left him in a deep sleep from which he awoke with the scent of roses surrounding him with their delicate invisible breath as an all-pervading sensation. Their scent was full and rich, sweet and aromatic. As he awoke his eyes focused on a deep red-coloured rose as he inhaled its fragrance. Its petals were full, heavy and at a stage just before they might droop but showing the beauty of a life attained to the full. The outside edge of each petal showed some early darkening, almost black, while the rest, rich and red, spoke of maturity. They were open just enough to see the carpel within awaiting pollination in the swirling warm red softness of the flower which exuded the scent of re-creation, the scent of love.

George thought of Anna and of their afternoon on the river the previous week, the day before the earthquake. He remembered the green willowy arbour and the pink fireweed, the scent of the river and of her. He remembered the sandy bank, of reaching out to touch her rounded fullness, which like the rose was beauty itself, but which responded to his lips with a firm warmth from her softness. And he remembered that later ultimate sensation, an escalating ecstasy of feeling coloured by mutual love and followed by rest and fulfilment, just as the rose, with its carmine colour and exotic scent, might be complete and fulfilled after pollination.

—

The sound of the front door opening interrupted their thoughts. Anna had returned. Watson, in a lull in their conversation had been thinking about the secret life of James Plunkett while George's concentration was centred on roses and he had to make some degree of mental effort to offer, "Shall I make some coffee?"

"You see, I knew there was a reason why you're here." Anna laughed as she said it and the worn out look of tiredness which had shown when she came into the room faded into that smile which George had known now for over thirty years. He kissed her and called downstairs to Maria's basement apartment, "Dad, do you want some coffee?"

"No thank you My Dad. It's too late at night for me. I'll see you all tomorrow," she called back and they both smiled at their banter. Georgi made them laugh even when she was no longer there with them.

Watson looked at Anna. He could see how George would have been drawn to her with her warmth of personality pervading the room, her intelligence, her undoubted beauty still now at the age of forty eight and that smile. "It must be hard, being on call so much," he said having noticed her look when she had first come in.

"It's part of the job," she told him with a shrug and Watson thought of parts of his own job that had been hard, but they had not been there all the time, day and night, week in and week out.

"Well, it does get you down now and again," she admitted, "but it's funny that just as soon as you get exhausted and feeling low, something happens that makes you think it's all worth while. I might spend hours at night helping someone and get only complaints in return and then someone else who I have almost forgotten will tell me in passing how something small I have done, perhaps years in the past, had changed their life and made them remember me. So I keep going, but sometimes I do wonder if perhaps I should be a journalist like George." She brightened again with that smile, "or just retire like you."

"Why don't you retire then?" The question wasn't serious but she answered.

"We have to see Georgi through university. Then we'll see."

Watson changed the topic of their conversation.

"I went to the village today to see Dave Wilson. Now there's someone who thinks a lot about you. He says he's going to smoke some salmon for you. I think he would do anything for you if you asked him."

"Well, it's mutual. He once saved my life, and Georgi's. We were in our boat, trapped by the tide and likely to be swept under a log jam and he got us out at considerable risk to himself."

"He didn't tell me," Watson told her, "but then he doesn't talk a lot about that sort of thing does he?"

Anna thought and then said, "He doesn't talk much anyway but we seem to understand each other. No he wouldn't talk about it. He's a special sort of person." She nodded for emphasis as she said this and Watson wondered what she would think of Dave being the only keeper for many years of her father's secret, until he and Maria found out. He looked worried for a moment, concerned about that secret and whether it was right to keep it so.

"Did you know his parents or grandparents?" he asked.

"Yes I met his father once when he was up from Vancouver, but I knew the grandparents best. Sadly, she was killed in the tsunami wave after the earthquake and he died soon after of a broken heart."

"Do people? Do people really die of broken hearts?" Watson was intrigued.

"The death certificate usually records something else, as if we're afraid to admit it for some reason, but I think so, yes." Anna knew that she would have died from a broken heart if George had not recovered after being shot that day by the river.

"What about your parents and family? I hope you don't mind my asking." Watson wondered what she had been told about her father.

"Well, my father died in a train accident when I was only a few months old so I don't remember him of course, but my mother died when I was older, although still a child and, as well as remembering her well, I remember what she told me about him. She told me that he was a good man, hard-working and considerate and likely, in due course, to take over the business where he worked. I wish I could have met him."

"Me too." Watson interjected. He had intended to sound sympathetic but his policeman's mind added an enquiring edge to the words. Anna was only momentarily confused by it and continued, "She never got over his death. I think she died of a broken heart as well as from her illness. She did her best for me and I'm grateful to her and to him of course. It wasn't only a small thing he did for me was it, giving me my life?"

Watson nodded agreement while he thought to himself, 'No I can't tell her. Dave's right, she shouldn't know. But how did Dave know that?' However it was against his nature, this secrecy. He didn't feel comfortable with it and it showed.

"You look thoughtful," Anna said.

"I was thinking of Dave Wilson. He seems to think of things clearly, not 'through a glass darkly' like most of us," he said as he took his coffee from George and nodded to him as he did so, acknowledging their earlier conversation.

"As a matter of fact I've been invited to go fishing with Dave and Jonas this weekend. They say the chinook are coming in." Watson was delighted with his promised weekend on the water.

"Well, we'll all be travelling. I'm going with George to Keemanu in the boat. I have a clinic to do there," Anna told him, "and Georgi, who's coming back tomorrow, is hiking over the power line trail with three of her friends, two men and another woman. They'll meet us there and come back with us in the boat. They'll have to cover nearly fifty miles in two days so I expect they'll be tired when they get there. George said he wouldn't go in case they thought he was some sort of chaperone but I don't think he's fit enough and he knows it." She hugged him as she said this but George's dismissive denial of his wanting to act as chaperone would have had less credibility to anyone who might have been able to hear his later enquiry from Anna about Georgi's knowledge of birth- control.

After Watson's departure Anna told him. "She told me

she's been on the pill for over three years."

"Well, I had to ask. There is a family history you know..." he said grinning, perhaps sheepishly, or was that simply Anna's interpretation?

"Thank goodness there was. Come on, I might get called out of bed soon. There's someone in the maternity ward, but who knows, it might not happen until the morning."

"Times change," he said.

"Thank goodness," she repeated.

—

Frank Watson looked a little uncomfortable carrying a bunch of flowers, but it seemed the right thing for him to do when he was invited back to Anna's house the following evening after his talk with George, to meet Georgi on her arrival back from university. It was she who opened the door for him, saw that the flowers needed redirecting from their unlikely bearer, took them from him and said, "Flowers? For me?" She pretended to accept Watson's gift with mock pleasure.

"You could share them with your mother," he said diplomatically. "I'm Frank Watson. You must be...?" He saw her mother's brown eyes and wide smile and knew without doubt who she was, but she interrupted him with, "Hello, I'm Georgina. They used to call me Georgi when I was young, but now I'm old I'm called Georgina. Can I call you Frank?"

"Frank would be fine." He smiled at the twenty year old who didn't think she was young any more while her youth, obvious for all to see, was declared by its own exuberance.

She called out, "Mum, My Dad, It's Frank. He brought flowers."

She ushered him into the room. "You know my mother and this is My Dad. He's George and he refuses to call me Georgina. Says that he's too old to change but I love him anyway. Don't you think he should learn to call me Georgina, Frank?"

"Well, Georgi, Georgina both sound good to me. Good solid names like George. We met yesterday by the way." He attempted to mediate in this major life crisis of hers and saw that he had done so when she agreed with him.

"That's right. Solid, substantial George." She poked in fun at his belly, which admittedly was just a little bigger than he might have wished, hugged him and told him not to change. "If you promise not to, you can still call me Georgi. But only you, Mum and 'Dad' and no one else." And Maria, Georgi's 'Dad' sitting in the corner, looked several years younger for being included in this inner sanctum of recognition.

Watson tried a hurt look for being excluded but he was no actor and simply looked as if he might have a headache. Georgi was adamant, the rules had been established. He would have to make the best he could of it all.

Brian Philpott arrived with Jim Sanders and his wife. "I've got you that book, 'Future Shock' by Alvin Toffler," Brian had found a copy for Georgi.

The evening promised to be memorable. Watson introduced himself to Jim Sanders and talked about the years gone by in Bishop Falls.

"Time here is divided into two distinct periods; before and after the earthquake," Jim told him. "I saw it all happen you know. Just happened to be there on our deck looking down the Douglas Channel when it hit. It was just before half past seven when I got back from work and the electric clocks all stopped at seven thirty four. There was a loud crack, as if something massive had broken deep in the earth and a sort of rolling vibration followed, travelling at the speed of lightning up the valley and toward the town-site. Trees fell over in waves spreading up the valley and the power lines went down as well as some of the houses built on the ridge. There were arc flashes from the transmission lines and the relay stations at the works. The ground began to shake and the house followed its movement. Some chimneystacks went and brick buildings were badly damaged but the wooden houses weren't affected so much unless they started on fire. It was strange to see that some buildings were totally unaffected while others nearby were damaged. The hospital was not as badly hit as it might have been and its main structure stayed up although there was a fair bit of internal damage. The post-office went but fortunately there was no one in it at the time. There were several fires breaking out in homes around the town and the Fire Department couldn't use the telephones or the water system as the mains supply had been breached. They could have done with the water from the dam but that all went into the sea. The tsunami did some damage at Kitamaat and the docks but fortunately it was played out before it reached the town-site." He stopped, realising that he was reliving it, as he had done so often before and turned to George, "And this guy, would you believe, slept through it all and wondered what all the fuss was about!"

"Were many people killed?" Watson asked.

"It could have been much worse, but yes, Maria Harris' husband," he nodded towards the corner of the room where Maria still sat talking to Georgi, "that Kitchener fellow, several people at the village, six at the works. There were fifteen in all and a lot of injuries. The town recovered quickly, but of course those families didn't."

"What about the dam failing. It looks all right from

here." Watson was intrigued to know if that particular structure built under the control of the unqualified Harris had been stable under the influence of such a catastrophic force.

"It didn't fail. It did look at first as if it had, but they had built in some pinning into the rock that added stability; some new idea of Harris'. What happened was that an old fault in the mountains above gave way under the influence of the earth movement and the whole mountainside collapsed into the reservoir, pushing the water over the top. Quite spectacular; I saw it happen; looked like Niagara Falls. The dam itself didn't give way though so it must have been well designed although the inquiry people didn't like it. It was an untried design made up by Harris himself. I bet it won't be long before someone else copies it and gets the credit for it."

"Why was it built anyway? The main dam is near Keemanu isn't it?" Watson asked.

This one was built as a reserve power source in case the main dam or the transmission line failed. They used tidal power to pump water up from the next inlet to add to the smaller supply from the watershed above the dam. It would have produced enough power to stop the aluminum pots from freezing until repairs were done. You probably know that the aluminum smelting process is an electrolytic one that takes place in lines of tanks or 'pots', each half the size of this room. They are all filled with molten metal, alumina or bauxite that would freeze solid if the power was interrupted and it would take months to start up again. They were lucky they got the power back quickly after the quake so that Harris' dam wasn't needed anyway." He looked across the water at the dam, remembering.

"So how's London? Smoky as ever? I haven't been there for years." Jim Sanders had finished his story and Watson answered, "Not like it is here, that's certain. But it's not as smoky as it used to be and I couldn't think of living anywhere else".

—

Two days earlier, after he had spoken to Maria, Watson went back to see Dave to let him know what had happened. As he had suggested he would, he went also to see Jonas and there he learned that the run of chinook or spring salmon was under way.

"How d'you know the run has started?" he asked.

"Killer whales 're coming up the chuck looking for dinner," Jonas told him. The northern pods of orcas usually stayed out of the narrow coastal inlets but the exception to this rule always happened when the salmon migrated to the rivers to spawn. Then they followed them up the inlets almost as far as the fresh water. Dave had seen this happening several times in past years. He was obviously excited when he said, "Jonas and me are going fishing to Allan Reach to get some salmon for the smoke house."

Watson had seen the smoke house, a wooden hut about ten feet wide by twenty feet long with fish drying and being smoked from wood chips burning slowly on the floor, their position being changed regularly to get maximum exposure to the smoke. The fish were soaked first in brine to dry and kept in the smoke- house for several days or even weeks.

"How big are the salmon?" he asked.

"Chinook get up to sixty pounds but the record's closer to a hundred," Jonas told him. "Come along if you like."

Watson didn't need to be asked twice and that was how he arrived there three nights later, forty miles down the channel, lying on his back and looking at the stars. 'Can this really be me here?' he asked himself, on the deck of

Jonas' boat. It lay at anchor in Bishop Bay, the moon new and the water calm since there was no wind and the boat simply drifting, swinging slowly on its anchor-line with the current. Above them the stars and planets seemed to move, wheeling slowly past their view with a brilliance Watson had never seen before, as the tide swung the boat gently in a circular movement. There was no reflected light nearby to mask the contrast between the darkness and even the faintest stars in that part of the night sky above them and an overwhelming sensation of peace and an appreciation of the magnitude of the universe silenced all three of them with its beauty.

As the boat drifted, the nearby mountains moved across the lower part of their field of vision, appearing as an insubstantial obscuring darkness against the background of stars. And in the water below, phosphorescent sea organisms traced the movement of the anchor rope along the radius of an arc described by their boat in response to the sea current. A waterfall splashed softly into the water across the bay and the magnificence of their surroundings seemed to insist on silence so that no one spoke for several seconds. Watson then became aware of Dave shaking with silent laughter next to him.

"What's so funny Dave?" Jonas asked him.

"It looked just like him. The way he walked, but that hat..." Dave stopped talking as another paroxysm of laughter took hold of him, yet his face still presented its usual serious expression and this started Jonas and Watson laughing as well until they were all too weak to continue.

"Kitchener's dead," Jonas reminded him at last.

"Perhaps it was his ghost." Dave was in fine form. "Do you think it was Frank?" He looked as if he was about to start his laughing again but was able to stop.

Watson hadn't seen the man with the hat. He had been

too fascinated by the appearance of the ship that had carried the ghostly Kitchener, the source of Dave's mirth, to notice anything unusual.

They had caught four big salmon that afternoon as well as several smaller jack-springs that were thrown back, to 'try again next year', to use Jonas' expression.

"You should have fished lower. We'd have caught ten or more by now," Dave advised Jonas who answered, "And lose my down-rigger weight on those rocks I suppose." The down-rigger carried their nylon fishing line down to a selected depth. Its lead weight, about five inches in diameter, held down a wire line to which the fishing line was attached with a plastic peg. This could be released as soon as a fish struck their lure, trailing behind a stainless steel plate that was so constructed that its movement in the water appeared like one injured fish about to seize another.

Later in the afternoon Watson had become aware for several minutes of a distant drumming sound coming across the water. It sounded like the bass speaker of a music player.

"Someone playing music down here?" he asked.

"Killer whales 're having a party to celebrate the fish coming." Dave was in a good mood. He always was when he was on the water. He felt at home there.

"Come on you guys," Watson was feeling at home too. "What is it?"

"Wait and see. Look!" Jonas told him. It was still in that half-light when the sun had set behind the mountains and the colours of the trees and slopes were moving through a range of tones, darkening slowly in the tranquillity of the evening. The regular sound was now obviously caused by the propellers and diesel engines of a large ship, and as the sound became more pronounced, they could hear the wash breaking from its bow even before it rounded the point by the disused cannery at Butedale. It suddenly seemed to appear close to them, immense, white and with lights glittering along every deck. Music came to them across the water and Watson noticed the name on its bow with a start.

"That's the Pacific Queen. I'm going on it in Alaska next week. If you stay here I'll throw you that can-opener we forgot when I go past," Watson told them with obvious excitement at the prospect.

The ship looked impressive in the failing evening light, its own lighting contrasting with the dark blues and black of evening. People walked the decks wearing suits, ties and dresses. It was as if they were actors on a stage in another world that moved closely in front of their eyes, gliding past with themselves as an unseen audience. After it had gone it would have been easy to think it had all been imagined; difficult to believe what the eyes had seen.

"Look! He looks like Kitchener. The one with the hat there, see?" Dave noticed him but the other two did not.

"Perhaps Queen Victoria's there with him too," Jonas teased him and as by then the ship had passed them by, they had only to deal with its wake as their boat bobbed around and they grabbed for the cups, plates and bottles which seemed to have taken on a life of their own for a short while. Their fishing over for the day they moved on to Bishop Bay to anchor for the night. As they dropped the anchor Dave said, "This was my grandfather's favourite place. He said he'd come back here when he died. Hey! Henry, You out there?"

When silence followed his last echo, he wished he hadn't called out like that and kept quiet for some time while he looked out into the darkness. He remembered then some words from Henry's funeral service; 'Lord now lettest thou thy servant depart in peace; according to thy word. For mine eyes have seen thy salvation, which thou hast prepared before the face of all people.' Dave remained quiet then for some time. He missed Henry a lot.

—

"You can't read someone else's letter!" The young woman who said this was just as interested in their find as was her friend and also the two men with them, but knowing they would read it anyway her protestation afforded her conscience the justification of virtue denied when she joined them.

"Come on Ginnie, this letter's seventeen years old. It's postmarked the fifteenth of March nineteen sixty. If you don't want to read it you can go outside while we do if you like." The speaker, a young man in his early twenties had his name, Roger, labelled across his back-pack that he had just put down when they all agreed that this was the place to stop for their night's camp. The protester, a young woman with auburn hair and bright eyes, said to be rather similar to her mother's, was a person who thought that she was too old at the age of twenty to be called Georgi. They, all four, were dressed and equipped with what the second man in their party, who for some reason they called Socks, called 'the gear'. He referred to the preponderance of brand labels emblazoned across their clothing, climbing equipment, plastic water bottles, belts, boots, woollen hats, ropes, toggles, tents, gloves as well as the rest of 'the gear'.

They had stopped by a dilapidated wooden cabin in the forest half way between the town of Bishop Falls and the hydroelectric generating station at Keemanu. There, much to the relief of Socks who was not 'into' hiking and felt exhausted, the fourth member of their group suggested that she was getting tired and that here was the best place to stop. Heather had prevented him from having to be the first to give in.

As it happened they all went outside to see what the letter was about since it was too dark anyway to read it inside the cabin, which although it lacked windows, did boast a rusted wood-stove which had obviously not been in use for many years. The letterhead was from the Government of Ethiopia, Department of Education and the letter read: 'Dear Mister…son.' (A stain through the envelope and the letter itself obscured the full name of the addressee.) 'In recognition of your generous contributions made regularly over the past twenty years for the benefit of children in this country, the Minister has recommended that a new school being built at Ras Dashen be named after you. We trust this is satisfactory to you. Your contributions have enabled hundreds of chil…' The rest of the letter was unreadable as it had for the most part, been eaten by ants, while the part they had read had been protected by being placed under a wooden block on a shelf.

"I wonder who he was?" The conscience-stricken Georgina now wanted to know more.

"He was probably some rich guy wanting to hand over some of his ill-gotten gains as a sop to his conscience." Roger was not prepared to be as generous in his interpretation of the letter as its addressee must have been to merit the recognition to which it referred.

"You're such a bloody communist Roger," Socks told him, "Can't you give credit where it's due? He obviously did more to help them in Ethiopia than any of us are likely to in our lifetimes. You always see things the same way; 'Money equals capitalism equals evil.' You can't see the wood for the trees."

"And talking about trees," Heather interrupted them, "we're not quite half way yet so we'll have to get an early start tomorrow, so let's eat, sleep and get going early."

They decided to sleep in the cabin and lit the stove. It smoked as it had always done in years gone by as Scratchy Stubbs might have recalled, but its heat was not as necessary on that balmy Summer night and by leaving the door open, they were at least able to vent the smoke enough to see across the room.

"From the map it looks as if we have about a mile to go to the hanging platform. Then we climb until we get over that ridge, following the power lines all the way and we'll be there about five o' clock if we're lucky." Roger-the-socialist planned their next day's activities while the others did useful things until sleep carried each one of them quickly through the night to their morning start.

Despite the cabin's obvious disuse over a long period of time, there were well worn bear paths around it in three directions which made the going easy when they started off at the order given by Socks of, "Wagons roll!" A mile onward the platform suspended across the valley between the transmission towers came into view.

"How'd you like to climb up there? Or down again for that matter?" Georgi asked the others who agreed that they were probably better to keep going as time was moving on. Even on that summer morning the practicality of such a venture seemed doubtful. It looked to be an impossibility in winter.

"What's that you've got there?" Heather asked Socks who had seen something glinting in the morning sun close to a cleft rock beneath the platform.

"It's a watch. No strap on it. A cheap one. It won't work. There's some rust in it and, Oh! There are some initials on the back. 'L McQ'. I'll leave it in case he comes back," he joked placing the watch, balanced on the cleft rock, so that the initials could be seen as if they declared ownership over the rock itself. In the undergrowth around, had they looked, they might have found a few bone fragments showing on them scoring made by the teeth of wild animals. But they were preoccupied with other matters and Georgi picked some wild flowers and placed them in the cleft of the rock. She didn't know why she had picked them. She could hardly carry flowers with her all day, but she thought they just seemed to look to be in the right place there in the cleft in the rock by the watch when she looked back a few minutes later as they re-entered the forest. Then she lost sight of them and they were, perhaps, forgotten.

"Look at that then!" Roger looked back from the top of the ridge before their descent into Keemanu and they all stopped to see the view of mountains, still with last years' snow on their northern slopes and now in September awaiting the first new fall of winter, even now overdue. "You know when I die..."

"Don't be morbid!" Heather stopped him, "Whatever you say now you'll change your mind in sixty years so why bother?"

"No seriously, when I die I'll have my ashes spread somewhere like this. I can't think of anywhere better to be. I thought of it back there when you put those flowers on that rock Ginnie I don't know why."

"I think he needs a beer urgently." Socks' contribution to their philosophical discussion which might have developed had, they all agreed, a practical appeal which superseded the urgency of the topic previously under consideration.

Heather interjected, "I've just thought of something. That letter last night. It was never opened. The top and sides were sealed and we took it out of the envelope through an opening in the corner made by ants or whatever else had eaten it."

"You're right. I wonder why he didn't read it." Georgi looked pensive for a while and then said, "Well let's go.

We'll be late for Mum and My Dad if we don't get going now."

Anna asked them two and a half hours later, "Well, did you find a pot of gold at the end of the rainbow up there?"

"No, but Roger found an old letter, Socks found an old watch and Ginnie found some flowers." Heather told her.

"And what did you find Heather?

"Blisters."

—

The following day Frank Watson called to say goodbye. He was leaving the next day for his long-awaited cruise and would not be back afterwards. His arrival was interrupted by a voice that didn't sound as if it belonged to an older person, "Mum, My Dad, can you see if you can find... Oh, hello Frank." Georgi grinned when Watson replied, "Hello Georgina." and then continued, "Can you see if you can find a job for me to do this summer. I need cash. I'm going to Europe next year... Oh, if that's all right with you two. I'm going to look into Grandad Plunkett's family history; about his home, the railway accident and all that family stuff when I'm over there."

"At your age I would have gone to London to have a good time and never mind about that sort of thing." Watson's unlikely advice stemmed from his concern about what she might find if she searched too diligently into her family's history and he wondered again as he said it, whether he and Dave had done the right thing with their secrecy about it all. 'But then,' he thought, 'no one's right all the time are they?'

10

He that dies pays all debts.'
Shakespeare – The Tempest

A policeman's ambition and a busman's holiday, winners and losers, an ending.

They were an odd couple; a strange caricature of people who might have lived in a bygone age but who still apparently existed as if nothing had changed, forty years or so after their time, The first, wearing a dark suit and striped tie, was obviously a manservant who arranged chairs, clothing and personal effects for the other who, sitting with his back to Watson at the cruise ship's bar, had his face hidden from him. He could see that he was slightly built, somewhat stooped and that he was attired in an expensive white suit and a Panama hat, beneath which the grey hair of a man in his late sixties extended down to a thin wrinkled neck. This particular anatomical feature was being pampered as Watson watched, by being wrapped by the manservant with a black fur stole to keep out the evening's cold. This climatic inconvenience however was not otherwise noticed to be sufficient to necessitate closing the sliding doors between the bar and the deck area, where a game of cards was in progress. The owner of the fur-wrapped neck seemed to impatiently reject the attentions of the manservant who withdrew to the other side of the table, apparently watching attentively for any opportunity to assist his employer further. The latter meanwhile continued his concentration on a card game he had started with three American ladies.

"His name's Conrad Murgatroyd. He's English. One of your lot. Rich and related to the aristocracy.You should go and talk to him." The bartender spoke in Watson's ear. The latter's response however was less than enthusiastic as he had seen a slip of paper change hands when the collar was being adjusted. The bartender continued, "It's no wonder he's rich. He has the luck of the devil; always wins in the end even though he usually loses at first."

'They always do' Watson thought and wondered how many people worked the cruise ships for a living and how many were taken in before their game was exposed. He would see the purser and let him know, but first would watch to see how far they would take their game.

"I'm on a winnin' streak. You'd best give up now before you lose more than you can afford." The warning sounded friendly but the other players responded as intended, by refusing to admit to each other to any financial embarrassment they might have by withdrawing from the game if their losses continued. The speaker's accent was not entirely consistent with the persona described by the bartender as Conrad Murgatroyd. He rose from his seat as if to stretch his legs, turned to face Watson, whose presence he had sensed and needed to assess, nodded to him and with an inclination of his head towards the group at the table, invited him to join their game.

'It can't be, surely. But it is. I know it is. I wouldn't forget a face like that.' Watson talked to himself as he wrote a note which he handed to the bartender for the purser and scribbled also on two small pieces of note paper before joining the group at the table. The new game was soon underway and Watson deliberately avoided being seen watching the manservant's activity in order not to draw attention to himself and so the 'Panama hat' seemed to be confident when he said, "Two aces and a queen. I think it's mine is it not?" and reached for his winnings.

"No it's mine I'm afraid." Watson noticed the look of enquiry directed to 'the striped tie'. Had he missed telling about Watson's hand? The look was brief but telling. The man was no expert. Watson handed his cards to 'the hat' without showing them. There were a queen and two jacks and the initial sneer beginning on the pointed face beneath its brim stopped and transformed itself into a friendly smile of resignation when he noticed a piece of paper attached to the queen. On it was written, 'Hector sends his love'.

"Oi can't argue with that." He said. "Oi think it's time for me to go to bed so oi'll love you and leave you." His accent seemed to change still further from that which he had affected before as Conrad Murgatroyd. He reached for his remaining winnings but Watson shook his head and they were returned to the American ladies who had yet to understand what was happening. The purser and two sailors in uniform seemed to be in his way when he wanted to leave, so he was there to see Watson pass a card to his 'manservant', saw what happened next and knew that this particular career was finished for both of them. He would soon find another. He was a survivor.

The card was the joker. Watson was playing a hunch. He had never seen the man before yet there was a familiarity he recognised, or perhaps he just imagined it.

"I think you dropped this?" he said as he passed it to the

'striped tie'. Attached to the card was a piece of paper. On the front was printed the name James Plunkett, while on the back, the name McQuaid was added with the letters R.I.P. following it.

The reaction from James Plunkett was such that Scratchy Stubbs' departure from the deck to a room below was not even noticed by the others. As James Plunkett read the names he went pale and clutched at his chest over his striped tie, falling into a chair close by, where he sat still staring into the distant darkness outside. His pallor increased as pain, similar to that which he had experienced in Vancouver years before, again pressed heavily and inexorably on his chest, arm and jaw. His lips went blue and beads of sweat appeared on his forehead. He seemed to be elsewhere in his mind and didn't respond to questions put to him. A doctor was called and he was transferred to the ship's infirmary.

—

James Plunkett or Richard Harris, had lived his life of lies and deceit for so long that he was not always certain of his own identity and this confrontation on the ship exacerbated his pre-existing thoughts of persecution. He couldn't think clearly because of the pain; couldn't speak out and in his mind incidents from his past appeared and then vanished in a chaotic confusion of images, threatening, terrifying and guilt-ridden which then assembled themselves into his own visual and emotional representation of his past tawdry life.

There, he saw a flat in Gloucester where his crying wife and ugly baby made his life unbearable. His employers failed to kill him in a train crash so that he was able to put their money to good causes when his unrecognised engineering abilities were put into practice. He saw Scratchy Stubbs who had started all the trouble with his greed. McQuaid was a problem but he had gone away. (Harris' denial refused to acknowledge his part in that event.) He remembered that time seven years ago, seeing Scratchy talking to McQuaid and then some months later to that doctor friend of Anna's and he was certain he knew, when he followed her to the river that day, that she was going to talk about his secret. He couldn't remember why he had his hunting rifle with him but knew he had to keep the doctor from talking to her. He had been certain that she already knew about him and was planning to denounce him. The possibility had seized him with panic. He decided that he had to act. He pointed the gun at Anna who bent over as he squeezed the trigger so that the shot hit George Mandleson who fell to his knees. There had been confusion in his mind afterwards and there were shouts, other cars, a man with a fishing rod and he even thought he saw Maria in their camper. They all seemed to be converging on him at the riverbank. He ran back to his car. He had not been seen. No one followed him. He drove to the work site and the dam where he threw the rifle into its depths and lay down, exhausted, on the bed in the watchman's hut. In the distance he could hear an ambulance's siren and wondered where it was going. He had imagined that someone had been shot.

He had slept well later that night after drinking half of a bottle of cognac to overcome insomnia and awoke later in the afternoon of the following day. He had been unable to remember details of the events of the previous day, but knew he had to leave Bishop Falls as soon as possible. He hadn't eaten for nearly twenty-four hours. It was after seven o' clock in the evening and his legs felt weak beneath him, trembling as he walked. The sensation then became like the one he had felt during the rail accident many years in the past, a lifetime before.

A rumbling noise in the ground increased to a violent shaking which threw the hut up and down and eventually tipped it over, so that he had had to scramble out with the ground still rolling beneath his feet. The sand on the ground seemed to move and flow like water as rocks churned to the surface and sank again. A small landslide nearby almost buried him while boulders fell down from the hillside above. It seemed to last for an eternity but in fact was over in fifteen seconds.

He was unhurt. He looked across at the dam in time to hear a roar and to see millions of gallons of water flow from it into the ocean below, washing away buildings roads and cars as it went. He immediately assessed the effects that the disaster would have on him; The dam must have failed. There would be an inquiry and he would be found out. He had to leave and knew he had to go right away.

He scrambled towards his car, downhill near the water. Rocks and debris slowed his progress and a heavy pain developed in his chest that increased as he ran. He felt a need to see Maria to tell her, to see Anna, to tell her and to tell the world about it all, what he had done and how he wanted forgiveness. Then he saw, as he rounded a rocky outcrop fighting for breath with the chest pain increasing, that the water was flowing over the top of the dam and not through it.

"The dam hasn't failed," he shouted aloud at the surrounding mountains, "not failed, not failed!" A huge pressure then built up in his chest, crushing and pounding and yet at that moment he knew; knew that he could survive and carry it all through. No, he had done nothing wrong and would not have to tell anyone anything. He collapsed on the road where a momentary awareness caused him to look up in time to see a fifteen foot high wall of water bearing down towards him as it rolled along the ocean-side road. A tsunami wave, generated by the earthquake, had flowed up from its nearby epicentre in the ocean growing higher and faster as it reached the narrower and shallower parts of the inlet. There it attained an immense power, such that huge trees near the water were uprooted in a maelstrom of water, rock, wood, metal and other debris. His car was picked up by it and smashed under a pile of rock at the base of a cliff and Richard Harris, (or was he James Plunkett?), lay at the edge of this devastation, saved by the rocks that had slowed him down.

He had hidden overnight and then made his way to the railway line leading from Bishop Falls to Terrace. It was largely destroyed by the earthquake, with the bridges over the creeks broken and was certainly impassable for rail traffic. It did however present him with a route whereby he could leave unnoticed in the turmoil which followed the disaster. He had had to walk over thirty miles on a hot day before he reached the road near Terrace. The pain in his chest slowed him down. It recurred each time he tried to hurry. On the way he remembered another broken railway line, years before. That one had also seemed at first to be the means for him to escape to a new life, but had simply led him eventually to this new predicament.

"You wasn't thinkin' of leavin' so soon were you?" Where the line approached the road near Terrace, Scratchy Stubbs stopped his car and offered him a ride. He had been away doing some business related to banking and to making arrangements for the deposit of a large sum of money he was expecting to receive. "We still 'ave that small business item we discussed that we need to finish off before you go, if that's what you 'ad in mind."

Harris got in. "It's all done already, lucky for you. They

probably think I'm dead now so the cheque would be stopped today if it didn't go through yesterday. Look, I have to get away now. Perhaps we could come to some arrangement? I still have some offshore assets to call on and…," he looked significantly at Scratchy before continuing, "you don't want to have to go to London, do you?"

They had come to a new 'friendly arrangement'. It lasted from that time for seven years until the evening of the card game when Watson ended it. Neither Scratchy nor Harris had trusted the other during that time and they both lived in a state of chronic anxiety brought about by their balance of mistrust.

But the balance would be upset that evening. Harris knew he was dying and remembered there was something he had thought that he would want to do before he went on to the next life; something to do with some kind of redemption. But he knew he had done nothing wrong, so he forgot about it.

—

"There it is. The Railway Arms. Doesn't look anything much, but we can get something to eat there and someone might know about the crash." Georgi and Socks had splashed out and rented a new nineteen seventy-nine Volkswagon for their day trip from London.

It was true. The building didn't look very attractive. Had its owners been attempting to attract tourists, this particular inn with its unprepossessing exterior just outside the Cotswolds village of Charminster would have been unlikely to succeed. There were no black beams, false leaded-lights, garden tables with parasols, oak-veneered furniture and paintings of hunting scenes from times-gone-by which might attract such trade. The owners had resisted the pressure from the national breweries and existed still as a small enterprise selling local beer and cider on tap to people who lived nearby and who knew what they were buying. The building itself was square and brick-built with a frontal symmetry so absolute as to almost offend the eye. It was topped with grey slate which drained rainwater into two rusting down-pipes, one at either end. The bricks were weathered, the mortar cracked and in need of re-pointing and the paint-work on the window sills was no longer able to protect the woodwork from cracking.

Socks' initial observation that it 'didn't look much', seemed to be confirmed by the chicken-house and run at the side of the house which added country smells to the air pervading the small unpaved parking area. These followed the visitors to the front entrance where the smell of beer from over one hundred and fifty years of use became the more dominant sensation. Socks opened the door for Georgi to go in ahead of him.

The room was small and smoke-filled, with ten mostly occupied, small, wrought-iron tables in it and although no one apparently paid any attention to them as they chose an empty one, the level of sound softened a little as they were assessed by glances which were made discreetly during conversations. It was as if the obtrusion of the former might be softened by the apparent importance of the latter.

Socks nodded towards the local beer in response to the barman's enquiry and their acceptance there was confirmed by Georgi's decision to try the local cider when so advised. The conversation then returned to its pre-existing sound level despite Georgi's obviously foreign accent that was a cause for notice.

"You American?"

"Canadian."

"Same difference i'n' it?"

"Well...." It seemed rude to argue Georgi thought, shrugging her shoulder.

"'Ere, you don't know Royston Smith do you? We used to call 'im Smiffy. 'e went to Canada. Toronto."

"No, but we'll look out for him; tell him you asked after him," Socks offered to be helpful and added, "I'll have the toad in the hole. What about you Ginnie?"

"What's that? I don't think it sounds too good," she whispered, and then louder, "I'll have the shepherd's pie please."

They were both hungry and both enjoyed their meal and it was after that that Georgi asked Smiffy's friend if there was anyone he knew who might know about a train crash that happened nearby in nineteen twenty- nine.

The barman seemed to look sideways at an older man sitting alone at a nearby table before saying, "Probably all dead now. It was a long time ago. Why d'you ask?"

Georgi, who had been smiling encouragement and had seen his glance, let her smile fade so that Smiffy's friend was the more concerned when he heard, "My grandfather was on the train. He died but they never found him."

"Terrible business. It was before my time. They blamed Bill Matson. He'd left his shift before time and being foreman had to take the blame. Died soon after the enquiry, they say." The barman who had apparently finished all he knew, wiped the clean bar top vigorously and moved away to attend to the other tables where, at one of them he spoke quietly to the older man who had been the momentary object of his attention during Georgi's enquiry. He returned then and said, "Go and ask him over there what he knows. He might be able to help."

"Who is he?" Georgi asked, looking at the rather wizened and gaunt looking man who looked introspective and even guarded as he avoided eye contact with her. He kept looking downward at the newspaper cuttings which he referred to frequently, noting things down on a piece of paper as he shuffled through them. The paper seemed to be about horse racing, as far as Socks could make out from their table nearby.

"Alec Coles," the barman told them, "Made a fortune on a multiplier at Cheltenham years ago then lost it all in the next year. Never talks to anyone as a rule even though he spends most of his time in here. But you can talk to him. Told him you was askin'."

"Hello," Georgi went ahead of Socks, "I'm Georgina Plunkett. My friend's called Socks. It's not his real name, he..."

"Come with me. I'll show ee where it 'appened." He interrupted her and didn't ask anything about them but had obviously heard about their enquiry.

At his suggestion they drove for about a mile up a country lane before stopping near a gateway into a field. A harvester was dropping square bales of straw into a truck driving alongside as it cut and separated the wheat. A bird sang high overhead. A heat haze rose from a railway line that ran straight for half a mile from a disused signal box to a junction where a sideline left the main line. Their guide hurried on introspectively with only a brief word spoken or muttered quietly to himself; "signal box, Fred Oldsby, points, Cranbourne siding, Newent goods, apples, Cardiff, express, tighten bolts, switch points."

As he spoke his speech seemed to develop a rhythm which matched his gait as he increased his speed, almost running over the railway sleepers, his feet treading on every second tie with the left and every third with the right, so that this limping syncopation of gait that he created was reminiscent of the rhythm of a train's wheels speeding along the track.

He seemed to have forgotten their presence, driving himself to run faster, his breathing laboured, his eyes staring from side to side until he grabbed his file of newspaper cuttings from his pocket and threw them down an embankment as he screamed out, "My God, No, No," and sank to his knees at the side of the rails, covering his face with his hands.

"Ahem," Georgi tried to attract his attention when they had caught up with him, "we didn't want to upset you; to make you remember it all again." She touched him on his shoulder and looked at him anxiously. Socks stood by, embarrassed for the seventy year old man who had lost his self-control so completely.

Alec Coles looked up at them, as if he were surprised that they were there and then remembering why, and then recalling it all as he had done again and again for fifty years said, "I'm sorry. It 'appens every so often. Can't 'elp it." He was crying. Socks looked away. Georgi took his hands in hers and looked into his eyes. They were old, tired and now bloodshot from his exertion. She saw the pain he was suffering and smiled at him with the same smile of warmth, acceptance and healing that her mother might have given.

"It was a long time ago. You can let it go now," she said. "You don't need to tell us if you don't want to."

"I do want to tell ee," he paused and then said, "tis now or never. Come over 'ere and sit down." They sat looking down an embankment from the railway lines. A growth of sturdy alder trees grew up from below them, their branches now above eye level

"'tweren't Bill's fault." He seemed to take a deep breath, "'twere mine." Alec recalled all he could of that day in nineteen twenty- nine and recounted it for them.

"First thing I saw was the carriages bent up in the air,

then smoke an' fire an' screamin' an' when I ran up I saw a man down this bank tryin' to get up it. 'e fell back an' I thought he were dead but later 'e weren't there when I went to look for 'im. Funny the things you remember. He'd gone an' left some of 'is sandwiches. Jellied eel sandwiches! Couldn't never touch 'em after that. Never 'ave." He shuddered and stopped talking and they drove him back to the Railway Arms.

On their way back to London, Georgi thought of Harris back during those years of her childhood before My Dad had come to stay. She didn't know what had reminded her of him just then, since after Maria, her first 'Dad' had died, Harris' name was rarely mentioned and she had all but forgotten him.
